THE SILVER SPOON

THE SILVER SPOON

MEMOIR OF A BOYHOOD IN JAPAN

Kansuke Naka

translated by Hiroaki Sato
with illustrations by Sumiko Yano

Stone Bridge Press • *Berkeley, California*

Published by
Stone Bridge Press
P. O. Box 8208, Berkeley, CA 94707
tel 510-524-8732 • sbp@stonebridge.com • www.stonebridge.com

Originally published in Japanese as *Gin no Saji* by Kansuke Naka (1885–1965).

English text © 2015 Hiroaki Sato.
Illustrations © 2015 Sumiko Yano.
Cover design by Hisako Fujishima.

Book design and layout by Linda Ronan.

Printed in the United States of America.

First edition published 2015.

p-ISBN: 978-1-61172-019-8
e-ISBN: 978-1-61172-911-5

To Sondra
four decades later

Contents

Notes and Acknowledgments

In the notes, the following books may be cited by author's last name only:

Definitions of Buddhist terms: Burton Watson, tr., *The Lotus Sutra* (New York: Columbia University Press, 1993), and Philip B. Yampolsky, ed., *Selected Writings of Nichiren* (New York: Columbia University Press, 1990).

Social references: B. H. Chamberlain, *Things Japanese* (or *Japanese Things* in the reprint edition: Tokyo: Tuttle, 1971); E. Papinot, *Historical and Geographical Dictionary of Japan* (reprint edition; Tokyo: Tuttle, 1972). Both originally published early in the 20th century, they often provide just the right sort of information for *The Silver Spoon*.

Certain festivals: U. A. Casal's *Five Sacred Festivals of Ancient Japan: Their Symbolism and Historical Development* (Tokyo: Sophia University and Tuttle, 1967), a Swiss businessman's loving report on the *gosekku,* the five seasonal turning points. Casal arrived in Japan in 1912 and lived there for fifty years.

The translations of tanka from the *One Hundred Poems by One Hundred Poets (Hyakunin isshu)*: those by F. V. Dickins that appeared in the *Journal of the Royal Asiatic Society* in 1909. There are a number of English translations of this mini-anthology—Dickins (1838–1915) himself had made an earlier, completely different one, published in 1866. But his 1909 translations, complete revisions of his earlier attempts, came out about the time Naka wrote *The Silver Spoon.*

Terms related to traditional Japanese clothing: Liza Dalby, *Kimono: Fashioning Culture* (New Haven: Yale University Press, 1993).

Biographical details on Naka Kansuke and his relatives and friends, editions of *The Silver Spoon*, etc.: Watanabe Gekisaburō, ed., *Naka Kansuke zuihitsu-shū* (Tokyo: Iwanami Shoten, 1985); Tomioka Taeko, *Naka Kansuke no koi* (Tokyo: Sōgensha, 1993), and Horibe Isao, *"Gin no saji" kō* (Tokyo: Kanrin Shobō, 1993).

In this book all Japanese names are given the Japanese way, with the family name first, except on the cover and on the title and copyright pages.

I started translating *The Silver Spoon* toward the end of the 1960s with Sondra Meadow Castile; ten of the episodes we worked on were then printed in the March 1972 issue of *Doshisha Literature: A Journal of English Literature and Philology*.

I thank the late erudite scholar Kyoko Selden (1936–2013) for interpreting many expressions and passages of *The Silver Spoon* for me; the poet Ishii Tatsuhiko for information on the publishing history of the memoir from Iwanami Shoten and Hirata Shigeru and Kakizaki Shōko for acquiring necessary books.

The novelist Dianne Highbridge and the scholar Gustav Heldt read the translation and made suggestions. Jenefer Coates copyedited it with unusual meticulousness and thoroughness.

Hisako Fujishima designed the cover and Yano Sumiko worked out the many lovely illustrations.

I thank the late poet Robert Fagan (1935–2009) for reading my translations for nearly forty years and, above all, my wife Nancy, the primary reader of whatever I write in English.

HIROAKI SATO

Introduction

The Silver Spoon (Gin no saji) of Naka Kansuke (1885–1965), first serialized in a daily newspaper in 1913, is the most admired childhood memoir ever written in Japan. As the philosopher Watsuji Tetsurō (1889–1960) wrote in his afterword to it in 1935, "the child's world is drawn in a magically vivid way."[1] Reading the story in China the following year in order to translate select passages into Chinese, Zhou Zuoren (1885–1967), the younger brother of Lu Xun (1881–1936), complimented Naka on being an author who "was not influenced by his predecessors, did not care about the fads of the world, simply looked at things with his own eyes, felt things with his own heart."[2]

Translating several passages from *The Silver Spoon* into English two decades later, the American student of Japanese literature Howard Hibbett called it "an extraordinarily beautiful evocation of the world of childhood, which retains its freshness today."[3]

In Japan more recently, the memoir has been affectionately called "a children's story for adults" *(otona no dōwa)*. The characterization may stem from Naka's own term "children's stories for grownups" *(seijin no tame no dōwa)* for a group of his own fables gathered into a single volume in 1961,[4] which had been inspired by ancient Chinese legend, old Japanese poetry, the Bible, and so on, and required a certain amount of classical knowledge to understand. *The Silver Spoon*, in contrast, is a straightforward memoir with no overt intent to edify the reader.

1   Watsuji's afterword has remained part of Iwanami's paperback edition of *Gin no saji*. In the 48th reprint, in 1971, the words appear on p. 193.

2   Ryū Gan'i (Liu Anwei), *Tōyōjin no hiai: Shū Sakujin to Nihon* (Tokyo: Kawade Shobō Shinsha, 1991), pp. 145–46.

3   Donald Keene, ed., *Modern Japanese Literature* (New York: Grove Press, 1956), p. 254.

4   Naka Kansuke, *Tori no monogatari* (Tokyo: Iwanami Shoten, 1983), p. 375.

Changing Japanese Society and Naka's Memoir

Much of the world of childhood that Naka conjures up in *The Silver Spoon* has to do with festivals, fairs, and fête days, daily rituals and games, with people taking part in them as a matter of course, their age-old beliefs and superstitions untouched—the descriptions of which are, one must add, greatly enhanced by the presence of the author's exceptionally good-natured and eternally patient aunt who, as a semi-permanent member of the Naka family, took it upon herself to look after him. (The aunt was the eldest sister of Naka's mother Shō, 1849–1934. But as her name has not been fully ascertained, she must remain nameless.)

Such a focus on "tradition" may strike some of those who know Japanese history as a little strange. After all, Naka was born and brought up a few decades *after* the Meiji Restoration in 1868, which, in putting the emperor back as ruler, had ended the two-hundred-and-fifty-year-old Tokugawa shogunate and its semi-isolationist policy. The new government did not just open Japan to international commerce and diplomacy but also sought to adopt all things Western. The nation's greatest goal for the period was emulation of the West.

So, in 1883, just two years before Naka was born, the government had completed, at exorbitant cost, the Rokumeikan, "Deer Cry Hall," a large Italianate two-story building for balls and masques designed by the British architect Josiah Conder, with Minister for Foreign Affairs Inoue Kaoru proclaiming at its opening: "We have decided to make the Rokumeikan a place where from now on high officials and gentlemen from inside and outside Japan may meet and socialize, unaware that longitudes and latitudes ever existed, where they may form friendships and fellowships unlimited by national borders."[5]

In 1889, when Naka was four, the government, after years of deliberations, promulgated a new Constitution mainly

[5] Hiroaki Sato, with Naoki Inose, *Persona: A Biography of Yukio Mishima* (Berkeley: Stone Bridge Press, 2012), p. 278. The original of Inoue's speech is found in *Mishima Yukio zenshū*, vol. 22 (Shinchōsha, 2002), pp. 656–57.

modeled on that of Germany, thereby instituting constitutional monarchism.[6] In 1894, when he was nine, Japan, in its first open bid to compete with imperialist powers, went to war with China and won.

Yet most such epochal events did not affect Naka's childhood, at least as he remembered it—save the 1894–95 Sino-Japanese War just mentioned. As Naka tells it in one episode of *The Silver Spoon*, the sudden rise of jingoism and the almost instant racial denigration of a people whom the Japanese had admired throughout their history provoked a deep sense of indignation in the ten-year-old boy. Zhou Zuoren, the Chinese writer quoted above, was particularly touched by this episode: by the mid-1930s, when he was translating passages from *The Silver Spoon*, Japan's imperialist approach to China following the start of its westernization efforts had created an intractable quagmire in his own country.

In regard to "traditions," another government policy deserves mention. To promote the "civilization and enlightenment" that the West embodied, it early on declared the Five Festivals[7] and other traditional observances outmoded and pernicious. Here, the purpose was not so much to promote westernization as to strengthen emperor worship that till then had barely existed, as was clear in the new national holidays introduced to replace the festivals and events. Among them were the Tenchōsetsu ("heavenly-son's-longevity-event") to mark the Emperor's Birthday (November the third) and the Kigensetsu ("national-origin-event") to mark the day

6 It may be more accurate to say that Itō Hirobumi, the principal formulator of the Meiji Constitution, consulted the German jurist Rudolf von Gneist and the German scholar of public administration Lorenz von Stein to buttress the constitutional concepts he and Iwakura Tomomi had already developed. Also, Itō had the German legal scholar Karl Friedrich Hermann Roesler participate in the drafting of the Constitution. George Akita, *Foundations of Constitutional Government in Modern Japan, 1868–1900* (Cambridge, MA: Harvard University Press, 1967), pp. 58–66.

7 The New Year, Hina-matsuri or Girls' Day (Third Month), Tango no Sekku or Boys' Day (Fifth Month), Tanabata or the Star Festival (Seventh Month), and Jūgoya or Chrysanthemum Day (Ninth Month). All originated in China but were much modified in the process of being adopted.

Japan is supposed to have been founded (February the eleventh). That day, says the semi-mythological account of the *History of Japan* (*Nihon shoki*, compiled in 720), Jinmu ascended the throne as first emperor.

These high-handed impositions confused and puzzled the citizenry, and those who devised them knew it. In *Questions and Answers on Enlightenment* (*Kaika mondō*, 1874), one of the many books written to impress upon the populace the requirements of the dramatically new era, Kyūhei (or Dated Dave, we might say) is made to ask Kaitarō (Enlightened Ernest):

> Since the calendar was changed [from the lunar to the solar, in 1873], important event days such as the Five Festivals and the Bon have been abolished to celebrate incomprehensible days such as the Tenchōsetsu and Kigensetsu. That April the eighth is the Shakyamuni's Birthday and the sixteenth of the Bon is the day the lid of Hell's Cauldron opens, even infants who beat dogs know, sir. As to the origins of the Tenchōsetsu and Kigensetsu, even an old fogy like me, Dated Dave, who eats beef pots, doesn't know that, sir.

Dated Dave's reference to "beef pots" (*gyūnabe*; today's sukiyaki) is a wry comment on a dietary reversal. Buddhist Japan had not touched beef, but Westerners brought in the custom of eating it. Dated Dave is suggesting that he's been civilized and enlightened enough to eat meat, but he is not enlightened enough to comprehend the newly created holidays. He goes on to mock the Japanese flag, another new imposition on the people who did not have anything like a national emblem till then, with "lantern marches" now required on celebratory days.

> When it comes to the government forcing us to take out a banner, which looks like a shop sign for selling fire, and lanterns, so as to celebrate days such as these that don't exist in the minds of us ordinary folks, there's just no reason for it, sir. After all, celebration days are the days ordinary folks celebrate when they feel like celebrating together. In

the event, sir, I think forcing us to celebrate the days which we don't feel like celebrating is most unreasonable.[8]

Enlightened Ernest answers, with an air of authority, why the government's action is not at all unreasonable, and Dated Dave is made to appear persuaded. That, at any rate, is the setup of the book.

The "ordinary folks" were not so readily persuaded, of course. As is usually the case with any such period of upheaval, by the time of Naka's birth the pendulum had swung back and people had revived, even reinvigorated, many of the pre-Restoration customs and observances—assuming that they had ever abandoned them. As the professor and translator of English literature Baba Kochō (Katsuya: 1869–1940) noted as he fondly recollected what Tokyo was like during the Meiji period (1868–1912), they probably revived their old ways because the Meiji revolution was "a victory and conquest by an advanced few over the unadvanced masses" and those few in the vanguard did not give much thought to the fact that customs and similar festivities take a long time to take root.[9]

Ancestors and Family

Naka Kansuke's lineage can be traced to a physician named Kansetsu in the seventeenth century in a small fiefdom called Imao, in Mino (today's Gifu)—although Imao was officially recognized as an independent fiefdom only in 1868 as the Meiji Regime started. Because of his special medical skills, Kansetsu was given a respectable annual income, measured in rice, of one hundred and fifty *koku* or nearly eight hundred bushels. But the stipends so measured were deceptive, with the actual take far smaller, and his descendants' stipends were further reduced. In addition, the social and political upheavals in the last phase of the

8 Ogawa Tameji, *Questions and Answers on Enlightenment (Kaika mondō)*, 1874. Quoted in Inoue Kiyoshi, *Meiji ishin*, vol. 20 of *Nihon no rekishi* (Tokyo: Chūō Kōron Sha, 1966), pp. 222–23.

9 Baba Kochō, *Meiji no Tōkyō* (Tokyo: Shakai Shisō Sha, 1992; originally, 1942), pp. 98–99.

Tokugawa shogunate severely squeezed the samurai's economic life. By the time of Naka's father, Kan'ya (1842–1906), the family had fallen on hard times, with his income put at thirteen *koku,* subsistence level for a samurai.

The new government also took steps to reduce the status of the samurai as a whole, and that didn't help, either. In 1869, samurai stipends were drastically cut by decree. In 1872, the existing four classes—samurai, peasants, artisans, and merchants, in that order—were reclassified into three—nobility *(kazoku),* gentry *(shizoku),* and commoners *(heimin).* Although Naka Kan'ya belonged to the gentry class, which was made up of former samurai (except for those with an annual income of ten thousand *koku* or more, who were made to join the titled class), now there existed "no impassable barrier between the different classes," as the early Japanologist Basil Hall Chamberlain (1850–1935) put it.[10] That meant a greater easing of mobility among classes than had existed during the Edo period (1600–1867), although the sense of class remained strong until after Japan was defeated, in 1945, and the class system was abolished altogether. In 1876, the samurai were stripped of their sword-carrying privileges.

But Naka Kan'ya had a special relationship to the man he served, Takenokoshi Masamoto (1851–1910), the first (and last) lord-president of Imao, and that might have helped. Masamoto's wife was his adopted daughter. With the advent of the new regime, Kan'ya was given a high police rank of *gon-daizoku,* then *daizoku.* In 1872, he moved to Tokyo with his lord as his deputy house-administrator *(kafu).* The following year, Kan'ya and the house-administrator *(karei)* started an import company called Yōhakusha that dealt in German silver, nickel, and aluminum to help build the Takenokoshi family's finances. The company, with Kan'ya as its president, apparently did well.

When Kansuke was four, Kan'ya built a new house in the Yamanote, an area preferred by the gentry class, moving his family there for the health of his sickly wife Shō and his sickly son Kansuke. Much

10 Chamberlain, p. 95.

later, when Kansuke sold the house and other properties that Kan'ya had bequeathed, he made a sizable amount of money. Unlike many members of his former class, Kan'ya had the ability to deal with the profound social changes taking place at the time. His earlier poverty, in any case, had become part of family lore by the time of Kansuke's birth and was hardly a factor in his boyhood.

Naka Kan'ya Recalls His Past

In *The Silver Spoon*, Naka described how his father used to recall his past in the evenings, surrounded by his family and his carpenter—although, as we will see, he later revised his memoir extensively and in doing so, dropped the following passages along with many others.[11] This scene occurs in the new house in the Yamanote.

Headcarpenter Tatsu-san, who worked for us, moved into the small house on our premises. He was thirty-plus, a genuine Edo-ite male in his prime, and terribly tough-minded. His boastful talk was all about things like how in a worksite fight somewhere he took on three men and beat them all up by himself, or how when, at age sixteen, he ran away from his boss and went to Ise begging all the way,[12] he went over a mountain pass someplace with just a single cucumber to eat, or how, once, while he was doing repairs at his ancestral temple, the resident monk was so blatantly greedy that it made him annoyed and he removed all the nails from the ceiling he was making so that when the monk went, unwittingly, up to inspect it, he crashed right down with the

11   The original can be found in the first of the seventeen volumes of the "complete works" (*zenshū*) of Naka Kansuke: *Naka Kansuke zenshū*, vol. I (Tokyo: Iwanami Shoten, 1989), pp. 239–40.

12   Ise, Mie, is where the Ise Shrine is, and thus may be called Japan's Mecca. "Pilgrims come to this temple from all over Japan," João Rodrigues, S. J. (1561–1633), observed. Michael Cooper, comp. and ann., *They Came to Japan: An Anthology of European Reports on Japan, 1543–1640* (Berkeley: University of California Press, 1965), p. 298.

whole ceiling and was so dazed he couldn't stand up for a while.

"That damned monk came down with a fever and was laid up for three days," Tatsu-san said. He would wear layer upon layer of carpenters' liveries from several places like a formal twelve-layered garment[13] whenever he kept my father company during his evening drink; his party piece being mimicking Kinokuniya's voice, he'd do it for a while, then praise himself by calling out, "Kinokuniya!"[14]

My father, who sat in front of his *sturdy* tray[15] that was as large as 2.5 foot square with dishes and plates twice as large as regular ones lined up on it, would roll a hot piece of boiled tofu on his tongue, pour sake into his favorite thick cup and drink it down, then pour and drink again. Many of us were lined up around him, beginning with my mother and aunt, along with us six siblings, Tatsu-san, our nurse and maids. Each time Tatsu-san's vocal mimicking was over, my father would laugh loudly like a broad-minded man, "Ha-ha-ha."

On such occasions, he would also tell us children what things were like in the old days: how, close to the Imperial Restoration, when he was eighteen, all he received from his father upon his death was a single cabinet and a few pennies, the rest being debts, or how, after the replacement of fiefdoms with prefectures,[16] he, being no exception himself, became so destitute that when he had free

13 *Jūnihitoe*. Heian noble women's dress. Dalby, pp. 228–69. As Dalby explains, "twelve layers" is an exaggeration. Dalby was inspired to write this book by her interest in this elegant dress and its great range of colors.

14 "Kinokuniya" is one of the "house titles" (*yagō*) of kabuki actors: Here, Sawamura Sōjūrō VI (1838–86). In kabuki, an aficionado in the audience cries out the house title of the actor when his scene reaches a climax or when his acting is particularly good—à la "bravo!"

15 The tray (*zen*) described here is now used only on special occasions, but in Naka's boyhood it was used daily, with his father apparently using an exceptionally large one. Bernardino de Avila Girón, the Spanish merchant who visited Japan from 1594 to 1598, reported: "I will not praise Japanese food for it is not good, albeit it is pleasing to the eye, but instead I will describe the clean and peculiar way in which it is served. Usually each person eats at his own table. These tables are generally square in shape, measuring two spans either way; some are completely flat, while others stand on four short legs about two fingers long, with a ridge,

time from work for his lord, he moonlighted selling roof tiles and making kite frames. Whenever sake and smugness had produced their good effects, he'd start talking about the *hiiyari-dondoko-don* Western-style military drills [with fife and drum] that had been introduced around that time, even making us hear the odd Dutch words he said he used when commanding his men in front of his lord, dressed in his battlefield samurai jacket. At his side, my mother, who had been his loyal spouse throughout the miserable life of the past, would agree with him unreservedly at every point. My aunt, who had gone through similar circumstances but ended up a cruel loser, would listen with deep feelings as she recalled the past, while the head carpenter, as if plunged into a smoke screen, would single-mindedly keep marveling at everything he heard.

Kansuke's Older Brother Kin'ichi

In considering Naka Kansuke's life and writing, we cannot ignore his older brother Kin'ichi. Kansuke was Kan'ya's fifth son, but three of his older brothers had died young, leaving only the second oldest, Kin'chi (1871–1942), alive. Kansuke also had two older sisters and two younger sisters.

Kin'ichi studied internal medicine at the Imperial University of Tokyo. In 1902, the year he married Nomura Sueko, Viscount Nomura Yasushi's daughter, then nineteen years old, the government sent him to Germany to study medicine further and, upon his return, in 1905, he was appointed professor at the Fukuoka Medical School (upgraded to the Imperial University of Kyūshū, in 1911).

But less than four years after his return from Germany and at the height of his career, Kin'ichi suffered a severe stroke and, born bully that he was, became a half-crazed

also about two fingers in height, running along the sides," etc. (Cooper, *They Came to Japan*, p. 194).

16 Reform of municipal administration following the German model that the new government introduced in 1871.

invalid, speech-impeded and violent. For the next thirty years, he would wreck not just the life of his wife Sueko—the woman that Kansuke's friend, the eminent philosopher and educator Abe Yoshishige (1883–1966), described as someone "I respected and loved the most, who was attractive and at the same time admirable, in addition to being a natural person who was furthest from malice"[17]—but his brother Kansuke's life as well. With him incapacitated, Japan's family system then prevailing thrust Kansuke into the position of family head to take on what he called "the house burden."

Kansuke adored his sister-in-law Sueko—he simply called her "my older sister" *(ane)*—as sharer in this difficult situation, and he wrote heartfelt essays about her in diary style, among them *Breaking the Ice (Kōri o waru)*, which covered a period after a stroke—subarachnoid hemorrhage—had cut her down, in 1940, and *Honey Bee (Mitsubachi)*, which covered a period after her death, in 1942. He called her a "honey bee" for resolutely taking care of her husband while assiduously discharging domestic work despite Kin'ichi's "hostility, cruel treatment, and illness," and her "bleak solitude for forty years, her difficulties for forty years."[18]

Natsume Sōseki and *The Silver Spoon*

Naka went to the First Higher School, then to the Imperial University of Tokyo. His professor of English at both was Natsume Sōseki (1867–1916). Sōseki resigned from his university post in early 1907 and joined the daily newspaper *Asahi Shinbun* as an "associate" to write full time—with the agreement that he would write at least one full-length novel a year for the paper. Several months later, Naka switched from English to Japanese literature at the university. He graduated in 1909.

While Sōseki was still teaching, some of his students began to visit him, and these visitors, later to become prominent writers, scholars, and educators, would be called

17 Quoted in Tomioka, pp. 121–22.

18 Naka Kansuke, *Mitsubachi, Yosei* (Tokyo: Iwanami Shoten, 1985), p. 20.

Sōseki's "disciples" *(monjin, deshi)*. Naka, too, visited him, and also would become sufficiently well-known, but with his reserve, aloofness, and misanthropy, he kept out of the group, even though Sōseki played a pivotal role in his debut as a writer. According to *Natsume Sensei and I (Natsume Sensei to watashi)*, the essay Naka wrote for the November 1917 issue of *Mita Bungaku*,[19] he liked the three novellas collected in Sōseki's *Quails' Cage (Uzura-kago)*,[20] published in 1907, the one called *Grass Pillow (Kusamakura)* most of all, but he didn't like *I Am a Cat (Wagahai wa neko de aru)*, Sōseki's first work, which had won him plaudits and popularity. He found the title itself "repellent," he wrote. He made it plain in the essay, and probably in person, that he wasn't a good, let alone admiring, reader of his former professor's writings.

Still, it was to Sōseki that Naka sent the childhood memoir he had written and called *The Silver Spoon*. Sōseki, a remarkably tolerant man despite the periodically severe bouts of neurasthenia that he suffered,[21] was impressed, and pushed for its publication in the *Asahi Shinbun*. He wrote to an editor at the daily:

> . . . The other day I had requests to read two works. Both are interesting and the *Asahi* would in no way embarrass itself by carrying them with the thought of introducing unknown writers. One of them in particular, which is by a bachelor of arts, a man named Naka Kansuke, is a record of how he grew up until he was eight or nine, and it is by far the worthier for the *Asahi* to introduce in its pages, I believe, because his prose is equipped with freshness and dignity and also his way of writing is genuine. The only thing is that, unlike novels written to be illustrated, it doesn't have much drama *(henka)* or development *(shinten)*. . . .[22]

The *Asahi* accepted Sōseki's word and

19 Included in Watanabe.
20 Initially, the three novellas were not published as individual books.
21 Howard Hibbett, "Natsume Sōseki and the Psychological Novel," in Donald Shively, ed., *Tradition and Modernization of Japanese Culture* (Princeton: Princeton University Press, 1971), pp. 312–20.
22 Tomioka, pp. 171–72.

serialized *The Silver Spoon,* from April 8 to June 4, 1913. Sōseki, in fact, did not just recommend the memoir. He gave the young Naka a good deal of advice about his writing: spelling errors, the tendency to ignore paragraphs, to write interminable sentences in kana syllabary, not using kanji, "Chinese characters," appropriately.[23] In the Japanese writing system, kanji serve as distinct syntactical markers.

When Naka wrote a sequel the next year, Sōseki again "liked it very much," he wrote to Naka, even as he noted that it is "eventless *(jiken ga nai)* so that philistines may be unable to read it."[24] Again the *Asahi* accepted his recommendation and serialized the work, from April 17 to June 2, 1915, this time under the title of *The Contrarian (Tsumujimagari).* It would become Part II of *The Silver Spoon.*

When the second serialization was complete, Sōseki even offered to pen an introduction to the childhood memoir to have it published in book form. But Naka said it was too short and, when Sōseki suggested he add another piece to fatten the volume, he said he disliked the piece Sōseki named. So nothing came of it.

Publication in Book Form and Growing Popularity

In 1922, Naka's classmate Iwanami Shigeo (1881–1946) published the memoir through the imprint he had started, Iwanami Shoten, as a paste-up of the newspaper serializations, with some deletions. Four years later, the same publisher issued it as a regular book. For this edition Naka made extensive revisions and deletions to shape the story into its present form, cutting not only repetitions but also passages that placed him in an unduly favorable light. In doing so he reduced the number of installments or episodes in Part I from fifty-seven to fifty-three and in Part II from forty-seven to twenty-two—in the latter, practically obliterating the initial installment format.[25]

The readership clearly began to increase after 1935, when Iwanami included *The Silver*

23 Tomioka, p. 174.
24 Tomioka, p. 183.
25 Tomioka, pp. 240–41.
   Horibe, pp. 13–17.

Spoon in its paperback series and published it with Watsuji's afterword quoted earlier. The reprint history since then is proof of the book's steady popularity.

In October 1943, in the midst of Japan's war with the United States and others that was quickly turning into a colossal defeat for the nation, Naka wrote a poem called "Stamp" (*Ken'in*) and referred to the book's "unexpected twelfth printing," giving its run at 15,000 copies.[26] By then the publishing industry was under tight government control and paper shortages were mounting.[27]

More than a half century later, in 1999, when *The Silver Spoon* reached its 108th printing, Iwanami Shoten brought out a new edition. It, too, did well. By the end of 2006 it had seen eleven printings, selling a grand total of a million copies since the first edition came out, in 1935.[28]

The Silver Spoon has appeared in various other forms and editions, among them two sets of Naka's "complete works": the first set, in thirteen volumes, published by Kadokawa Shoten from 1960 to 1965, and the second, in seventeen volumes, published by Iwanami Shoten from 1989 to 1991. Publishers other than Iwanami have also published the memoir in paperback editions.

If *The Silver Spoon* did not sell particularly well for the first two decades or so, the main reason may well have been what Natsume Sōseki pointed out: lack of drama and development, and lack of events. As contrast, Sōseki could have mentioned one of his own earlier works, *Botchan*, popular since its first publication in 1907. Dealing with the narrator-protagonist's boyhood only at the very outset, the whole novella is meant to be satirical and comical. Still, it is written in terse, vigorous sentences, it is full of drama, it moves fast, and it is packed with entertaining events.

What then are the charms of *The Silver Spoon*?

26 Tanikawa Shuntarō, ed., *Naka Kansuke shishū* (Tokyo: Iwanami Shoten, 1991), pp. 23–25.

27 *Ken'in* refers to the practice in Japan's publishing world, continued until recently, of authors stamping their seal of approval on each copy of their book to confirm the number of copies printed.

28 Publisher's figures given in response to a private inquiry.

Again, Sōseki seems to have hit the mark. Naka recalled his former professor of English literature bringing up in conversation *Tom Brown's School Days,* Thomas Hughes's novel published in 1857, and *Peck's Bad Boy,* George W. Peck's newspaper series first collected in 1883, to observe that "the areas they write about are different." He also mentioned *Boys (Shōnen),* a short story by Naka's contemporary Tanizaki Jun'ichirō (1886–1965), to observe, again, that "it's a little different in character"— an understatement, considering that *Boys* concerns adolescent sadism and masochism. Nagai Kafū (1879–1959), the editor of *Mita Bungaku,* had praised the story extravagantly, along with four other pieces, among them *Shisei (The Tattooer),* putting the new writer Tanizaki in the limelight.

In the following passages in Naka's account, Sōseki is referred to as Sensei, "Teacher":

. . . I heard from a friend that Sensei was defending *The Silver Spoon* all by himself against people's criticisms of it. And I thought, It may be that Sensei likes *The Silver Spoon* more than I do.

I don't remember when, but commenting on *The Silver Spoon,* Sensei said,

"It's not what you'd call *sentimental.*"

Hearing this, I thought someone must have criticized the book using that word ["sentimental"].

. . . It is pretty (*kirei da*), Sensei said. Detailed descriptions, he said. He also said, It has originality. When I heard the word "originality," I thought, I haven't heard that word since my university days. Sensei said, It's a mystery to me that it is so well chiseled and yet that hasn't harmed the truth. I thought, It's no mystery that chiseling for truth shouldn't harm the truth. When talk turned to certain people who'd said *The Silver Spoon* isn't interesting at all, Sensei named some of those who'd said it was not interesting, and said, So-and-so finds interesting only things like the two people eating a single peach. Also he went so far as to say, So-and-so should be made to read something like this, as if it were terribly inappropriate that some should find uninteresting what others find interesting. . . .

One can well believe Sōseki's words as Naka recollected them because, as these passages indicate, Naka was a contrarian who would not hesitate to contradict to his face anyone offering words of praise. Sōseki called him a *henjin*, an oddball or eccentric, Naka admitted.

There is also a certain "nostalgic" purity to *The Silver Spoon*. This quality may have struck some of Naka's contemporary readers as mundane and unexciting, but it may be the most pleasurable aspect to the readers of later generations, as Iwanami's survey in 1987 showed. In that survey to mark the sixtieth anniversary of its launch of the paperback series, the publisher asked "readers representing various fields" to name the three books in the series that stayed in their hearts, and *The Silver Spoon* came out on top. (The number one cumulative seller was Plato's *Apology, Crito, and Phaedo of Socrates*.) Many of the three hundred respondents reported that the memoir depicts the child's world so sensitively, so beautifully, that it "purifies their mind." But they most commonly said that it revived for them their own childhood and boyhood.[29]

In this regard, Tanizaki Jun'ichirō's *Childhood Years (Yōshō jidai)*[30] presents an illuminating contrast to *The Silver Spoon*. Both cover about the same period in history and the author's life, from the second half of the 1880s to the early 1900s, from infanthood to boyhood. But the similarities end there.

Naka described life mainly in the Yamanote whose inhabitants were largely of the gentry class; Tanizaki, life in the Shitamachi whose inhabitants were predominantly commoners. Naka wrote his memoir in his late twenties to early thirties, apparently relying on memory; Tanizaki wrote his when he was seventy, relying not just on his own memory but also on the recollections of his relatives, acquaintances, and old friends, as well as records, historical commentaries, even

29 Tomioka, pp. 233–35.
30 Paul McCarthy, tr., *Childhood Years: A Memoir* (Tokyo and New York: Kodansha International, 1988).

classical texts. Naka, in reliving the past, limited himself to the immediate surroundings and the people that entered his sphere as a child and the senses and emotions they provoked; Tanizaki extended his interest to the overall setting and age to reconstruct his youthful days over a span of a dozen years.

But the most remarkable difference may be what Watsuji Tetsurō, in his afterword to the 1935 edition of *The Silver Spoon,* pointed out as "unprecedented": that it is "neither a child's world as a grownup sees it, nor is it anything like childhood memories recollected in a grownup's experience." Instead, it is a simple, precise record of things a child observed and perceived. *Childhood Years,* in contrast, is either or both of what Watsuji judged Naka's memoir was not. Tanizaki at times leaves a child's sensibilities and thoughts far afield, bringing in a retrospective view—e.g., "now that I think of it"—to reinforce what he thinks he felt, how he reacted to things and people. What he wrote is a layered account of *la recherche du temps perdu.*

The Silver Spoon in Naka's Oeuvre

Naka, as noted, has left us a sizable body of literary work. It includes fables collected in *Stories of Birds* and other fictions. A few of them are highly realistic. One of them, *Dogs (Inu),* which he wrote in 1922, was too much so for its time in its descriptions of sexual intercourse, albeit between dogs. The publisher of the story, Iwanami Shigeo, was summoned to the Metropolitan Police Department and agreed to censor certain descriptions, leaving them blank. The story was banned altogether anyway.[31] It dealt with an old Indian ascetic who, overcome by lust for a young beautiful woman, turns both her and himself into dogs so he may have sex with her to his heart's content.

Naka wrote this and a similar story, *Devadatta,*[32] when he was contemplating the

31 Tomioka, pp. 281–83.
32 The title of Chapter 12 of the Lotus Sutra. Naka's story is based to some extent on one of "the three Pure Land Sutras," Amitayurdhyana Sutra, or Sutra of Immeasurable Life.

choice of either "suicide or priesthood,"[33] and imposing a stoic's life on himself. For a period he ate such poor food that he suffered from severe beriberi. It was at this time that he told himself: "If being in love with someone aims at sexual acquisition or makes it a prerequisite, I do not have love nor do I want to have love. I am someone determined to control all lusts, purify them, make full use of them through wisdom, and turn them into material for moral improvement."[34]

Except for such fables and fictions, Naka's writings largely consist of what he chose to call *shōhin*, "small pieces," and what others character-ize as *nikki-tai zuihitsu*, "diary-style essays." They are both recordings of daily occurrences and observations shaped into essays. The Naka scholar Watanabe Gekisaburō has compared them to one large river called "life chronicle" that began with *The Silver Spoon*.[35]

These seemingly innocuous pieces were not without problems, how-ever. The novelist Nogami Yaeko (1885–1985), for one, noted in her diary, as early as 1935, that Naka's approach required him to constantly "ideal-ize" himself, turning him into "a kind of hypocrite." In 1951 she observed that she was "put off" by the way Naka "shut himself up in an egotistic, self-righteous shell . . . never forgetting to bemedal himself as a good boy whenever he talks about himself." In 1954 she found it "troublesome" that he so readily invoked his "admirers."[36] Indeed, not many writers would think of turning a collection of fan letters into an essay, as he did in *Yosei (Remaining Life)*, published in 1947. It was largely made up of responses by the readers of his *Honey Bee*. Some of them came from the front in wartime.

The scholar of French literature Ikushima Ryōichi also sensed Naka's "ego-tism" under the gentle exterior of his person-ality and writing, noting that he imagined Naka "always battling this *egotism* in the innermost part of his heart."[37]

Still, Nogami's criticisms are notable in part because she once confessed her love

33 Watanabe, p. 236.
34 Tomioka Taeko's after-word to Naka Kansuke's *Inu* (Tokyo: Iwanami Shoten, 1985), p. 128.
35 Watanabe, pp. 233–35.
36 Tomioka, pp. 343–55.
37 Ikushima Ryōichi's after-word to *Mitsubachi, Yosei*, p. 212.

for Naka and evidently remained fond of him, even after marrying his classmate, Toyoichirō, who went on to become a distinguished educator. Weakling that he may have been as a boy, Naka grew to be a tall, good-looking man: Kobori Annu (1909–98), a daughter of the great Meiji writer Mori Ōgai (1862–1922) and herself a writer, remembered him for his "deeply sculpted, Nordic-style, fine features and his towering, magnificent physique that placed him slightly apart from the Japanese."[38] He did not lack lady friends, for all his resolve regarding sexual desire. He remained unmarried until 1942, when he turned fifty-seven: his bride, Shimada Kazu, was forty-two years old.

The Style of *The Silver Spoon* and Its Translation

Perhaps to recreate the thought processes of a child, Naka often places amid short declarative sentences long, sinuous ones that take full advantage of the remarkable tolerance that the Japanese language has for sentences loosely linked by connectives. He uses direct and indirect speech, sometimes with quotation marks, sometimes without. He uses punctuation arbitrarily. Though these features are not necessarily what sets Naka apart as a writer, I have tried to reproduce them wherever possible; I have always tried to remain faithful to the original in translation. As a result, this translation in many places will not read well, though saying this reminds me of Vladimir Nabokov's caustic remark: "I constantly find in reviews of verse translations the following kind of thing that sends me into spasms of helpless fury: 'Mr. or (Miss) So-and-so's translation reads smoothly.'"[39]

Aside from Naka's style, *The Silver Spoon* has several further features that make its

38 Tomioka, p. 150. Kobori Annu's painter husband, Shirō, did a Naka portrait. It is used as the frontispiece of Iwanami Shoten's *Naka Kansuke zenshū*, vol. 1.

39 Vladimir Nabokov, "Problems of Translation: Onegin in English." Rainer Schulte and John Biguenet, eds., *Theories of Translation: An Anthology of Essays from Dryden to Derrida* (Chicago: University of Chicago Press, 1992), p. 127.

reading less than perfectly smooth—not just for foreign but also for modern-day Japanese readers. Naka is precise in recalling details. He names names—of trees, plants, and insects, not to mention festivals and such, along with their paraphernalia, all with vivid specificity. He introduces a plethora of historical and literary references. Little wonder that some years ago Iwanami decided to provide a couple of dozen endnotes in its paperback edition. In translating *The Silver Spoon*, I have expanded the scope of items to be annotated because things that may still be common knowledge among Japanese readers may not be so among English-language readers.

Finally: How reliable is Naka's memoir?

In his poem "Stamp," referred to earlier, Naka spoke of *The Silver Spoon* as an assemblage of "old remembrances of untruths and truths" *(uso ya makoto no furui tsuioku)*. This description may indeed be true: in most instances, matters one recalls from the past tend to be vague, while things remembered are at best little more than patchworks of facts and nonfacts. What Nabokov said of his own autobiography, *Speak, Memory*, may also apply to *The Silver Spoon*: "The act of vividly recalling a patch of the past is something that I seem to have been performing with the utmost zest all my life," while he defined the process of doing so as "a form of magic . . . a game of intricate enchantment and deception."[40]

You might say Naka Kansuke succeeds beautifully in conjuring his own kind of magic in *The Silver Spoon*.

H.S.

40 Vladimir Nabokov, *Speak, Memory: An Autobiography Revisited* (New York: G. P. Putnam's Sons, 1966), pp. 75, 125.

PART ONE

I

In one of the drawers of the bookcase in my study that contains bric-à-brac, I have long kept a small box. Made of corkwood and with peony-design paper strips pasted at each of the wood joins, it appears to have originally contained tobacco imported from the West. There's nothing especially beautiful about it, but for the subdued tone and soft touch of the wood, and the warm puffy sound it makes as the lid is shut, it is still one of my favorite things. It is packed with a cowry shell,[1] camellia seeds, and other bits and pieces that were my playthings when I was a child, but I have never forgotten that among them is a curiously shaped silver spoon. It has a round bowl about half an inch wide and a short handle that is slightly curved. It is thick, so if held at the end of the handle, it feels unexpectedly heavy. From time to time I take it out of the box, carefully wipe off the tarnish, and gaze at it without ever growing bored. Looking back now, it was a very long time ago that I happened to find this small silver spoon.

From the beginning our house has had a cupboard. When I grew tall enough to reach its upper part on tiptoe, I would open its doors and pull out its drawers just for their different gives and squeaks. One of the two miniature drawers, side by side with tortoiseshell handles, was warped and hard for a child to open, but that only increased my curiosity until one day, after a struggle, I finally forced it out. My heart pounding with excitement, I tipped its contents onto the tatami and found, among weights for scrolls and netsuke, the silver spoon. For some reason I wanted it and immediately took it to my mother.

"May I have this?"

Mother, who was in the dining room working with her glasses on, looked a little surprised. "You must take good care of it," she said.

Such prompt permission was unusual, and I was at once happy and somewhat let down. The drawer had been broken when

---

1   Used as an amulet for safe childbirth.

KOYASUGAI: COWRIES

we moved from Kanda to the Yamanote and even mother had forgotten about the silver spoon and its peculiar history. This she told me while continuing to sew.

2

When I was born, my mother had a particularly difficult labor. Even the old midwife who was renowned at the time gave up, so they had to call in a doctor of Chinese medicine named Mr. Tōkei. Yet his decoctions just didn't seem to help my delivery at all, and my father, losing his temper, started to snap at him. So Mr. Tōkei, totally at a loss, read out this or that passage from his book of medicine, trying to prove that he'd made no mistake in his prescription, while desperately waiting for the tides to turn. After giving mother such trouble, I was finally born. But the way Mr. Tōkei, driven to distress, moistened his finger with saliva to turn the pages of his book one by one as he scooped various medicines from his medicine case remained in the realistic mimicry of the clownish aunt who brought me up, and for a long time afterward it afforded a never-failing source of laughter in my family.

Not only was I weak when born, but soon after birth I developed a terrible rash that covered my head and face, making me look "like a pine cone," according to mother. As a result I had to continue being cared for by Mr. Tōkei. To prevent the rash from affecting me internally, he made me take coal-black electuary and powdered rhinoceros horn every day. Since an ordinary spoon was awkward for scooping medicine into a child's small mouth, my aunt found this spoon somewhere and gave me the medicine with it throughout my illness. When I heard the story, though unaware of any of it until then, I developed something akin to a fond memory of the spoon and decided never to let it go.

Because I hardly slept night or day for the itchiness of the rash all over me, mother and aunt took turns tapping the scabs with a small rice-bran bag containing adzuki beans. When they did this, I looked happy, twitching my little nose, I was told. I remained weak and hyper-sensitive until I was quite a bit older and had headaches as often as every three days. So my family would tell visitors that I'd suffered brain damage because they'd tapped my head with a rice-bran bag. I caused a lot of trouble coming into this world. And partly because my mother didn't fully recover from child-birth and partly because there was then no other help available, it was decided that my aunt, who was living with us at that time, would take care of me, apart from when my mother breastfed me.

3

My aunt's spouse was called Sōemon and in their province was a samurai, though of low rank. But both husband and wife were such good-natured, good-for-nothing people that with the coming of the Meiji Restoration they fell on hard times. Subsequently, after Sōemon died during the cholera epidemic in a certain year of Meiji,[2] it became even more difficult to keep the household going, and in the end my aunt had to place herself in the care of my family. Back in their own

2 The outbreak in the tenth year of Meiji (1877) claimed 6,817 people. It came a few months after the government promulgated the Cholera Prevention Law. But whether it was the one that killed Sōemon is not clear, for cholera outbreaks were rather common. For example, Clara Whitney (1860–1936), in her diaries, noted that Ulysses S. Grant, visiting Japan in 1879, had to avoid Kobe because of an outbreak there, which is said to have killed more than 100,000 people, and that in 1890 her dear friend Mrs. Murata died in the epidemic. See *Clara's Diary: An American Girl in Meiji Japan* (Tokyo and New York: Kodansha International, 1975), p. 251 and p. 171. In September 1886, there was another outbreak in Tokyo. This one also killed more than 100,000 people. (Modern researchers think those tolls are way too high.) One of the earliest recorded cholera out-breaks in Japan may have occurred in 1674. Maruya Saiichi, *Chūshingura to wa nani ka* (Tokyo: Kōdansha, 1984), p. 127. A worldwide outbreak reached Japan in 1822. The cholera out-break in 1858 killed 28,000 people.

OFUKUSAMA: MR. AND MRS. GOOD LUCK

province, not only those who were hard-pressed but also those who were not would take advantage of my aunt and her husband's good nature and borrow money from them, and the two of them would make a loan even when they had hardly a thing to eat themselves. As a result, they were soon almost bankrupt. At which point, those who had borrowed money didn't hesitate to laugh at them behind their backs.

"They're just too good-natured for words, aren't they," they'd sneer.

It wasn't that the couple, once they became really hard up, didn't go to those who might have been compliant and ask for a repayment of their loan. But they'd then get all teary-eyed at the least pitiful story the borrowers told them and would come home again repeating, "What a pity, what a pity!"

Also, they were terribly superstitious. Once, they bought a pair of white mice somewhere, saying they were the messengers of the Lord Daikoku,[3] and bred them with extreme care, calling them Mr. and Mrs. Luck.[4] The mice multiplied, as you'd expect mice to do. Finally, swarms of them were scurrying about the house. This the couple regarded as a great blessing, and on any commemorative day they would cook rice with adzuki beans or pile roasted beans high in a square wooden measure and offer them to the mice. And so, when people had borrowed what little money they had and the carriers of good luck had eaten all the rice they kept in their rice casket, my aunt and uncle, with no possessions beyond the clothes they were wearing, and now counting on my family, came to us all the way from their own province—we having moved here to accompany our lord. Soon afterward, Sōemon died of cholera, leaving my aunt an utterly indigent widow. Speaking of that time, my aunt explained that

[3] One of the Seven Deities of Good Luck, he embodies wealth and prosperity. He is usually shown as a figure carrying a large bag on his left shoulder and a magic mallet in his right hand, standing or sitting on rice bags. Mice often accompany him to suggest that his supply of rice is inexhaustible and can accommodate any number of them.

[4] The white mice here are probably a variety of what later (in Episode 1.23) are called "Nanjing mice," having originally been bred in China as pets. In Japan breeding them became very popular in the mid-18th century.

korori—"dropping dead"—raged in Japan because Christians in a foreign country had sent an evil fox over the waters to kill off the Japanese, and that that had happened twice, "the one *korori*" and "the three *korori*."[5] Sōemon came down with "the one *korori*" and was taken to a quarantine ward where they just let the patients, who had turned black with the *korori* fever, die, without even allowing them to drink water. All the patients died with their intestines burned, she said.

For my aunt, bringing me up was the only pleasure she had in life. Indeed, it may well have been because she had no house, no child, was old, and had nothing to look forward to, but there was another, mysterious reason she cared for me to such a superstitious degree. When my brother, who'd be just a year ahead of me if he were still alive today, died of epilepsy soon after birth, my aunt grieved as if her own child had died, weeping aloud and wailing, "Be born again, be born again!"

So, when I was born the following year, she believed that with the grace of the Lord Buddha the deceased child had been reborn and decided to take inordinately good care of me. Indeed, how happy and moved she must have been to think that this child, covered with dirty scabs though he was, had not forgotten her prayers and had abandoned his house on the Lotus of Paradise just for her! Accordingly, after I turned four or five, when she gave offerings to the Buddhist altar—the happy role of my devout aunt every morning—she would from time to time take me to the altar and try to make me, a child still unable to read the first letter of the Japanese syllabary, memorize my brother's Buddhist name, Ikkan Soku'ō Dōji, or The Boy Who Responded to a Single Call, which was, according to her thinking, nothing less than my own name while I was in Paradise.

5   Another name of cholera after the non-endemic disease came to Japan. It cleverly derives from the pseudo-onomatopoeic adjective *korori*, which describes a ready submission or death. What "one" and "three" mean is not clear, although cholera was also called *mikka-korori*, "three-day death," because of its swift effect.

4

Perhaps not inside the house, but every time I went out of it, even by a single step, I would cling to my aunt's back. But my aunt must also have been reluctant to let me go, even while moaning that her hip hurt or that her arms were going numb. I probably did not step on the ground until about five, and when I was put down to do things like adjusting my sash, I felt as if the earth was swaying and had to hold on for dear life to the hem of her sleeve. In those days I had a pale green sash tied high on my chest with a small bell and a Mount Narita[6] amulet hanging from it. That was my aunt's idea. The amulet, of course, was so I wouldn't be injured, wouldn't fall into a ditch or a river. And the bell was so she might hear it if I was separated from her and got lost, so she could come to find me. Her eyes were hazy and couldn't see far. But for the child who never left her back all year long both the bell and the amulet were utterly pointless.

Because I was sickly, my intellect was slow to develop. Also, I was prone to extreme depressions and seldom showed a smile, except to my aunt. I hardly spoke and barely responded even when a family member talked to me, merely giving a silent nod and then only when I was in the best of my moods. I was such a weakling and so shy that just the sight of a stranger's face would prompt me to hide my face on my aunt's back and weep. I was so thin that my ribs showed, and the only big thing about me was my head. And because my eyes were so deep in their sockets, everyone in my family called me

6   A city in Chiba famous for its Shinshō temple, which, in turn, is famous for its statue of Fudō (Acala). Papinot: Fudō is a "Buddhist divinity (probably the same as Dainichi) which has power to foil the snares of the devils. Fudō is represented with a dreadful expression and surrounded by flames; in the right hand he holds a sword *(gōma no ken)* to strike the demons, the left hand, a cord *(baku no nawa)* to bind them." Emperor Suzaku (923–52) is said to have presented Fudō with a sword, and "the touch alone of this sword is said to cure insanity and deliver from the possession of the fox."

AUNT CARRY KANSUKE

PART ONE | *11*

Octopus Boy, Octopus Boy. For myself, I corrupted Kanbō and called myself Kanpon.[7]

7 The author's given name
was Kansuke, abbreviated
to Kan, but since that is
too short in Japanese,
his family is likely to have
called him Kanbō, "Kan
Boy" (like calling William
"Billy Boy"). However,
little Kansuke was unable
to pronounce it, so he
called himself "Kanpon"
instead, "pon" being the
sound of a drum, like
"bom" in English.
8 Red and white sugar-
coated beans; also called
Genji beans. Hōrai (Peng-
lai in Chinese) is a mythi-
cal island east of China
where the inhabitants
maintain eternal youth.
Papinot: "According to a
Chinese legend, one of
the three mountainous
islands of the Eastern
Sea inhabited by genii
(tennin). This tradition
probably has its origin in
the vague notions of the
Chinese concerning the
existence of Japan."
9 Kulika in Sanskrit. Here
it refers to the Dragon
King as the manifestation
of Fudō, who is usually
presented as a dragon
coiling around a sword
erected on a boulder
and trying to swallow
it from its tip—all in
flames. Also see note
6 on Mount Narita in
Episode 1.4.

5

I was born in the most Kanda-esque part, as it were, of Kanda, where fires, fights, drunks, and burglars were daily fare. The houses in the neighborhood that left an imprint on my sickly brain were those on the other side of the street—the rice shop and candy shop, then the tofu shop, the public bathhouse, the lumber yard, and the like. Above all, the black fence of the physician's house further away and the gate to our lord's estate on which we lived were especially conspicuous.

On fine days my aunt would go outdoors with me clinging to her back like a monster from the *Arabian Nights* and visit as many places as she thought I might like or her old legs could manage. At the end of the lane right behind us was a house where Hōrai beans[8] were made: men with Kurikara[9] tattoos wearing only loincloths would pop the beans, singing, headbands gallantly tied around their heads. But I didn't like it there because I was afraid of those demonic men and the rattling noise they made got on my nerves. Whenever I was taken to an unpleasant place like that I would immediately start to snivel, squirming on her back and, without saying a word, would point in the direction I wanted to go. My aunt, who understood her little monster very well, would then never fail to take me to the place I had in mind.

I liked best the fox shrine[10] which still stands at Izumi-chō by the Kanda River. Early mornings when there was no one around I often amused myself throwing stones into the river or pulling the ropes attached to the bell that looked like a huge nut. My aunt would choose a clean stone for me to sit on or simply put me down on the steps of the shrine before offering prayers. The way the perforated coins clattered down the alms box was fun. Whatever god or Buddha it might be, she would first pray: May this child grow strong.

One day, I was looking at the river, clutching the wooden fence while my aunt held my sash from behind. White birds were going back and forth, fishing. The way they flew silently about, gracefully fluttering their long, soft-looking wings, seemed a sight specially arranged for a weak child so susceptible to pain. I was uncommonly elated. But, unfortunately, a woman peddler carrying eggs and wheat cookies on her back came by for a rest, so, as always, I at once clung to my aunt's back. The woman put down her burden, took off the towel from her head, and, as she wiped her neck with it, chatted pleasantries so cleverly that she managed to charm even a coward like me. By the time I had made the timid decision to get down again from my aunt's back, she was opening a box filled with alluring wheat cookies. Picking up a particularly fragrant

10 *Inari*: though two Chinese characters meaning "rice" and "load" are applied to it, the word may derive from *inanari*, "rice growing." Originally it referred to a shrine dedicated to the deities of the "five grains," i.e., rice, wheat, millet, beans, and barnyard grass. At some point in history, however, the female deity of food, Miketsu-kami, was mixed up with the fox deity, of the same name, and, in consequence, *inari* shrines became strongly associated with the fox. In Edo, in particular, *inari* worship was so pervasive that a proverbial saying went alliteratively, *Ise-ya inari ni inu no kuso*, "Ise-ya, inari, and dog shit are everywhere." *Ise-ya* was a shop name most favored by people from Ise Province. In Japanese belief the fox has the magical ability of transforming itself into anything and can be an agent of evil or goodness.

one shaped like an elongated gold coin and, twirling it at the tips of her fingers, she placed it on my palm, cooing, "Good boy, good boy."

My aunt could do nothing but pay for it. Even today, when I see a woman peddler wearily take down from her shoulders a basket pasted over with tanned paper and begin to show me white, reddish eggs half buried in husks and wheat cookies whose fragrance pleasantly assails my nose, I feel the urge to buy all that the poor woman has. The fox shrine has been renovated into a more presentable state and draws many more people today, yet the same willow that was there then still streams in the cool wind.

6

On days when she did not take me to the fox shrine, my aunt would take me to the Field of the Jail, putting enough money for offerings and admissions in her grubby wallet. This was where the famous Tenma-chō Jail[11] used to be—but now there were various sideshows. Also, small merchants would set up rows of booths selling horned turbans cooked in their own shells, popped beans, orange water,[12] and, in season, corn, roast chestnuts, and pasania nuts. At the entrance to a makeshift playhouse with a red-and-white striped curtain around it, a man sitting cross-legged holding wooden clappers and tabs for wooden clogs would occasionally cup his hands around his mouth and call out, *"Hōban! Hōban!"* Another man would hold a chicken right under the snout of a chained wild dog from time to time just to make it squawk. A suspicious-looking *kappa*[13] with a plate on his head splashed

11 From 1677 to 1875, the largest prison complex in Japan. Among the many executed there was the scholar patriot Yoshida Shōin (1830–59).

12 *Mikansui*: sugar water boiled down and then mixed with water flavored with a couple of drops of lemon, grape, or (as here) orange juice.

13 "River kid": an imaginary

about in a pool of water. *Deroren* sermon-givers[14] just blew on the conch and jangled metal sticks, at times reciting, *"Deroren! Deroren!"* These were utterly uninteresting to me, but my aunt liked them and took me to see them often.

Once, a rare thing, a puppet theater was playing, with the billboard picture showing someone looking like the princess I'd seen in picture books dancing with a drum on a grass hill covered with cherry blossoms in full bloom. Elated, I got to go inside, but immediately there was a horrible clanking noise and a creature, face and limbs all red, with his sleeves tucked up with a twisted sash, jumped out, shocking me into tears. Later I was told it was meant to be Tadanobu the Fox of *The Thousand Cherry Trees.*[15]

One of my favorite shows was a wrestling match between ostrich and man. A man with a twisted headband and in body armor of the kind used in fencing would prance out like a challenging bird, and the ostrich, annoyed, would kick at him. Sometimes the ostrich would be wrestled to the ground, his neck held down; sometimes the man, kicked about, would run away, crying, "You got me! You got me!" Once, when the latter had just happened, the man whose turn was next was eating from his lunchbox in a corner when the ostrich, now lingering nearby with his human opponent gone,

water creature that resembles a human boy four or five years old except that his face is like a tiger's and he has a beak as well as a turtle-like carapace on his back. Another of his distinctive features is a plate-like dent atop his head; while out of water he can be active as long as water remains in that dent. He is said to play all sorts of nasty tricks on human beings, especially in the water. It is interesting that later on Naka uses the word "hatch" to describe the creature's birth.

14   *Deroren saimon*: originally minstrels who recited simple sermons as they went from house to house for money. From Edo to Meiji, some of them became stage performers.

15   *Senbon zakura*, more fully *Yoshitsune senbon zakura* or *Yoshitsune and the Thousand Cherry Trees*, a *jōruri* written by Takeda Izumo (d. 1747) in collaboration with two other playwrights. The story combines the love affair between the warrior-commander Minamoto no Yoshitsune (1159–1589) and the dancer Shizuka with the episodes pertaining to some of the vanquished members of the Taira clan. In this typically convoluted *jōruri* play a fox transmogrifies himself into Satō Tadanobu (1141–86), one

sneaked up and suddenly lunged out to snatch the whole lunchbox. The way the man jumped away in consternation was funny and the spectators burst out laughing. But my aunt shed tears.

"The ostrich is starving but can't even get his own meal," she said. "I'm so sorry for him."

of Yoshitsune's staunchly loyal soldiers, to follow the drum originally given by the Emperor to Yoshitsune, now in Shizuka's possession. The reason: the drum uses the hides of the fox's parents who were selected because they had "accumulated virtues for a thousand years" and acquired magical powers as a result. Made during the rule of Emperor Kanmu (737–806) for the imperial ritual of calling forth rain, the drum is named Hatsune, "First Sound," the first cry of joy when it was struck and the rain came down. For a production of a kabuki version of this play, McCarthy, *Childhood Years*, pp. 107–10. For an early account of the relationship between Yoshitsune and Shizuka, Hiroaki Sato, *Legends of the Samurai* (Woodstock, NY: Overlook Press, 1995), pp. 144–50, and for descriptions of Tadanobu, pp. 132–52.

16 Short socks with a separate big toe and hooks above the heels. They were mostly used on formal occasions.

7

For me to be born in the midst of Kanda was as inappropriate as for a *kappa* to be hatched in a desert. All the children in the neighborhood were brats training up to be Kandaites. Not only would they not play with a wimp like me, but they never missed a chance to torment me. In particular, the son of the *tabi*[16] dealer across the street would, if my aunt wasn't very careful, suddenly materialize from behind me, slap me on the cheek, and run away. I was so frightened, I grew afraid of going outside.

When I stayed inside, my aunt would put me up to the high window facing the street, make me clutch the grille, and holding me in that position from behind, tell me the names of the things that came into view—the horse, the cart, and so forth. One of the chickens belonging to the rice dealer across the street was crippled, having once been run over by a cart. Whenever she saw it out on the street, with one leg always tucked up, wing and tail feathers tattered and dusty, my aunt never failed to say, "Poor chicken!" so that I gradually came to dislike seeing it.

Usually I played in a very gloomy three-mat room where the Buddhist altar was. At night it became my bedroom, but sometimes my older sisters worked in it. My two sisters, twelve or thirteen at the time, were grammar school pupils, and I still remember how they used to produce black books from their Western-style envelope-shaped bags, spread them out on the old wooden desks, and practice writing. One of the desks was about three feet wide with two drawers that had brush handles, coiled in paper, stuck into the holes of its two missing knobs. The other one, with shallow drawers, was so small that it could barely accommodate a child's folded legs underneath. These desks, handed down from my brother to these sisters, went on to be handed down from them to me, and then from me to my younger sister, for decades.

If my aunt stood me on the smaller desk to look out the window facing the garden, I could see big azalea bushes growing close to the black fence. On summer days, they swelled with fabulous red flowers and, though in the midst of the town, they enjoyed the occasional visit of butterflies who came to have a meal of honey. The way the butterflies fluttered their wings as if in a great hurry was entrancing to watch. At such times, my aunt would pop her head round from behind my shoulder and say that the black butterfly was the grandpa of the mountain house and the white ones and yellow ones were all princesses. In fact, the princesses were lovely, but the Old Man of the Mountain House looked scary as he flew about, flapping his big coal-black wings.[17]

Also, my aunt would take out for me various toys from a basket with a lid that was meticulously covered with pages from children's books. Of the many toys I had, I loved most a clay dog painted black that we had picked up from the ditch in front of the

17 Japan has several large black swallowtails in the tribe *Papilio*. Which one of the following three species is meant here is not clear: "Black Swallowtail" (*kuroageha*), "Long-tailed Swallowtail" (*onagaageha*), or "Crow Swallowtail" (*karasuageha*).

house. His face had a suggestion of gentleness that I liked. Aunt called him Divine Dog, made a shrine from an empty box and other things, installed him in it, and offered prayers. I also treasured the clumsy Rouge Ox.[18] In fact, these two were the only good friends I had in the whole world.

8

Besides these toys, we had all sorts of weapons such as swords, halberds, bows, and guns. My aunt would turn me into a perfect warrior by equipping me with things like a lacquered helmet and an armor-piercing dagger. Then she'd put on a headband tied at the back and pick up a halberd herself. We'd then each deploy ourselves to either end of the long corridor to engage in mock battle. Now ready, we approached each other slowly, warily. The moment we came face to face at the center of the corridor, I'd call out,

"Are you Shiōten?"

To which the enemy would respond:

"Are you Kiyomasa?"

Then the two in unison:

"Splendid we now meet!"

Then simultaneously we made clattering sound effects with our voices, "*Yā, takatakatakataka!*" jabbing and slashing at each other, the outcome of the fight undecided for a while. This was a scene in the Yamazaki Battle, and I was Katō Kiyomasa, my aunt Shiōten, Governor of Tajima. In time, we'd throw away our weapons and grapple. After some spectacular fighting,

18   *Ushibeni,* literally "ox rouge": red ointment that used to be sold for lip sores during the period called *kan,* "cold," which designates about thirty days before the *setsubun,* in early Second Month. For the purchase of this lip medication on the Day of the Ox, a crudely made bull-shaped toy was given free.

Shiōten would see that Kiyomasa was tired, mutter an indignant "Darn!" and fall. I would then proudly sit astride her back, pressing her down. Profusely perspiring, she played Shiōten to the hilt.

"Don't take me prisoner!" she begged.

"Cut off my head!"

So Kiyomasa would draw his short-sword and try to saw through her wrinkled neck, Shiōten grimacing as she bore it. The fight would end when she closed her eyes, pretending to expire, her body, all strength gone, turning into a rubbery mass. But on rainy days I would insist on repeating the same thing seven or eight times until Shiōten could hardly stand from exhaustion.[19] My aunt nonetheless kept it up, even while whimpering, "Can't do anything about it! Can't do anything about it!" until I became bored with the game and offered to quit. At times, too exhausted, my aunt couldn't get up for a while after she was beheaded. When that happened, I'd fear she might have really died and would gently shake her.

9

During the Myōjin Festival,[20] our neighborhood, because of what it was, would become awfully boisterous, the young men of the town making the rounds of houses, decorating the eaves with red and white paper flowers

19 On the 13th of Sixth Month 1582, Toyotomi Hideyoshi (1536–98), one of the commanders under the warlord Oda Nobunaga (1534–82), defeated another warrior-commander, Akechi Mitsuhide (1526–82), in Yamazaki, between Kyoto and Osaka, following the latter's sudden rebellion and assassination of Nobunaga. The combat between Katō Kiyomasa (1562–1611), a warrior-commander under Hideyoshi, and Shiōten Masazane (d. 1623?), a warrior under Mitsuhide, is likely to be largely a tale imagined by professional narrators and kabuki writers. The name Shiōten (Yomota) Masazane usually comes with the court title Governor of Tajima.

20 *Myōjin*, "bright god": any of the deities so designated by the Engi regulations of 927, or any shrine where one of them presides. Before the end of the Second World War there were at least four *myōjin* festivals a year, but here Naka refers to the Kanda Myōjin Festival, which in his days was held in mid-Ninth Month; today it is held in May.

KANDA MATSURI: KANDA FESTIVAL

and hanging lanterns marked with *tomoe*[21]
or the circle of the sun. I was happy that the
eaves of my house were also decorated with
flowers, with lanterns hanging. On days such
as these some stores would cover the floor
with a carpet and set up the Shijinken.[22]
Two gaudy heads were reverently placed on
a platform along with a large divine sake
bottle offered to them in which forlornly
stood a rolled dedicatory sheet[23] shaped like
a sharply cut bamboo. The golden lion had
glaring silver eyes and was crowned with a
jewel ball,[24] while the scarlet *komainu*[25] had
glittering golden eyes with a wild mane. My
aunt, exercising the same skill that she used
in making the Divine Dog and the Rouge Ox
my friends, made the lion and the *komainu*
friendly to me too, and I didn't burst into
tears despite their scary faces.

Young males of the town, from youths
to children who could barely walk, all in
yukata uniform, headbands stylishly tied
around their heads, sleeves tucked up
smartly with a saffron-colored hemp cord—
I love those hemp cords adorned with bells
and tumblers—wearing no footwear except
white *tabi* and showing off their bulging
calves, strutted about, each waving the
largest *mandō*[26] he could manage. Candle
flames flickered both in the lanterns under
the eaves and in the *mandō* lights that flew
about through the town. From the tips of
the top-heavy *mandō*, dyed red and white,

21 A tadpole-like represen-
tation of water rising in
the middle and flowing
away centrifugally. A cluster of two, three, or four
such figures in a circle is
common.

22 According to some,
shijinken means "four
deities' swords," and it
is also called *shijinki*,
"four deities' flags." These
swords or flags symbolize
the four deities in Chinese
tradition representing the
four corners (directions)
of heaven and the four
seasons: Seiryū (Blue
Dragon, representing east
and spring); Suzaku (Scarlet Sparrow, south and
summer); Genbu (Turtle
or Half-turtle, Half-snake,
north and winter); and
Byakko (White Tiger, west
and autumn). The names
shijinki and *shijinken*
were used interchange-
ably because the tip of
each flag was adorned
with a sword blade. As
Naka, who originally had
shishi komainu, "lion and
koma-dog," goes on to
describe, by his
time the *shijinken* referred
to two gaudily painted
lion heads made of wood.
For *komainu*, see this Episode's note 25, below.

23 *Maki-hōsho. Hōsho* here
refers to white quality
paper used for ceremo-
nial purposes.

24 *Hōshu* or *hōju*: a ball
with a pointed head
with flames rising from
the tip of the head and

LANTERN WITH *TOMOE* DESIGN

hung ample clusters of votive paper. It was pleasing to see them sharply twirled about in the air. At each strategic point of the town a group of adults and children gathered around their barrel *mikoshi*[27] to work out fighting tactics.

My aunt, who was fond of all such things, once took me out as well, after tucking my sleeves up and fitting me with a headband to look like everyone else. With my red flannel pants showing under the tucked up hems of my kimono and my long sleeves tied up with a cord, I was carried on her back, holding a small *mandō*. Unfortunately, one of the brats who had clustered around their Barrel King spotted me and suddenly threw a couple of stones at me.

"Damn!" he shouted. "He's on a woman's back and holding a *mandō*!"

My aunt was struck with fear.

"Please be nice to him, he's a sickly child!" she cried out, and tried to hurry away. But a couple of kids scrambled up to us, grabbed my legs, and tried to pull me down. At once I, clinging to my aunt's neck, burst out crying as if torched. Almost strangled, trying to remove my hands that were tightening around her throat, my aunt eventually managed to get back home. When she regained her breath, she noticed that I had lost the *mandō* she'd gotten me, as well as my wooden clogs—the clogs that I'd treasured, for I could tie them to my feet with pale-blue cords.

two sides. Endowed with magical powers, it produces whatever you wish to have.

25 "Koma dogs": a pair of leonine dog statues placed as talismans at the entrance of a shrine. What *koma* means or refers to is subject to debate. Some say the idea of setting up a pair of guardian lions or lion-headed dogs originated in Egypt and the Middle East.

26 A box-shaped lantern held up with a pole.

27 *Taru-mikoshi*. A *mikoshi* is a portable shrine carried by a group of men on certain festive occasions. For boys, sometimes a sake barrel is substituted for the shrine.

IO

I was so sickly, I seldom stayed away from a doctor for long. Happily, though, Mr. Tōkei of the powdered rhinoceros horn soon died and I began to be cared for by Mr. Takasaka, the "Western doctor." The rash Mr. Tōkei had tried so hard to reduce was beautifully washed away with a Western medicine and I was cured in no time. Despite his fearful face, Mr. Takasaka was very good at charming a child. I had developed an acute distaste for Mr. Tōkei's electuary, but it was with joy that I took to the sweetened liquid medicine the new doctor offered. In time, Mr. Takasaka suggested that, for my mother's health and mine, we move to some place in the Yamanote where there was fresh air. Luckily, because my father had finished most of his work with his lord and had time on his hands, he transferred his duties to someone else and decided to move to the Koishikawa heights.

When at last the day for moving arrived, everyone kept telling me again and again that we would never return to that house. But I was fascinated by all the hubbub made by the people we'd known who came to help. Also, I was happy to share a cart with my aunt in the procession, and I cheerfully prattled on. After a while, the road gradually became less crowded and eventually, after climbing a long clay slope—until then I didn't know what a slope was—we arrived at an old house surrounded by a cedar hedge, which was to be our new residence.

II

In the new neighborhood everyone lived quietly in old houses with cedar hedges encircling them. Most of them were gentry who had lived there for generations, since the former shogunate period. These were people whose status had declined as society changed but who had escaped the misery of falling to a hand-to-mouth existence and led modest but peaceful lives. In this rural district where there weren't many houses, neighbors not only recognized one another, but knew as well how someone's house looked inside. They were that friendly.

Inside the cedar hedges, which were left ragged and untended, there were always vacant lots where fruit trees grew, and the spaces between houses were cultivated either for vegetables or tea, making good playgrounds for children and birds. The vegetable gardens, hedges, and tea plants were all new and delightful to me. The house we moved into was to be only temporary, until a new one was built in a spacious adjacent lot. By the dark, gloomy foyer there grew a "yielding-leaf" tree,[28] whose leaves and red leafstalks I very much liked. Sometimes I would take a slippery leaf from the tree and place it on my lips or cheek. The day after we moved in, someone caught a cicada and gave it to me in a bird cage that happened to be lying around. I had never seen or heard a cicada before and was curious, but whenever I drew near it, it turned violent and made such a jarring noise that I caught a fright.

Every morning I was awakened very early and made to walk barefoot in the grassy lot. For me it was a big job just to memorize the names of the plants growing there, such as shepherd's purse and galingales. My grandmother, then nearly eighty, walked in the dew with me, leaning on her cane, wearing a satin cowl on her hairless head. One morning she buried three choice chestnut seeds in the mound along the backyard fence and said that by the time her grandchildren grew up, they would be able to enjoy the chestnuts. After she died, we called them Grandmother's Chestnut Trees and took very good care of them. They have now grown into magnificent trees, and in autumn we shake down several basketfuls of chestnuts and peel them for our own children.

Soon the construction began. On my aunt's back I went, though somewhat scared, to see the horses and bulls that had brought the lumber and were now tied to the fence. The horses breathed rods of steam out of their large nostrils as they bit off leaves from the cedar, while the bulls vomited up something with a belch and munched and munched on it. I preferred the placid round-faced bulls that kept licking their slimy muzzles to the

28 Yuzuriha, called "yielding-leaf" because the old leaves drop only after the new leaves have fully grown. Its Latin name is *Daphniphyllum macropodum.*

restive, long-faced horses. In the workplace, chisels, adzes, and broad axes made all kinds of noises, exciting even a depressed, sickly child. Among the artisans, Sada-san was a gentle-hearted soul. Whenever I stood beside him, mesmerized by the shavings that smoothly rolled out of his plane before falling to the ground, he would pick up the beautiful ones for me. If you put the shavings of cedar and cypress, as red as blood, into your mouth and sucked on them, you got a taste that made you feel as if your tongue and cheeks were being squeezed. Also, it was delightful to scoop up a puffy mass of sawdust with both hands and spill it, letting it tickle the fingers.

Sada-san always stayed on after the others left. Then he would clap his hands to offer prayers to the moon. I liked hanging around the work site to watch him do this, but his co-workers nicknamed him "Oddball" and used to swear that he would die young.

Then I would look around the worksite after it had been neatly cleaned up, with broom marks, and where now, in contrast to the bustle and din of the day, the evening mist was quietly beginning to settle. Reluctantly I allowed myself to be called back in, to wait for the morrow. I was intoxicated with the fragrance of the wood and felt refreshed as I watched with wonder the new residence growing more complete day by day.

12

29 The name comes from the Chinese temple Shaolinsi that is famous as the place where the Dharma faced the wall for nine years and where karate originated. But it is a common temple name both in China and Japan. Horibe Isao thinks Naka used the name for the temple called Ryūkōji.

Neighboring us to the south, separated by a patch of tea shrubs, was a Zen temple called Shōrin-ji.[29] Because it had large precincts, and perhaps because my devout aunt felt more at home in a temple, she took me there from time to time. Along both sides of the path from the gate to the entrance of the main hall, which was about forty yards long and paved with two rows of stones, there grew tea shrubs that were untended, with cedar and other trees rising up here and there. I often asked my aunt to pick me a tea blossom. The blossoms, not being well attached to the branch, would fall to the ground, many of them all at once, when one was picked. After rain, every tea shrub contained a great many raindrops, sparkling. There is nothing remarkable about a tea blossom itself, yet it has a suggestion of loneliness that is appropriate for childhood memories. The roundish white petals generously enclose yellow stamens, and it blooms in the shade of roundish dark-green leaves. I made a habit of covering my nose with one and smelling it.

To the left, by a well, there was a magnolia tree that, when it bloomed, filled the air with a sweet scent. The squeak of the well's pulley carried over the quiet tea shrubs to my house. On the huge screen placed in the foyer of the main hall there were peacocks painted in brilliant colors. Next to the male bird who was perched up on something, with his tail drooping like a straw raincoat, the somewhat smaller female bird stooped in a pecking position. Around the various wildly blooming peonies surrounding them frolicked several butterflies.

Also occasionally, my aunt took me to the Lord Dainichi[30] close by to play. As I shook the thick, twisted rope to strike the "alligator-mouth" gong at its top, my aunt threw in coins and prayed. Then she would alternately touch my head and the Lord Pindola's[31] head so my brain disease might be

30 "Great Light": Mahāvairocana in Sanskrit, the pantheistic main deity of esoteric Buddhism who embodies the universe. Here it is a temple enshrining the deity. Horibe thinks it was Myōsoku-in.

31 More fully, Pindolabhāradvāja in Sanskrit, called Binzuru in Japanese. The best of the Shakyamuni's sixteen disciples, he was reprimanded for using the divine power he acquired after he took Buddhist vows. As a buddha with the ability to cure all sicknesses, his figure—represented in Japan as an old man with white hair and white eyebrows—used to be placed at the forefront of a Buddhist hall to enable people to do the kind of thing that Naka's aunt does here, so he was popularly called "the rubbing buddha," but for that very reason the placement of the figure at an accessible spot was later banned to prevent contagious diseases.

cured, before lightly rubbing her own eyes. The wooden base of the Pindola was exposed, made shiny and grubby with finger marks, as he glared with large eyes, sitting cross-legged on the dais. In that temple, as in any other temple enshrining the Dainichi, there was a well over which hung offertory towels in persimmon and flower colors. It also had a dipper made by warping a piece of wood floating in its basin, the same kind that was held by O-Tsuru of *Awa no Naruto*[32] in my picture book. My aunt would gratefully draw water from the well, cool her small eyes with it, and, as she opened them, say, "Gracious Dainichi, I think my eyes can see a bit better."

It was believed that this particular Dainichi's oracles were very accurate, and there were people who came great distances to draw one. One day my aunt decided to find out what the Dainichi had to say about my illness. She went into the wing of the hall where a paper screen was erected.

"Excuse me, sir." When she said this, from inside there was, a "Yes, ma'am," and a young monk whose head was freshly tonsured popped out his face. My aunt told him the whole story in great detail and asked for an oracle. The monk went to the front of the principal image, offered prayers for a while, and shook the box many times with a big, rhythmical rattle. Then he drew out an oracle, came over to us, and carefully copied what it said on another sheet of paper for us. Since my aunt could not read "square characters,"[33] he explicated each one for her. In effect, the oracle said this child would become healthy in the future and lead a happy life. On our way home my aunt was all happiness.

32 There are a number of *jōruri* and kabuki plays called *Awa no Naruto mono,* all of them with convoluted story lines. In one, *Keisei Awa no Naruto,* the samurai Awa Jūrobei, who has ruined his life through his infatuation with a courtesan and turned into a robber, kills O-Tsuru, a girl pilgrim, without knowing that she is his own daughter. The kind of "picture book" Naka mentions here obviously may have left out the more lurid part of such a story.

33 I.e., Chinese characters.

13

━━━━

About a hundred yards away toward a more deserted area, there lived an old man and woman who raised several chickens in a vacant lot encircled by an althea hedge. They sold cheap candies. I became terribly fond of the straw-thatched roof, the first I'd ever seen, the torn mud walls, and the well-sweep that made a grinding noise. Going there with my aunt to buy candies was one of the things I really looked forward to. The old man and woman were both hard of hearing and were slow to come out. If you called out to them a number of times, one of them would trudge out and open the lids of candy boxes here and there. *Kinkatō, kingyokutō, tenmontō, mijinbō.*[34] If you hold in your mouth the bamboo tube filled with bean jelly, you smell the fresh bamboo before the jelly slips out onto your tongue. The Ota-san[35] in a candy laughs and cries, turning her face this way and that. If you bite apart the one with blue and red stripes and suck, a sweet wind comes out of its spaces.

The one I liked best was called the cinnamon stick. It was an *aruhei*[36] stick coated with powdered cinnamon and had, within its rich sweetness, a provocative smell of cinnamon. One terribly rainy day, for some reason I felt a sudden pity for the old man and woman and at the same time wanted

34 *Kinkatō* were candies made of white sugar formed into fish and other shapes then colored. *Kingyokutō* was a transparent summer candy made of gelatin, sugar, and spice, coated with granulated sugar. *Tenmontō* may have been asparagus roots pickled in sugar. *Mijinbō* was a candy shaped like a twisted stick made of baked rice-granules and sugar. For pictures of the kinds of cheap candies Naka is talking about, see "Naka Kansuke to dagashi" http://www.toraya-group.co.jp/gallery/dato2/dato2_047.html (retrieved Summer 2014).

35 More fully, *O-Tafuku-san,* "Miss Many-Blessings." A smiling female face with a high brow, small nose, and fat cheeks. Here Naka is talking about the O-Tafuku-ame, a stick-shaped candy that incorporates the face in such a way that it shows no matter where you break it.

36 Derives from the Portuguese word *alfeloa.* A candy brought to Japan during the second half of the 16th century. It was made of sugar and wheat-gluten and came in the shapes of flowers and fruits or, as here, stick-shaped.

a cinnamon stick. I was so insistent that my aunt took me out, carrying me on her back covered by a half-coat. Unfortunately, they had no cinnamon sticks that day and I was so disappointed that I wept all the way home. If I drank "cow's milk"[37] without protest or when I spent the whole day playing without whimpering, she would buy me a rattler[38] as a reward. It was shaped like a peach or a clam and dyed in red and white stripes. I would come home on my aunt's back, shaking it, enjoying it, and crack it open when we reached the house. A little drum made of paper or a flute made of tin would come out. I would treasure them as if they were the most valuable things in the world. Some of them came in triangular wrappings of mud-colored leather, their joins sealed with a portrait of an actor.

37 In quotes because in those days milk was still regarded as a kind of medicine.

38 *Garagara.* More fully, *garagara-senbei,* "rattling cracker," so called because its hollow inside contained a tiny toy that rattled when you shook it.

39 The most important Shinto shrine, whose presiding deity is Amaterasu-Ō-Mikami or Tenshō Daijin, the so-called Sun Goddess. Luis Frois, S. J. (1532–97), who thought the deity was male, reported: "An almost incredible number of people flock from all the kingdoms of Japan in pilgrimage to this *kami* for he is the principal one; this multitude includes not only poor and lowly folk but also many noble men and women who have taken a vow to make the pilgrimage. And it even seems that he who does not go there cannot be counted among the ranks of men." See Cooper, *They Came to Japan,* p. 299.

14

Born feeble and lacking exercise, I was dyspeptic and prone to forget about eating until, as if I were a queen bee, food was brought to my mouth, giving a great deal of trouble to my aunt. Sometimes she put rice balls in a box that had once contained bean paste and, pretending we were on a pilgrimage to the Ise Shrine,[39] she would lead me round and round the mountain-shaped mound in the garden, finally clapping her hands and offering prayers in front of the stone lantern, then sitting me down on a stone under a

TAKENOKO: BAMBOO SHOOTS

pine tree to eat from the lunch box. Once she took me, along with my younger sister and her wet nurse, to a field where evening primroses were in bloom, and we ate the rice rolls wrapped in seaweed that we'd brought along. From the cliff where stands of large cedars, Chinese hackberries, and zelkovas rose up, we had a sweeping view of glowing Fuji, Hakone, Ashigara, and other mountains. Unusually happy, I was eating my lunch when, with unfortunate timing, someone came walking toward us. I immediately threw out my chopsticks and said I'm going home. Of all living creatures, human beings were the ones I disliked the most.

So I did not find any food tasty, but my aunt, with her unique powers of persuasion, could impart a fine taste to anything. I liked clam preserves because those lovely clams were supposed to crawl, with their tongues out, before Princess Oto in the Dragon Palace.[40] And I liked bamboo shoots because the story of Mōsō's filial piety[41] was interesting. If you wash off a chubby bamboo shoot, around the culm toward its base there are rows of short roots and purple warts. If you hold its skin up to the sun, you can see golden down, and white stripes like ivory on the other side. If the skin was large, I put it on my head as a cap; if small, the bristles were removed to wrap pickled plums. If I sucked on the latter for a while, the skin turned red as if dyed and the sour juice seeped out. I also liked black bamboo. Watching these shoots boiling in an earthen pot, turning round and round, looking truly delicious, and seeing my aunt tasting them, even my queen bee self would feel saliva flowing near my back teeth. If I sometimes acted spoiled, refusing to take up my chopsticks, she would put a tiny painted bowl to my mouth to feed me, saying, "You are a baby sparrow, a baby sparrow."

The red sea bream looks beautiful,[42] and

40 An imaginary castle at the bottom of the ocean ruled by this goddess. Famous for the legend of the fisherman Urashima Tarō, who went down to the underwater palace and married the princess.

41 One of the Twenty-Four Greatest Tales of Filial Piety in China, originally compiled during the Yuan Dynasty by Guo Jujing (dates unknown), but there are variations. Mōsō (Meng-sung in Chinese) once found a bamboo shoot in the snow, a rarity, and was able to feed his starving parents.

42 The red sea bream (*Pagrus major*), which

that its head carries the seven tools[43] and that Lord Ebisu[44] holds the fish in his arm makes a child happy. Its eyeballs are delicious. The outer layer is crumbly, but the core is soft yet unyielding, and no matter how long you chew on it, you can't chew it right up. When you spit it out, a semi-transparent ball drops on the plate with a clink. That its teeth are white is also good.

15

In those days there was a madman called Mr. So-and-So. Old folks said that when young he was obsessed with learning and always read books. Then he grew boastful of his scholarship, and went out of his mind. He let his hair grow wild and wore scorched rags on his body that looked almost scaly with grime and soot. Leaning on a thick bamboo cane, deep in thought, he quietly wandered about barefoot in winter or summer. When someone who remembered his past gave him rice balls and such, he would carry them home on his open palms as carefully as a priest holding an alms bowl. But if someone happened to give him something to wear, he would put it on with visible reluctance for one or two days, only to discard it for his rags.

He lived in a cave he had dug out near a farmhouse about two hundred yards away from us, and he kept a fire burning inside

can grow to be more than 3 feet long, has been prized in Japan as "the king of fish" because of its pretty color, shape, and taste. It is also prized because of its name, *tai*, which is part of the word *medetai*, "propitious," "felicitous."

43 Because the sea bream has large bones, an old saying had it: "The sea bream is equipped with all the agricultural tools in its bones." Evidently, "the bones" referred both to those of the head and those of the whole body. The "seven tools" are sometimes specified; "seven" can also mean "all the necessary."

44 One of the Seven Deities of Good Luck, he is the deity of marine transportation, fishery, and commerce, usually presented as a figure sitting on a rock, holding a large sea bream on the left side and a fishing pole in his right hand.

all year round. He would come out of the cave as he pleased and walk as far as he liked in whichever direction caught his fancy. When bored, he would simply turn on his heels to go home. Come rain or wind, he would be seen walking about in the neighborhood. As a result, when nobody saw him for a whole day, they said he must be in a bad mood, and when he didn't come out for three days, four days, they would wonder if he was well. Oddly, if he encountered a woman on the street, he would take a couple of steps back and spit as though he had seen something vile. My aunt, who was fastidious, had been concerned about the grubby, smelly man ever since she first saw him, and would hurriedly turn away before he had time to take his three steps back. One day, when on our way to the cheap cookie store we bumped into him, she couldn't take it any more.

"Would you kindly wash your face for me? I'll give you five pennies." With these words she started to pull out her purse from her sash. The man looked taken aback and stopped. Then, shaking his head with great disgust, forgetting even to spit, he strode away.

This madman lived until I grew to be a normal kid. Then one day the rumor spread that he had been burned to death during the night. Although I was a bit afraid, I went to his cave, but all I saw was his bamboo cane and unburned kindling.

16

Saying she'd let me play Which-Nut,[45] my aunt would knock down nuts from a white camellia tree, although because she had poor eyesight and not much strength, she mainly slapped down twigs and leaves. Which-Nut was a game from her province; you chose camellia seeds of a certain shape, with players all putting out the same number, then taking turns to shake all their seeds in their hands before throwing them

45 *Kinomedochi.*

KINOMEDOCHI: WHICH-NUT

out on the tatami. The person with the greatest number of seeds with white bud spots showing won the round and all the seeds. Each seed had strengths and weaknesses depending on its shape and center of gravity. Some people, I was told, lacquered their seeds for adornment or slyly poured lead into them to strengthen them. You collect the nuts that were knocked down, and crack open their shells to find seeds shaped like a boat or a turnip, and sometimes shiny, all packed snugly into their compartments. They are called *mō, jā, toko, kai*,[46] and such, according to their shape. I recall spending a whole quiet rainy day playing Which-Nut with several dozen seeds.

Come summer, my aunt would point to clumps of clouds of various shapes that moved in the glittering sky overflowing with sunlight, telling me, as if it were all true, that that one was Lord Monju[47] or that one was Lord Fugen Bosatsu.[48] One day, tired of playing, I was lying by myself, waiting for a cloud shaped like a Buddha who would protect me to come along. However, the cloud that happened by, which looked like a Buddha lying supine, suddenly collapsed into such a terrifying form that I decided that a monster, assuming the form of a Buddha, had come to get me, and ran off to my aunt. From then on, I named the cloud of that particular shape a Dead Man's Buddha and, whenever I saw it, promptly hid myself.

Besides the weapons for the Yamazaki Battle, the leather basket also had toys in it, of which the drum and the *shō*[49] were my special treasures. The black-painted pot of the *shō* had an arabesque lacquered on it. The long and short tubes arranged in a ring made soft, varying whistling sounds that gave my feeble nerves a pleasant sensation.

46 Comparable to breaking up a sentence "Well, now, where, are you?" into individual words.

47 Mañjusrī in Sanskrit. His name meaning "deep virtue" or "great fortune," he is the symbol of wisdom. Normally seen accompanying the Shakyamuni, along with Avalokitesvara, riding upon a lion and holding the delusion-cutting sword.

48 Samanthabhadra in Sanskrit: All-Compassionate One of Perfect Activity. Often seated on a white elephant.

49 A musical instrument used in the imperial court dance Gagaku; it consists of a pot into which are fitted seventeen bamboo tubes. A type of free reed instrument.

The drum was small enough for my shoulder, and I liked everything about it, including its scarlet tuning cord and the interesting shape of its body. My invaluable aunt, who had dabbled in almost everything, would make me play the drum, while she herself played a larger drum on her knee in nice accompaniment.

Small items, such as a rabbit's paw made into a makeup brush, the "crane's beak" for rubbing the throat when a bone got stuck, and the brass mallet used to do something with sword-hilt ornaments, were all kept in what was called Kanpon's drawer in the cabinet with the many small drawers. I never volunteered to name which one I wanted. My aunt would take them out one by one while I whimpered, shaking my head, until she hit upon the right one. Even so, in most instances, if she took out the Divine Dog and the Rouge Ox, my mood would change for the better. Sometimes I would develop a dislike for something and toss it any which way. Even then she wouldn't lose her temper but, concerned that something might be wrong with me, put her hand on my forehead. If I had a temperature, I was taken to the doctor at once. I didn't like that, so if she put her hand on my forehead, I would visibly lose heart and grow quiet.

During the chrysanthemum season, she would pick chrysanthemums in the backyard and make a "chrysanthemum rug" to calm me. You spread on a sheet of paper various petals of different chrysanthemums like an Arabian design and press them. After a while you remove the press, and you have a fragrant rug. I liked chrysanthemum rugs very much.

At times I would dump out all the picture books filling my bookcase and make my endlessly patient aunt tell me one story after another. If I'd been scolded for something, after a good deal of weeping, I would then sulk. Angry at even those who, making an excuse of one kind or another, came to comfort me, I would console myself in a corner of a room, spreading picture books around me or playing with toys. At such times the Divine Dog, the Rouge Ox, the magic mallet, and the princess in the picture book, though they didn't say a word, soothed me with their kindness. Then I would become sorry for myself for having stopped weeping and tears would start flowing again. Sobbing, I would tell myself, "I don't care. I have all these friends," while resenting everyone else.

17

At night I played with toys dumped in the dining room where my family was gathered. As you become sleepy, everything starts to get on your nerves. So if I began rubbing my eyes and fretting, it was time for my aunt to take me to bed.

"My, you've gotten sleepy," she'd say and put away the toys littered all around and push my neck down to have me bow on the floor and say to everyone: "Be well and happy."

I would resist, protesting that I didn't want to sleep, yet I would eventually be pulled into the bedroom where my aunt used to sleep with me and the wet-nurse with my younger sister. At sunset the *andon* lantern[50] in the room was lighted and the bedding prepared[51] so that I could go to sleep as soon as my bad mood began to show. In winter my aunt would take a night-robe from the several that had been left over the foot-warmer until they were almost warm enough to emit steam and exaggeratedly blow on it before tenderly wrapping my thin body in it. One of the coverlets had chrysanthemum figures, and another, probably imported from the West, the figures of golden-crested wrens and twigs on a maroon calico background. These coverlets held the fragrance of sunlight, and I loved to smell them, burying my face in their fluffy abundance.

50 *Andon*: with a wooden frame and paper for the shade, the lamp used rape-seed or some other vegetable oil. Because of its economy, stability, and safety, it was used long after the Western-style lamp using petroleum was introduced to Japan and gained popularity. In certain areas, it continued to be used well into the 1920s, even though by then electricity was available.

51 The bedding is put away in the closet in the morning so the room may be used for some other purpose during the day.

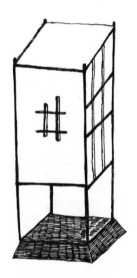

ANDON: LANTERNS

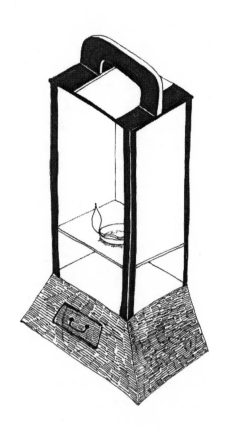

Since I was afraid of the dim light, after putting me into bed my aunt used to take out a new wick from the drawer attached to the lantern and add it. As she dipped the end of the new wick in the oil and put it next to the old one deeply sunken in oil, it would sparkle crisply and catch fire. Her hands would tremble as, with some difficulty, she pulled in the other end of the wick, which tended to stick out over the rim on the other side of the oil plate. Then from the spout of the oil pot she would pour amber-colored vegetable oil into the plate. The fluffy wick, the way it absorbed the oil, the shape of the wick holder, the smell of the burning oil, all such things. More than anything I disliked the corpses of insects lying black at the bottom of the oil and the burnt-out tip of the wick sticking to the rim of the plate. So, every day, after disposing of the used oil, she would scrape off the black wick tip with a blunt, broad-blade knife.

To this coward, the lantern was a little weird. From my bed where I lay with my sleepy eyes wide open, the spindle-shaped flame with the wick tip at its core looked like a goblin with a single long, narrow eye. As my aunt stuck her head inside the lantern to stir up the wick, almost burning her nose with the flame, her gigantic shadow reflected on the lantern paper made me wonder if she herself wasn't some kind of goblin.

Then my aunt, while putting the matches back in the drawer, would offer prayers for the souls of the insects who were lured to the light and burned to death. Once I couldn't sleep for fear that the Devil was lurking in the alcove ceiling where the light didn't reach. My aunt struggled to her feet and raised the lantern toward that part of the ceiling.

"See? No one's hiding up there." In those days I believed the Devil was something scary-black with wild hair falling over itself.

"Call me if you get scared during the night," my aunt would say. "You know I'm fierce. They'd all run away."

Then she would tell stories until I fell asleep. She may not have been able to read any "square characters," but she had heard and memorized an astonishing amount and knew an almost inexhaustible number of

52 Sai no Kawara; also, Sanzu no Kawara. Sanzu no Kawa, "Three-way River," is the river that dead souls must cross to go to the netherworld.

It corresponds to the Styx in Greek mythology. As Naka goes on to explain, its riverbed is the limbo where the souls of dead children are made to suffer, their task of building cairns constantly frustrated by demons. This folkloric notion, which became widespread during the Edo period (1600–1868), is said to have originated in a passage in "Expedient Means," of the Lotus Sutra, which reads: ". . . even if little boys at play / should collect sand to make a Buddha tower, / then persons such as these / have all attained the Buddha way." Watson, p. 39.

53 Ksitigarbha in Sanskrit: the bodhisattva who is given the task of giving salvation to every being during the period from the death of the Shakyamuni to the advent of the Maitreya. He has six manifestations. In Japan the worship of Jizō as the savior of wayfarers and children—especially children who died young—became popular during the Heian period (794–1185). Stone statues to him are found all over Japan. Papinot: "He is represented by the image of a bonze with shaved head, holding a gem in one hand, and a staff (*shakujō*) in the other, at the top of which metal rings are attached."

stories. Also, she had the knack of smoothly filling in the parts she'd forgotten with her own fanciful imagination. She gave different expressions and voices to different people, whether samurai or princesses, and would even put on the face of a monster for me which, in the dim light of the lantern, looked very real.

18

Among the most pitiful were the stories of the child who piles stones on the Riverbed of Sai[52] and the Hatsune drum of *The Thousand Cherry Trees*. My aunt would sing a snatch of that pilgrim's song in a sorrowful tone before adding explanations. I could not understand the whys and wherefores adequately, but a child who has troubled his mother just by being in her womb but has died before doing anything to repay his indebtedness is building a cairn to atone for the sin, piling stones forlornly on the Riverbed of Sai, when a demon comes along and harasses him by destroying the cairn with his iron cane. But then the gentle Lord Jizō[53] protects him by hiding him under the sleeve of his robe. Each time I heard this story, I was oppressed with a suffocating gloom, the thought of the fate of the poor child making me sob uncontrollably. Aunt would rub me on the back, saying, "Don't worry, don't worry. There, we have the Lord Jizō."

I always thought that the Lord Jizō was a Buddha who looked exactly like the stone buddha who stood at the roadside with his staff.

Brought up solely by my aunt who was born Buddhist, I made no discrimination between animals and humans, and I heard the story of the pitiable baby fox whose parents were skinned alive as if it were happening to myself. The white parent foxes cried out, "Our poor baby! Our poor baby!" even as they were being skinned, I was told. This was the most pitiful of the three stories about a drum that I knew. It was not the drum that fell from heaven, wrapped in a mysterious cloud,[54] or the soundless drum that a cruel person is said to have made from brocade,[55] but an ordinary drum made from the skins of foxes living in a field of Yamato Province that cried out of love for their child. Even now, when I think of this story, the feeling that I had then stirs my heart.[56]

My aunt also had all the poems of *One Hundred Poems by One Hundred Poets*[57] committed to memory and, after we lay down in bed, would recite them in her uniquely sorrowful tone, patiently making me memorize one or two every night.

"*Tachiwakare,*" she would say.
"*Tachiwakare,*" I would follow.

54 Originally a nō play called *Heavenly Drum (Tenko)*. After dreaming that a drum has descended from heaven into her womb, the married woman named Ōbo, "King's Mother," gives birth to a boy whom she names Tenko. Later a real drum also descends from heaven and when Tenko plays it, the sound is so heavenly every listener is filled with joy. Hearing the story, the emperor orders submission of the drum to the Imperial Court. Tenko hides himself with his drum but is captured and drowned in a river. The drum, taken to the court, refuses to make any sound. Chikamatsu Monzaemon (1653–1724) wrote a convoluted *jōruri* play out of this story.

55 Originally a nō play called *Brocade Drum (Aya no tsuzumi)* that tells of an old gardener who falls in one-sided love with a court lady. The lady, learning this, sends him a drum made of brocade with the instruction that if he beats it and she hears the sound in the court, she will appear before him. The old man beats it all night, but because of its material the drum makes no sound. Despairing, he drowns himself.

56 The stories Naka's aunt told were clearly variations of the original plays

that had been further modified for children. One idea expressed by Tadanobu the Fox in *Yoshitsune and the Thousand Cherry Trees* is a variation of the concept embodied in the Sai no Kawara story. In revealing his true self, Tadanobu explains that he has followed the drum because when his parents were killed, he was "an ignorant baby fox" and as a result "he didn't have a single day to look after them" and that "in failing to return the obligations to his parents," he was "inferior to pigs and wolves."

57 *Hyakunin isshu*: an anthology of a hundred tanka, each by a different poet, which was originally compiled by Fujiwara no Teika (1162–1241). It was adopted as a canonical text by the Nijō school of poets and during the Edo period it was turned into a card game. The game is played with two sets of a hundred cards, each card in one set carrying an entire poem with an appropriate picture— normally an imagined portrait of the poet—and each card in the other set carrying the lower hemistich of a poem. The latter set is spread on the floor and competitively grabbed up while poems are read aloud from the former set.

58 *Tachiwakare Inaba no*

"Inaba no yama no."
"Inaba no yama no."
"Mine ni ouru."
*"Mine ni ouru."*⁵⁸

In a while, I would fall asleep. If I memorized a poem well, she would stroke me to sleep, saying, "I'll give you a reward. Now you may sleep."

Because I memorized the poems rather quickly, my aunt thought I was a great child.

"Last night he memorized *two* poems in no time," she would proudly tell my mother the next morning.

Without understanding much, I would gather together only the words I knew in each poem and imagine its overall meaning, dimly. Along with the feeling generated by the way it was recited, I was deeply affected by it all. In those days I had an old set of poem cards, each with a poem and a painting. Though the cards were frazzled and the paintings faded, I could still make out, however vaguely, the snow piled on a pine tree⁵⁹ or a deer standing below maple leaves.⁶⁰ There was also a book of *One Hundred Poems by One Hundred Poets.*

My liking and disliking of poems was also determined by the picture on the card, the figure and the face of the poet. Among the poems I liked were *Sue no Matsuyama,*⁶¹ *Awaji-shima,*⁶² and *Ōe-yama.*⁶³ The *Sue no Matsuyama* poem conveyed to my ear an indescribably gentle, lonesome sound, with beautiful waves rolling on the piney shore in the picture on the card. The *Awaji-shima* poem invited tears. There was a boat on the sea, with plovers flying. Each time I heard the *Ōe-yama* poem, I couldn't help remembering a story from a picture book in which a princess, captured by a demon, was taken into the depths of that mountain.[64] I intensely hated the wrinkled-up monks such as Abbot Henjō[65] and Former Archbishop Gyōson,[66] but I thought Semimaru cute partly because of his name.[67]

19

On snowy nights my aunt, stirring up the charcoal-balls in the foot-warmer, would frighten me by saying that the Snow Monk in a white robe was standing right outside the door. When it was hot, she would fan me because I had a hard time falling asleep. I had preferences even for the pictures on the fan. Inside the fragrant mosquito net, listening to the mosquitoes flying about outside, I would sometimes break a rib of the fan just for the fun of it. A horned owl might come to the bush in the next-door temple and hoot. Then my aunt would say, "I hear the hooter is an evil bird and spits out a thousand mosquitoes in one hoot. We'll have

yama no mine ni ouru matsu to shi kikaba ima kaerikomu, by Arihara no Yukihira (818–93): "Upon Inába, / that tells us of our parting, / the pine-trees cluster, / should they 'she pineth' whisper, / I will return to love thee."

59 No poem in this anthology verbally combines a pine tree with the snow. Possibly, *Asaborake ariake no tsuki to miru made ni Yoshino no sato ni fureru shirayuki*, by Sakanoue no Korenori (dates uncertain): "At dawn of day / meseemed there lay the hamlet / 'neath the moon's bright shimmer / upon fair Yoshino shining: / but 'twas the snow new-fallen!"

60 *Okuyama ni momiji fumiwake naku shika no koe kiku toki zo aki wa kanashiki*, by Sarumaru Dayū (dates uncertain): "Whenas men hear / the cry of wandering deer / the red leaves trampling / upon the lonely hillside / 'tis known sad autumn's near."

61 *Chigirikina katami ni sode o shiboritsutsu Sue no Matsuyama nami kosaji towa*, by Kiyohara no Motosuke (908–90): "Our sleeves with tears / were drenched as each we promised / the sea-waves o'er / the Pines of Suye should, ere / our love died down, be breaking!"

62 *Awaji-shima kayou chidori no naku koe ni*

SANGOJU, SUZUME: "CORAL TREE" AND SPARROWS

plenty of mosquitoes tomorrow, I'm afraid."

As the cool winds rise, crickets begin to chirp. Once I thought of taking good care of them and put some in a firefly-cage, but after chirping a couple of times they fell silent. I looked in and saw they had all escaped through a hole they made in the silk gauze around the cage. Listening to them, even a child senses that the solitude of autumn has arrived. My aunt said they were saying, "It's gotten cold, now mend the tatters," while the wet-nurse told my sister they were saying, "Suckle me, suckle me, suckle me, and I'll bite you."

At times, I would wake early enough in the morning to hear the cawing of crows nesting in the black pines in the Shōrin temple. When that happened, my aunt wouldn't allow me to get out of bed.

"They're the first risers. You must sleep more."

She would allow me to get out of bed only after the second or third risers cawed. That was her way of keeping me in bed until an appropriate time.

Come evening, a great many sparrows returned to nest in the mound-shaped growth of the "coral tree"[68] that was in front of my bedroom and made a din, shaking their heads, sharpening their beaks, and pecking at each other as they vied for better branches. When the sun hid itself and the lingering light faded, even the one or

ikuyo nezamenu Suma no sekimori, by Minamoto no Kanemasa (dates uncertain): "Night after night must / Suma's tired warders / lie list'ning wakeful / to the mournful cries of sea-birds / across the waters flitting!"

63 *Ōe-yama Ikuno no michi mo tōkereba mada fumi mo mizu Ama no Hashidate*, by Koshikibu no Naishi (d. 1025): "Or hill of Ōye / or road o'er Íkuno's moorland / too far for me are— / nor foot nor scroll of mine hath / seen Amanohashidáte."

64 Ōe-yama, or Mount Ōe, designates two places in Kyoto, one close to the city and the other farther northwest. Though Koshikibu's poem refers to the former, Naka, as a child, mixed it up with the latter, the hideout of the legendary Shuten Dōji (Drunken Boy) who kidnapped people and did other evil things— the mix-up probably occurring because the poem seems to say something like "Mount Ōe is far away, and I haven't seen letters." The warrior-commander Minamoto no Raikō (also Yorimitsu: 948–1021) famously went there with his four "guardian kings" and subdued him. Shuten Dōji is thought to be a collective name for a bunch of marauding bandits.

65 Or Yoshimine no

two who, slow to sleep, were still chirping, would fall silent and become quiet. I thought they were my good friends, and when I found myself still in bed even after the third risers among the crows cawed, their chirps as they left their nests sounded as if they were laughing at me for being lazy, and I would hastily get up.

The "coral tree" does not betray its name and bears scarlet seeds. It is a pleasure to pick them after they've fallen and are lying on the soft moss.

20

The space behind our house, about fifty square yards, was half for growing flowers, half for vegetables. In early summer a seedling vendor used to walk by our fence hawking his wares in a cool voice. From time to time my aunt called him in and bought some vegetable seedlings. The boxes he carried were made of straw and stuffed with moist, crumbly earth in which various plants were lively sprouting pairs of leaves. The vendor, a man wearing a sedge hat, scooped them out as if he were handling something very valuable. Each time, my aunt bought a few seedlings of things like eggplants and melons and planted them in the vegetable patch. As the purplish seedlings

Munesada (816–90). His poem: *Amatsukaze kumo no kayoiji fukitoji yo otome no sugata shibashi todo-men*: "O winds of heaven, / waft clouds to bar the sky-paths, / a moment would I, / these maids angelic staying, / their graceful dance admire."

66 (1055–1135). His poem: *Morotomo ni aware to omoe yama-zakura hana yori hoka ni shiru hito mo nashi*: "O cherry-blossom! / our lot alike is mournful, / no other friend thou, / thou has but me, none other / but these, alas, have I!"

67 Semimaru means "Cicada Man" or "Cicada Boy." Though Semimaru, usually presented as a monk, has spawned a number of legends, some regard him as a non-historical figure. His poem is homiletic and reads: *Kore ya kono yuku mo kaeru mo wakarete wa shiru mo shirazu mo Ōsaka no Seki*: "'Tis steep Ōzaka / men call the Hill of Meetings, / where to and fro / the endless throng is passing, / of friends and strangers passing."

68 *Sango-ju*: sweet viburnum. Called "coral tree," because it produces coral-like clusters of flowers and berries. Its Latin name is *Viburnum awabuki*.

of eggplants and the seedlings of pumpkins and dishcloth gourds with fine white powder on them stirred their sprouting oval leaves, the two of us sprinkled water on them mornings and evenings. Each time I looked, they had grown, putting out vines and leaves, finally thrashing all over the place, dangling huge fruit. I liked to go out to inspect them.

My aunt, who loved to take care of them, while complaining, put up bamboo sticks to help the vines. Then they spiraled up the sticks one or two twirls a day, and soon among their coarse leaves they put out yellow and purple flowers. Roundish horseflies would come and fly about as though the world were all theirs, before diving into them.

While abortive flowers tumbled down, the bases of the real ones swelled, becoming flat or long and thin, in the end taking the shapes of the so-called "Chinese eggplants" or pumpkin. Eggplants grew like pouches, dishcloth gourds shaped up like blind snakes. Cucumbers had hateful grainy bumps. How happy I was when I brushed aside the leaves and found pods with unexpected seeds in them. Sword beans, kidney beans, scallion flowers resembling a worn-out brush tip.

Once, the "Chinese eggplants" seedlings she bought and planted gradually took on a different appearance, and they finally grew into gourds. I was overjoyed to see the gourds dangling in countless numbers, but my aunt was angry that she'd been duped by the seedling vendor and she would not take proper care of them. So, eventually all of them dropped to the ground. From then on, she decided to get seedlings at a downtown vegetable store. But no matter what the seedling was, she suspected everything was a gourd and would declare to the storekeeper that if it grew into gourds, she'd come back with it, roots and all.

On the mound along the cedar hedge surrounding the vegetable patch, grandmother's chestnuts and the walnuts I'd picked up some place and thrown out there were sprouting up. Also, the impatiens she loved and had planted had scattered their seeds and bloomed on various parts of the lot. Though they are not particularly attractive wildflowers, I too like the impatiens. For the fun of it I used to take a few flowers and dye my fingernails with them. It was amusing to crush the seeds of four-o'clocks and get white powder.[69] Apricot flowers, scarlet peach blossoms. There was an old almond tree that put out pale blue blossoms like a puff of cloud. My older brother and I looked forward to them above all else and were very eager to chase away the crows. Its large fruit grew in such clusters that the lower branches bent and touched the ground. Picking the ones we could reach, knocking down the higher ones, we'd carry home the heavy basket between us.

In the flowerbed bloomed tiger lilies and white lilies. Bright or overrich colors used to oppress me. In the case of flowers, one example was the dark-brown pollen thickly covering the heads of the lily stamens.

69 *Oshiroibana*, "cosmetic flower": so called because its pods contain white powder, the nutrient for its seeds. The English name derives from the fact that it starts to bloom late in the afternoon. Also called "the afternoon lady." Its Latin name is *Mirabilis japala.*

70 Yama in Sanskrit. The "commander-in-chief" of the netherworld, according to the *Zengaku dai-jiten* (Taishūkan Shoten, 1985); the supreme arbiter of sins and crimes of human beings. Some say he is a manifestation of the Ksitigarbha (for which see note 53 on Jizō in Episode 1.18).

71 In Buddhism the lid of Hell's Cauldron is lifted on the 15th of First and Seventh Months to release the sinners from tortures temporarily.

72 Chamberlain: "the great Buddhist festival . . . is often termed by foreigners the Feast of Lanterns, but might better be rendered as All Souls' Day. The spirits of dead ancestors then visit the altar sacred to them in each household, and special offerings of food are made to them. The

21

━━━

Very close by there was a temple for the Lord Emma.[70] When the day the lid of Hell's Cauldron[71] and the gloomy bell started to toll as though to lure people, my aunt would dress me—how reluctant I was—in a light blue hemp kimono, tie a sash made of Chinese silk crepe high around my chest, and take me out to offer prayers. Since she dressed me in the same kimono at each Bon,[72] eventually the light-blue color itself came to depress me. The space between the narrow precincts and the main gate was closely packed with stalls selling a cup of ice for a nickel, *oden* stew, and sushi. The peepings of balloons and the calls of vendors created an unbearable din in the dust. The shop boys in aprons shrieked as if the Lord Emma were their own. They were the kind of humans I especially disliked.

You went up the few stone steps and entered the red gate that had "thousand-shrine bills"[73] pasted all over it. There on the right was a small Emma hall in which the Lord Emma with a rustic face presided as he was expected to. Inside, the incense was stifling, and the constant clanging of the gong that the town children struck was so painful that I felt my head might shatter. But my aunt had to make me strike the gong a couple of times with a wooden hammer, and would not leave until she had made me look closely at the Lord Emma's face. Then, scarcely giving me pause for breath, she would take me to the main hall where there was the Old Woman of the Three-way River.[74] The pale old woman, eye sockets hollow like copper pots, sat with many folds of red and white cotton on her head. The unpleasantness of it all and the exposure to the burning sun never failed to give me a terrible headache. But my aunt was superstitious and every year found one excuse or another to take me to the temple.

On the day of the Nirvana Rite,[75] my aunt hung a sooty picture scroll of the Shakyamuni lying on his side and in front of it put a small desk with incense and flowers on it. This worm-eaten scroll and the statue of the black Lord Daikoku on the altar were the only two possessions left to her. As she sat in front of the desk and offered prayers, she would make me light a stick of incense

living restrict themselves to *maigre* dishes as far as possible." Used to be held from the 13th to the 15th of Seventh Month; today during the same days in August.

73 *Senja-fuda*: bills carried by people visiting a thousand shrines; they have the carrier's name, the province of his birth, and the name of his store.

74 See note 52 on Sai in Episode 1.18. As folklore has it, an old "clothes-stripping" man and an old "clothes-stripping" woman live by the river, robbing the dead people of their clothes before they cross it.

75 *Nehan-e*: on the 15th of Second Month, a rite is held to mark the anniversary of the entrance of the Shakyamuni into Nirvana. Nirvana: "The word, which means 'blown out,' indicates the state in which one has escaped from the cycle of birth and death. In Mahayana Buddhism, it is taken to mean awakening to the

and then would tell me various stories about the Lord Shakyamuni. Those who gathered around him were elephants and lions, asuras, kimnaras, dragons,[76] and heavenly beings, all of whom, through the skillful narration of this venerable, superstitious woman, would come alive and start shedding tears. The beautiful person who was looking down from the cloud floating above the paired sāla trees[77] was called Lady Maya, the Lord Shakyamuni's mother. The medicine bag she threw down from the Heavens caught on one branch of the sāla trees but no one noticed it, my aunt told me. The Lord Shakyamuni's entrance into nirvana sounded as if it were a parting with a parent, and I wept, feeling sorry for him.

true nature of phenomena, or the perfection of Buddha wisdom."

76 Asura: "A class of contentious demons in Indian mythology who fight continually with the god Indra. In Buddhism the asuras constitute one of the eight kinds of nonhuman beings who protect Buddhism." Kimnara: A "heavenly being who excels in singing and dancing." Dragon: "One of the eight kinds of nonhuman beings who protect Buddhism."

77 The tree "grows in northern India, reaching a considerable height and bearing light yellow blossoms. Shakyamuni passed away in a grove of [sāla] trees on the outskirts of Kushinagara."

78 A traditional jacket which, "once reserved by law to upper-class males, enjoyed a sudden and widespread popularity among men and women in all walks of life" during the Meiji period. Dalby, p. 64.

22

Unless it rained my aunt never failed to take me out on the fête day of the Lord Dainichi that was held three times a month. Because I walked clinging to her sleeve, her *haori*[78] often became lopsided and she had to stop in the middle of the road to adjust it. Sometimes, especially on a crowded street, my grip was so desperate she had to loosen my fingers one by one. I would tie the strings of her *haori* lightly, and she mine somewhat tightly.

At the Lord Dainichi's she would make me throw in coins, and call inside, "May we offer a candle?"

From a glittering corner of the hall would come a response, "Yes, ma'am," and a young monk would light a candle and put it before the principal image. After mumbling her prayers devoutly, my aunt would announce, "Now we're done," and make me hold onto her sleeve before we came out of the gate.

What she asked of the Lord Dainichi were things like "May this child be cured of his sickly body" and "May he not get hurt on the road," which she would think of in advance for each date bearing the number eight.

On the fête day a host of beggars appeared and lined up along the temple fence. At the early hour we arrived, not all of them would be out; only a couple of quick ones among the cripples and the legless would be getting out thin straw mats and such. Slowly influenced by my aunt, I came to feel a vague but profound satisfaction with my childish compassion after giving them alms. Among the beggars was a good-looking blind woman who played the koto. Unlike now, not many people owned a koto back then, and my aunt and our wet-nurse often gossiped about her, saying that she must be what was left of someone who had once served a shogunate aide-de-camp or else a daimyo in the old days. She sang koto songs in a voice so crushed as to be almost inaudible. The way her plectrums skimmed and rolled over the strings with a light susurrus, and the way the bridges shaped like wild geese scattered over the wooden koto showing its cloud-like grain, were all new to me and beautiful.

23

If you went a little early, you could see the showmen setting up booths like spiders. Around them lay tools and boxes containing the creatures for the shows, which you looked at full of curiosity. Soon the picture boards would be put up. Most of them were eerie affairs like a goggle-eyed merman swimming in the sea and a large snake with a forked tongue about to swallow a chicken. But sometimes you saw a picture showing, on the blue board, numerous mice in kimono of different colors performing various tricks, holding in their hands fans with the rising sun painted on them. I liked that picture very much and went in to see the show each time it was put up. Many Nanjing mice came out to pull a cart and operate a well pulley. At the very end they carried tiny rice bags out of a papier-mâché storehouse and made a neat pile of them. The brown-mottled ones and snow-white ones scurrying around pell-mell were so cute. The trainer was a woman of about thirty, dressed like a female Westerner, with her hair bundled up and wearing a hat, still a very rare sight in those days. Every time a mouse carried out a rice bag, she would say rhythmically,

"Heave ho! Little one, bring it out!"

When a rice bag tumbled down from the paws of a hasty mouse toward the spectators, one of the children would pick it up at once and throw it back. The woman would say, "I thank you," with a gracious smile and bow.

A rice bag often tumbled down toward me. I wanted to pick it up for her, but each time, though agitated, I could never put my hand out. The mice tricks done, the woman would produce a parrot from a red and blue striped cage and make him mimic her words. Usually the parrot would sit tamely on her palm and say whatever she wanted him to say. But when he was in a bad mood he would bristle his crown feathers and do nothing but screech. When that happened the woman would cock her head, looking lost, and say, "I don't know what's the matter with my dear Tarō today."

It was with regret that I would leave the booth, thinking about the picturesque parrot, his hooked beak, and his clever eyes.

79 As Naka goes on to explain, there are two kinds of *hōzuki*: marine and land. Marine ones are usually egg cases of whelks; land ones are the fruits of a variety of Chinese lantern plants (Physalis alkekengi var. franchetii).

24

Among the night stalls, the *hōzuki*[79] vendor was one thing that drew my heart. He would swivel a bamboo tube with a cogwheel attached to it, making a dull squeak.

MUSHIKAGO: INSECT CAGES

"Hōzuki yaa-i! Hōzuki!" he would call.

On the coralline leaves spread upon a lattice lay red, blue, white, and various other *hōzuki* dripping water. Round, fan-shaped *hōzuki*, soul-shaped Korean *hōzuki*, goblin *hōzuki*, halberd *hōzuki*—these were all *hōzuki* from the sea, each leathery bag carrying bilge that smelled of the beach. Tanba *hōzuki*, thousand-cluster *hōzuki*. The old man would swivel his bamboo tube and call out: *"Hōzuki yaa-i! Hōzuki!"*

Since I couldn't make a sound with any of the plant *hōzuki*, I always had them buy me the marine ones, which I would carry home, carefully clutched in my palms. The Tanba *hōzuki* looks like a monk clad in a scarlet robe. When she peeled one and found a mosquito bite, my older sister would get mad and dash it to the tatami. The mosquito is an evil fellow. While the plant is still green, he secretly sucks out its sweet juice. One so damaged has a tiny star on its head, and while you knead it, its skin breaks.

In summer the stalls of insect vendors bewitched me. In cages shaped like fans, boats, and waterfowl, each with a scarlet tassel dangling beneath it, they kept pine insects[80] and bell insects[81] chirping, trilling. The katydid[82] chirps like someone pulling a sliding door, and the horse-bit insect[83] like a rustle of dead leaves. I wanted a pine insect or bell insect, but my aunt always bought me a katydid. Once to spite her I bought a rattler[84] which she hated, and she didn't sleep a wink that night. Rattlers came in a coarse bamboo cage, the four corner bars painted red and blue. If you put a slice of melon in

80 *Matsumushi (Xenogryllus marmoratus)*: a variety of cricket. Prized for the twinkling sound it makes.

81 *Suzumushi (Homoeogryllus japonicus)*: a variety of cricket. Prized for its quiet, limpid sound. In Japan it's called "King of Singing Insects."

82 *Kirigirisu (Gampsocleis buergeri)*. The famous singing insect that is identified by this name in classical Japanese literature was probably what is now called *kōrogi*, cricket.

83 *Kutsuwamushi (Mecopoda niponensis)*. May correspond to the "fork-tailed bush katydid." Because the next insect mentioned is another name of this insect, Naka might have meant *umaoi*, "horse chaser" *(Hexacentrus japonicus)*, a variety of katydid.

84 *Gachagacha*: another name of *kutsuwamushi*, a large variety of katydid. Its onomatopoeic name is said to derive from the noise a horse bit makes and is sometimes described as "noisy."

the grille, they'd nibble on it, shaking their long antennae. They have puzzled expressions, and their incongruously long legs attached backward are funny.

Sometimes we bought pots of wildflowers. When bedtime came, my aunt would put them out under the eaves to expose them to the night dew. How can I describe a child's feelings as he looked at those flowers? It was a pure, innocent joy never to be felt again. Incited by the flowers, I would get up early the next morning and, still in my nightrobe and rubbing my eyes at the dazzling light, I would have a look. With tiny dewdrops lodging on the flowers and leaves, the velvety flowers of China pinks, heart's-ease with hairdo-shaped flowers, and pot marigolds were wide awake.

If you bought a picture book, they used to roll it and tie the middle with a strip of paper. Carrying it as if it were something fragile, I would take an occasional peek into the tube on my way home. Everyone would insist on seeing how beautiful the book was, and how important I felt as I slowly unrolled it for them. Everyone would marvel and say, I want it! I want it! Outside the picture frame on the cover, and in red ink, something like *Animals: New Edition* would be written. The smiling elephant with a long nose, the rabbit with pursed lips, the deer, and the sheep were all lovely. Though most of them were alone and looked quiet, the bear wrestled with the red Kintarō,[85] and the wild boar whose snout thrust out like a bamboo shoot was held down by Shirō, of Nitan.[86]

85 The childhood name of the warrior Sakata no Kintoki (dates uncertain). One of the four "guardian kings" of Minamoto no Raikō (see note 64 on Ōe-yama in Episode 1.18). As legend has it, Kintarō was born of the Old Woman of the Mountain and a red dragon and was brought up playing with bears and other animals. His ruddy-faced boyhood figure, wearing only an apron and carrying an oversize ax, is still used as a symbol of health, strength, and courage.

86 Nitta Tadatsune (d. 1203). A vassal of Minamoto no Yoritomo (1147–99), Tadatsune killed Soga Jūrō Sukenari after the latter, along with his brother, Gorō Tokimune, carried out a vendetta, in 1193. Later, at the instigation of Yoritomo's son, Shogun Noriyori, he tried to assassinate Regent Hōjō Tokimasa (1138–1225), but failed and was killed. In children's books, Tadatsune used to be depicted as a valorous warrior who could subdue anything.

After proudly showing the book to all, I would say, "Be well and happy," and go into the bedroom where my aunt would tell fabulous stories about the pictures. Finally I would look at the pictures all over again before putting the book near the pillow and falling asleep.

25

I was so timid I couldn't speak up when among people, and if I saw something I wanted all I did was stop walking, still holding onto my aunt's sleeve. My aunt, who knew this, would look around and ask questions. Until she hit upon the right thing I would simply go on shaking my head, but when it took too much time I would reluctantly point at what I wanted, only to put my finger shyly in my mouth. I loved the toy called "three scares,"[87] but my aunt disliked the snake and soon put it away when I wasn't looking. The bamboo rabbit jumped. On warm days its glue loosened and the rabbit, instead of jumping, would slowly raise its bottom and fall on its side. Besides these, the toys I liked were the bird in a cage that turned round and round, peeping, if you blew on the handle attached to its cage, and the "bream bow"[88] on which a fish slid down, its tail quivering delicately.

On windy winter nights, the fire of the *kantera* lamps in the roadside stalls sputtered desolately and the wicks looked like bloodshot eyes. At such times the person I pitied the most was an old woman selling raisin cakes. What the raisin cakes were I don't know. A shriveled-up woman of about seventy, she had a faded lantern with *Raisin Cakes* written on it and a few paper bags laid

87 *Sansukumi*: an object consisting of three magnetic parts representing a snake, a slug, and a frog. As common belief in Japan has it, the snake is afraid of the slug, the slug of the frog, and the frog of the snake.

88 *Tai-yumi*: A simple bow-like toy with a small bream shaped in clay attached to its string so that when it was held up vertically the clay bream may descend, trembling, as if alive.

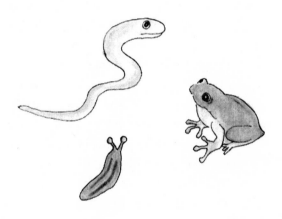

SASUKUMI: THREE SCARES

out on the small counter, but I never saw anyone buying them. I was truly sorry for her and pleaded with my aunt, but it was all so grimy that she wouldn't buy from her. Some years later when I was able to go out on fête days by myself, the old woman was still there, with her stall on the same corner near the noodle diner. Whenever a fair was on, I walked in front of her stall, back and forth, back and forth, tears brimming in my eyes. But each time I was unable to buy from her, and returned home, against my wishes. One night, however, I finally mustered my courage and approached the *Raisin Cakes* lantern. The old woman took me for a customer and picked up a paper bag.

"May I help you?"

I did not know what to say, and before I knew what I was doing, I had thrown a two-*sen* coin on the counter and then ran to the shrubbery in the Shōrin temple. My heart was pounding and my face burning.

I had no intention of going to "the fools' festival" at Lord Hachiman's.[89] This was because the fool's mask with a crushed nose, the *hyottoko's*[90] face whose eyes are topsy-turvy, and the too insistent, vulgar clown would sicken me. However, in their ignorant kindness, hoping it would cure my depression, my family, with even my aunt on their side, would try by any means to get me there. After I turned nine or ten, I would plead with them, saying it was painful to go to such a place. But they all thought it was just an excuse and would push me out of the house. When that happened, I went to a nearby field and, lying on my back on a cliff covered with large trees, spent my time watching the mountains.

89 Papinot: "Hachiman under which the emperor Ōjin (201–312) is honored as a god.... Hachiman was the tutelary god of the Minamoto." Also: "The name of the temples dedicated to the god of war." The dates Papinot gives for Ōjin are in doubt, but Ōjin, who in semi-mythological accounts is the fifteenth emperor, is today recognized as the first emperor likely to have existed.

90 The mask of a male face with one eye exceedingly small and the mouth shaped like a crooked tube. The word derives from *hi-otoko,* "man on fire."

26

────

Compared with the Kanda brats, the children in the new neighborhood were, as you might expect, much calmer, and the streets quieter, a world more suited to someone like me. So, my aunt tried very hard to find me a playmate, which she eventually did in O-Kuni-san, a girl on the other side of the street. (I have only recently learned that her father had been a samurai of the Awa fiefdom and a well-known loyalist[91] in those days.) Before anyone knew about it, my aunt had found out that O-Kuni-san was weak and quiet, even the fact that she had chronic headaches. She decided that therefore the girl could be just the right sort of friend for me. One day, she took me to an open area inside the gate of O-Kuni-san's house, where she was playing with some children, and, even though I resisted, put me down near them.

"He's a good boy. Would you play with him?"

For a moment the fun seemed to go out of the children, but soon they resumed their play with cheer.

That day it was for an "audience" only. Clinging to my aunt's sleeve, I watched them play for a while and came home. I was taken there the next day, too. In three or four days the children and I became used to each other somewhat, and when they laughed at something funny I showed a smile of sorts.

O-Kuni-san and her friends always danced "The Lotus Flower Has Bloomed."[92] So my aunt patiently taught me the song and made me rehearse at home. When she decided I had mastered it, she took me inside the gate and, though I fretted, installed me

91 Okamoto Kansuke (1839–1904): explorer of Karafuto (Sakhalin) and Chishima Rettō (Kurile Islands), educator, and author of sixty books.

92 One of the "ring-play" songs, which originated in Edo and was most popular at the start of Meiji. After it appeared in textbooks, the song came to be known throughout Japan. Children make a ring and, turning round and round, imitate the way the lotus opens and closes. One child stays at the center.

beside O-Kuni-san. Seeing us two timid children shyly holding back, she tactfully inveigled us into placing our hands together, one palm upon the other, made our fingers bend, and then, giving them a squeeze from above, she finally succeeded in linking up the two hands. Until then I hadn't had a stranger hold my hand, so I was a bit afraid. Also, worried that my aunt might sneak away, I kept my eyes glued on her. The addition of this inharmonious newcomer totally spoiled the children's fun, and they wouldn't start turning. Observing this, my aunt joined the ring and, clapping her hands cheerfully, moving her feet rhythmically, and turning, she sang,

Oh, it has opened, it has opened,
What flower has opened?

Slowly the children responded to her and began singing in whispers. Prompted by my aunt, I too started to follow the song secretively, while eyeing all the faces.

It has opened, it has opened,
What flower has opened?
The lotus flower has opened!

As soon as the small ring began turning, my aunt doubled her effort. The song grew louder, the ring turned faster. I'd not yet done any normal walking, and my heart began to pound, I felt dizzy. I wanted to let go, but everyone was absorbed and kept pulling me round and round. At long last the children said,

We thought it just opened,
But it has closed just as fast!

and all at once closed around my aunt. My aunt said,

Oh, I'm sorry! I'm sorry!

and got out of the ring.

It has closed, it has closed,
What flower has closed?
The lotus flower has closed. . . .

Hands thrust forward, still linked, they shook them in rhythm with the song.

We thought it just closed,
But it has just as quickly opened!

The closed lotus flower suddenly opened, jerking my arms apart, almost taking them off. After this was repeated several times, I was tired out by the unaccustomed exercise and the mental exertion. My aunt had to loosen my fingers before taking me home.

27

O-Kuni-san was my first real friend. At first, I couldn't play unless my aunt stayed with me, and stay she did, fully aware I'd been plopped down into that place, as it were. But having made sure that the neighborhood was, unlike Kanda, a world created for a child like me, quiet and safe, she began to leave me alone, after telling me in detail, over and over gain, to go inside the gate when the cart came by, not to go near the ditches, and so on.

When O-Kuni-san and I were face to face, she followed the usual children's formalities on becoming acquainted and asked questions, starting with my father's name, my mother's name, down to the year, the month, and the day of my birth. And when she asked my zodiacal year, I obediently said the Year of the Rooster.

"I was born in the same year," she said.[93] "Let's be good friends."

Then we walked about, fluttering our sleeves like wings, saying, "Cluck-a-cluck! cluck-a-cluck!" There's something gratifying about sharing the same birth year, as if you were reliving the past together. O-Kuni-san also complained that her family called her Skinny or Longlegs and I, being sour myself about my family calling me Octopus, sympathized with her. As we talked about various things, we agreed on everything, and it didn't take long for us to become good friends. O-Kuni-san was tawny and thin, with a distinct, shapely nose, and she had bangs, her hair neatly gathered behind and tied with a red piece of cloth.

Sometimes leaning on the worm-eaten gate post, sometimes squatting to play with mud, our faces so close as to make our heads almost touch each other, we chatted away about silly nothings, such as the tooth one of us lost yesterday and a finger pricked on a thorn. And when we became totally content with each other, we just laughed out loud. One of her eyeteeth, I think that was it, was missing, and whenever she laughed, the spot looked like a cave. Having had only my aunt as my companion at home, I quickly began, after I became O-Kuni-san's friend, to acquire ideas about things like what was good and what was bad. But since I, though of the same age, was far behind her, I followed her every word in everything.

In the neighborhood was a girl called O-Mine-chan who was one year older than us. She was not only mean but extremely jealous, so everyone disliked her. But since we met every day, children's courtesy sometimes made it necessary to let her join us. One day O-Kuni-san and I again talked about the Year of the Rooster and were fluttering about, cock-a-cocking, cock-a-cocking. When O-Mine-chan saw this, she declared, "Oh, I was born in the Year of the Monkey!" and, squealing like one, she scratched us.

93 Her real name was Okamoto Take (1883–96). That is, she was actually two years older than Naka, but, unlike Naka, she died young.

28

O-Kuni-san's comb was painted red and had a chrysanthemum design lacquered on it. She also had a hairpin with a scarlet and aquamarine crepe ball at its end. Every time she got something new, she showed it to me boastfully. But if I tried to look at it closely, she teased me by hiding it in her sleeve. At such times I regretted I wasn't born a girl, and wondered why boys didn't make themselves as pretty as girls.

When we played Hide-and-Seek, O-Kuni-san would first scare me with stories like "Yesterday the Three-eyed Boy appeared in the bush in the backyard" and "I saw a coiled rock snake." Then she would make me close my eyes under a damson plum and hide herself. I had to go around the house to the backyard to look for her. Near the corner toward the garden, inside a bamboo fence, they kept two geese that I was intensely afraid of. I tried to sneak by, but they always saw me and, pushing up their heads like the Lord Ebisu's crown, guacked after me. I would finally pass them and walk toward the tea bush, but then there was the next-door neighbor's milk cow, who would stick her head over the fence and moo. Since I was afraid of her too, I would only look halfheartedly in the tea bush and go on to search in the garden. There were many big trees there and it was difficult to find my friend. Looking around, I couldn't see anyone, and I knew the cow and the geese were waiting for my return.

"Are you ready?" I would call tentatively.

In the utter silence, there was only the sound of my voice and nothing else. Did she cheat and go off somewhere? I would begin to wonder, my sense of loneliness increasing. I'd wish that my aunt would come to get me.

"Are you ready?" I would call again. I knew my voice trembled with tears. Then, somewhere near the bamboo bush, a small voice would say, "Ready."

There she is, I would think, and go near the bush. But just behind the fence the ginkgo trees of the temple rose up black, and among the bamboo

O-KUNI-SAN'S COMB AND HAIRPIN

stood a confusion of camellias and honey locusts ominously dark. As I stood stiff with fright, wondering if it was true that the Three-eyed Boy had appeared, I would hear a giggle in the depth of the bush. Encouraged, I would go in. But bamboo stumps and roots stuck up everywhere and "it-hurts-it-hurts" grass[94] grew all over the place. So for me, whose aunt meticulously cleared the way of every pebble, it was like the Needle Mountain of Hell, impossible to walk. Besides, I imagined snakes coiling all around me. And it was all so eerie. Step by fearful step I pushed myself forward. When I went near enough, O-Kuni-san would jump out of the dark corner, rolling her eyes and crying, "Boo!"

I knew it was O-Kuni-san, but all the same I would get gooseflesh all over and run away desperately, shouting, "Stop it! Stop it!" That amused her, and she would chase me as if to the end of this world.

Then it would be my turn to hide. But I couldn't hide in the bush, and she knew her grounds well, so she would find me in no time. Sometimes, though, when for some reason she couldn't locate me, she would go into the house and eat cookies. I didn't know that, so, after waiting for what seemed to be an eternity, I would go out and say, "O.K., it's daybreak now!" Then, she would say, "I found you!" and come out munching.

"Here's something for you, too," she'd say and give me the crumbs of her *kinkatō*.

29

We were both very fond of decals. Their oily smell was indescribable. Racing to get the pictures, we would spit on them stickily and, while rubbing them with our fingers, say, "Hurry up and stick, hurry up and stick!"

Then we would place our hands side by side and enjoy stretching and pinching up

94 *Itai-itai-kusa* or *ita-ita-gusa*; another name of *irakusa*, stinging nettle.

the skin on the backs of our hands now tattooed with variously colored birds and animals. In a while the decals became dry and our skin itchy, but we would carefully scratch around them. Once we put the same picture on our upper arms to see which of us could keep it on longer. I took care lest my sleeve wear out the picture, but the next morning I saw only the incoherent fragments of it. Breakfast over, I went to see O-Kuni-san with much trepidation.

"I'm sorry, mine's become like this."

O-Kuni-san indignantly tucked up her sleeve as if to show she was different, only to discover that hers was a mess, too. Widening her eyes, she said, "So has mine!" and laughed merrily.

When the cherry blossoms scattered, we competed in stringing as many petals as we could on a thread.

One day we were playing house in front of O-Kuni-san's foyer with bowls of red bean rice, pretending that wood-sorrel leaves were cucumbers, when O-Mine-chan appeared and said, "Let's play." At once O-Kuni-san whispered to me, "I don't like her. Let's be mean to her."

She sneakily collected the catchweeds growing by the fence and suddenly threw some of them at O-Mine-chan, shouting,

"Catchweeds, catchweeds, catch the devil!"

O-Mine-chan wasn't about to be beaten so readily, and threw some back at us. O-Kuni-san gave me half of the ones she was holding, and I threw them at the girl as best I could in retaliation for the daily ill feelings.

"Catchweeds, catchweeds, catch the devil!"

"Catchweeds, catchweeds, catch the devil!"

"Catchweeds, catchweeds, catch the devil!"

Because it was a surprise attack and her force was inferior in number, O-Mine-chan began to run. We chased her and continued to throw wildly. In no time the catchweeds were stuck all over her back. She turned around angrily and glared at us before starting home with the catchweeds hanging onto her. I watched her go, fearful that she might tell her parents, but then she turned back again, stuck out her chin hatefully, and ran away.

Broad-bean leaves swell like a tree frog's belly when you suck on them. This was fun and I kept plucking them in the garden, though I was scolded each time. If you put a petal of the sasanqua flower on your tongue and draw in your breath, it makes a sound like a *hichiriki* flute.[95]

Come spring, the damson plum[96] in front of the foyer emulated a Confucian scholar and put on blossoms like a puff of cloud, and the clear fragrance of the pale blossoms, dazzled by the sun, lingered around it. The children of the neighborhood would gather below and play various games. When we heard them, my aunt would take me out to them and, after whispering instructions in their ears, go home. Though they were all three or four years older than I, they became attached to my aunt, who loved children, and took to calling her Kan-chan's Aunt. They often played with me, protectively, and looked after me like the children that they were. It was odd that, though much bigger than I, they easily lost any game they played with me. When we played tag, no one could catch me, and when we played with tops, mysteriously, no one's hit mine. Before I knew it, I would find myself a winner. When I went home and talked about it proudly, my family would praise me, saying, "Attaboy! Attaboy!"

It took a long time before this dimwit realized they'd treated me like a ninny.

30

Nearby lived a man who peddled millet jelly half the time and did farm work the other half. If the weather was fine, he always came along pulling his cart, blowing his *chara-mela*[97] every now and then. The sound of that instrument, which seems to shatter the harmony of everything, was strangely

95 A small wind instrument made of bamboo; used in Gagaku.
96 *Sumomo*: *Prunus salicina*.
97 *Charumera*: a simple, small wind instrument that originally came from Portugal in the second half of the 16th century, though the instrument later used came from China.

AMEYA: LOLLIPOP VENDOR'S TUB

exciting to children, prompting those at home to rush outside, and those playing to stop playing and come, running. An assortment of kids, some sporting sticks on their hips as swords, some with muddy tops pushed into the front of their kimono, would noisily surround the cart. Besides millet jelly, the man carried lucky draws and cheap sweets, so for a while the children would be busily occupied with the red and blue tickets. The man would squish a wooden stick around in the amber-colored jelly stagnating in the tub and bring it up with a shiny ball of jelly on the end. You put it in your mouth and turn the stick, and the dense sweetness melts in your saliva and the ball gets smaller and smaller.

The "yummy-yummy lollipop" couple also came by. The man carried on his head what looked like a washtub bound with many brass hoops. It was rimmed with small flags, each tipped with a red and white wood-duck-shaped candy. Dressed in a yukata with the design of a carp leaping up a waterfall,[98] he swayed his shoulders and hip rhythmically as he walked, beating his drum *udo-dong*. He was followed by a woman wearing a towel on her head in "big-sister" style,[99] playing the samisen raucously. If you bought a lot, the man would put on an *okame* mask[100] and dance, and the children would all circle round and watch. He would twist his head, wave his sleeves, and, dancing in carefree fashion to the woman's samisen, he would come with odd steps after the children, who ran about squealing. The dance over, he would say, "Sorry we've been too noisy."

Then he would try to hoist his tub back on his head, but almost drop it to please the children, before going away, weeping.[101]

98 The carp (*Cyprinus carpio*) is usually regarded as a sluggish, bottom-feeding fish, but in traditional imagination it is a vigorous fish full of fighting spirit—the truth of which has been amply demonstrated by the carp from China accidentally introduced into the Mississippi River. As Chinese legend has it, thousands of fish and turtles tried to leap up the waterfalls of the Yellow River called the Dragon Gate, but only the carp managed to do so, and turned into a dragon.

99 *Anesan-kaburi*: a simple way of wearing a towel in lieu of headgear.

100 The face of O-Tafuku-san, for which see note 35 on Ota-san in Episode 1.13.

101 *Yokayoka-ameya*. These were often strolling performers who would visit cheap inns in the evening and do skits from the lives of famous people.

O-Kuni-san's father was a big-boned, powerfully built, scary person. Often he was away on official duty; when he was home, he confined himself upstairs all day, writing. Because he scolded us at the slightest noise we made, I wouldn't go to play when he was home, and O-Kuni-san would stay home, cringing. If I went without knowing he was there and called to her, "O-Kuni-san, will you play with me?" she would open the papered sliding door of the foyer just a little, stick her thumb in front of her nose, and shake it most frightfully.

Once her family invited me over on the day of the Peach Festival.[102] The doll dais was set up high on the formal side[103] of the sunlit guest room, and the dolls arranged on it were splendid. My family's set was so tiny "you could almost put it in your eye," but O-Kuni-san's was big, complete with all five shelves. Because I believed all the dolls were alive, I was cowed and bowed successively to each one of them, drawing uproarious laughter from everyone present. At that moment, quite unexpectedly, O-Kuni-san's father, who I had thought was not home, appeared. I didn't know what to do, and staring alternately at the dolls and at the man, I was about to start sobbing, cringing. Seeing I was scared, he smiled, something he rarely did, and wrapped popped beans for me, and asked how old I was, what my name was, and so forth.

"Who's the scariest of us all?" he said at the end. Honestly, I pointed at him. That drew another uproar from everyone. He too laughed.

"As long as you keep quiet, I won't scold you," he said.

When he went upstairs, I finally felt relieved and heaved a sigh.

102 *Momo no sekku;* also called *hina-matsuri* (doll festival), *jōshi, jōmi.* Held on the 3rd of Third Month (today March 3). Chamberlain: "On the 3rd March every doll-shop in Tōkyō, Kyōto, and the other large cities is gaily decked with what are called O Hina Sama, —tiny models both of people and of things, the whole Japanese Court in miniature. This is the great yearly holiday of all the little girls." Many households used to have a set of such dolls. See Casal for a much fuller account.

103 *Shōmen:* the side of the room equipped with a *tokonoma* (alcove) and a decorative closet.

31

How I miss the games we played in those quiet childhood days! The most enjoyable were those in the evenings. Above all, in early summer as the sun was setting, leaving red, red reflections on the clouds, the children, pressed by the thought that they'd have to go home very soon, became all the more absorbed in their games. When she tired of "Hide Quickly,"[104] Blind Man's Bluff, "Dare Not Catch,"[105] and Hopscotch, O-Kuni-san would brush back her bangs to let the wind cool her perspiring forehead.

"What'll we do next?"

"Let's play 'Coop-him-in,'" I would suggest, wiping the sweat off my face with my sleeve.

"Coop him in! Coop him in!

"Coop the bird in the cage!

"Guess when he'll dare come out!"

After a shower, the young buds on the drooping branches of the cedars by the fence sparkled with raindrops, and these, if you shook the fence, spattered down all at once, which was fun. In a while the raindrops would collect again as before.

At one corner of the playground grew a large silk tree that put out pinkish, feathery flowers. In the evening when the time came for the mysterious leaves to sleep, splendid moths flew in and, quivering their thick brown wings, ran madly from flower to flower, which was eerie. Once, in the belief that the trunk of the silk tree was ticklish, O-Kuni-san and I rubbed it so hard that the skin of our palms almost came off.

As the sunset reflections on the clouds faded, the moon that had been surreptitiously waiting for her turn began to cast a faint light. O-Kuni-san and I would look up at her gentle face and sing "Lady Moon, How Old Are You?"

"Lady Moon, how old are you?

104 *Chongakure.* A contemporary's account says it is a variation of blind man's bluff or blind man's tag.
105 *Oka-oni.* Another variation or name of blind man's bluff.

"Thirteen'n'seven?

"Still so young! . . ."

O-Kuni-san would make tubes of her hands, put them on her eyes, and say, "Do this and you can see the rabbit pounding rice cakes."

I would duly follow her example and peer upward. The idea that a rabbit is pounding steamed rice all by himself in the faint round land gives such delight to the innocent, curious mind of a child. As the moonlight became brighter, we would chase each other's floating shadows to play "Let's Catch Your Shadow,"[106] until my aunt came to get me.

"Come home, supper's ready."

If I held back, planting my feet on the ground refusing to go, she would deliberately wobble as she tugged, saying, "I'm no match for you! No match for you!" Eventually she would coax me into going home.

"Would you play with him tomorrow, too?" my aunt would call to O-Kuni-san. After saying goodnight to her, O-Kuni-san, now turning away, would repeat:

"The frogs are singing, we are going!"

Still reluctant to leave, I would call out the same note. And we would keep calling it out to each other until we reached home.

32

While we were spending such carefree days, a shocking thing happened to both of us. We both turned seven and had to go to school. As I had once been there on my aunt's back when she took lunch boxes for my sisters, I knew what school was like. How could I go to a place swarming with such mean-looking children? Every night when the time came for me to take out the box of toys and play in the dining room, my father and mother would explain at great length, but I kept shaking my head

106 *Kage ya tōro.* Translation tentative.

stubbornly. My mother said that if I didn't go to school, I wouldn't be able to become a great man. I said I didn't care about becoming a great man. My father said he wouldn't keep a son who didn't go to school. I said I would leave home with my aunt and my box of toys.

The protests wrung from my meager brain and sickly child's pleadings were greeted with generous laughter at first, but as the first day of school drew near, the torture became harsher, and soon I was weeping pitifully by the time my aunt took me to bed. In a while, against my wishes, a satchel was bought, then a cardboard pencil case, a large brush for calligraphy, and everything else that was necessary. My sisters said they envied me because mine were better than theirs, but I didn't even want to look at them. All I wanted was the Divine Dog and the Rouge Ox. And if I could play with O-Kuni-san when outside, and when at home play Which-Nut with my aunt, I would be perfectly content. Why did they have to force me to go to school when I didn't want to, I wondered.

I could not for the life of me figure that out. One day I told O-Kuni-san what was happening.

"I'm getting scolded every day myself," she said.

So my good friend, too, disliked school and was suffering the same gloomy fate. We both sat on the root of the damson plum and consoled each other, confiding our shame.

"I'll never go to school," she said as we parted. "Promise you won't, either."

I was glad to make a firm pledge.

33

Finally the day came, but from the morning onward I kept repeating, "I won't go unless O-Kuni-san does," and somehow the day passed.

That night I was pulled out of the bedroom, my hiding place, into

ICHINENSEI: FIRST GRADER

the dining room, the court. They threatened me, cajoled me, but I held out with grim determination. At one point, though, my brother suddenly grabbed me by the collar, threw me down violently on the floor by a strange trick, and gave me a series of slaps on the cheeks.

"What are you doing to this feeble child!" cried my aunt, shielding me with her body. "I'll talk to him," she said, and escaped to the bedroom with me. My brother was doing jujutsu at higher middle school.[107]

The next day, my cheeks swollen, I didn't even go out for meals, but stayed in the bedroom. Worried, my aunt secretly fed me the offerings to the Lord Buddha. Then I came down with an acute fever. Even under normal circumstances I was hypersensitive, so with the fever I scarcely slept all night. My aunt tended me without a wink of sleep, murmuring her prayers.

This lasted for four or five days, and while I stayed in bed no one talked about school. But the first night after I'd recovered from the headache and the fever had subsided, they resumed the torture. My determination was, if anything, firmer than ever, and I repeated that I wouldn't go unless O-Kuni-san did. This time, for some reason, they didn't put me to a painful test, but simply asked, "Are you sure you will if O-Kuni-san does?"

I replied firmly, "I sure will."

The next day, about the time school was over, my aunt carried my pale-faced self outside the gate of our house. The school was only about a hundred and fifty yards away. Soon after the clank-clanking of the bell reached us, throngs of children came out to go home. To my surprise, O-Kuni-san came out, too, in high spirits, carrying wrapped things like everyone else. And because my aunt praised her, "You're great, you're great," she boastfully told us all about school. On my aunt's back, I decided that my friend was terrible. That night I had no choice but to agree to go to school.

The next morning, in *haori* and formal

107 *Kōtō chūgakkō*: a prep school for an imperial (national) university. Shortly after this time, in 1894, the name changed to *kōtō gakkō*, "higher school."

trousers, I entered the school gate with my father. I was taken to the teachers' room where in the cabinets with glass doors there were globes, specimens of birds and fish, picture scrolls of unfamiliar animals, and many other things that attracted me. (These were all things whose names I learned later.) As my father talked in great detail about how my brain was in poor condition and how I was physically weak and timid, I felt totally embarrassed. The teacher listened to him, eyeing me rudely, with an occasional nod. At length, he asked me in a soft tone:

"How old are you?"

"What is your name?"

"What is the name of your father?"

"Where is your home?"

Since I had been taught the answers to all these questions long before and the teacher proved unexpectedly gentle, I managed to answer all of them without a mishap. Perhaps because he was told that my brain was in poor condition, the teacher thought I was dumb. He asked me some more questions as if to make sure of this and gave me permission to enroll, saying, "I think he'll manage."

That day I went home without doing anything else and spent the rest of the day with my sisters giving me instructions on manners at school, how to bow, how to fasten the buckle on my satchel, and so on. And the next day I put on a cap with a cherry-blossom insignia,[108] strapped across myself the satchel I'd never worn before, and went to school, feeling indescribably confused as my aunt led me by the hand. I was so embarrassed that people were looking at my own unfamiliar appearance, and the worry about the still unknown school life was so painful, that I crept along beside my aunt, eyes glued to my toes. At school my sisters led us to the classroom and seated me in the front row.

It was Class C of the first grade where the physically underdeveloped and the mentally retarded were gathered together.

108 The gold cherry-blossom insignia on the school cap was the norm.

34

The children who had enrolled before me were already used to school and since none of them was a weakling like me, they were carrying on, making lots of noise. Before long the usual bell clank-clanked. Heard at close range, the metallic noise penetrated to the core of my head and was extremely annoying. My sisters left saying that they'd come again in the next recess and so did my aunt, with a promise that she would stay outside the room until all the lessons were over. So, left alone, I looked fearfully around and saw the other kids, looking definitely strong and mean, eyeing me rudely. I cringed and was looking intently at the knothole in my desk when the teacher of our class, Mr. Furusawa,[109] came in. Because of the pockmarks that covered his face he looked scary, but he was a man known for his gentleness who was liked by all the children of the school.

The textbook was different from the illustrated story books such as the one with PEKINESE, BOW-WOW, CAT MEOW, SQUEAL,[110] that my aunt had taught me, or the picture books like the one showing DOG, CHOPSTICKS, BOOK, DESK,[111] but it was easy. So I hardly looked at it but kept my eyes on Mr. Furusawa's graying hair loosen, fluttering in the wind.

Soon the lesson was over. Brats avalanched out of the classrooms around ours and, under the wisteria trellises covering the entire playground, leapfrogged, played tag, played commander games. To me, who hadn't known any world other than the tiny one of O-Kuni-san's, the whole affair was unbearably dizzying. So I stood there looking this way and that like a nervous bird, when my sisters' friends ran up to me, as if to say, "So this is the brother we've heard so much about!" and in no time completely surrounded me. And showering me with pert ingratiating remarks, they assailed me from all sides with the usual questions: how old was I, what was my name, and so forth. A poor timid thing, I was as frightened as

109 May have been Yanagiwara Rokuzō at Kuroda Ordinary Higher Elementary School (Jinjō Kōtō Shōgakkō). Horibe, p.124.
110 *Chin, wan, neko-nyā, chū.*
111 *Inu, hashi, hon, tsukue.*

a donkey attacked by a pack of female leopards and could only nod or shake my head, unable even to look up.

Unfortunately, at that moment, a teacher showed up, suddenly grabbed my sash, and lifted me into the air with a shout. The tears that had been hiding behind my eyes all morning gushed out, and kicking my legs feebly, I burst out crying. He was taken aback.

"Oh my goodness! I'm so sorry!" he said and, putting me down, wiped my tears with his handkerchief. Later I learned that he was my older sister's teacher and had done it to please me. I was told not to cry if he did it again. I got the point finally, and was determined not to cry next time, but it seems that once was more than enough for the teacher. He never tried to pick me up again.

The commotion during the following hour of calligraphy was extraordinary. Here a kid upset his ink pot and began crying. There another drew nothing but dumplings in his exercise book and was scolded. Mr. Furusawa went among the children, attending to each problem as if he didn't know what the word trouble meant, and taught each child, occasionally stretching up to rub his back. When his hand all covered with white chalk dust grabbed my brush-holding hand, my whole being stiffened and my brush tip trembled so badly that he had to go over my *i-ro-ha*[112] again and again.

That day the too violent stimulation and totally unfamiliar tasks gave me a headache and nausea, so when the session was over I went home. My aunt cooled my head with water.

"You did fine! You did fine!" she repeated as she gave me a cinnamon stick from the drawer in my wooden pillow, and my sister made me an amulet bag from Nanjing beads as a reward. My headache was gone in no time. All the other members of my family also praised me. "You did fine! You did fine!"

About the time school was over I went to O-Kuni-san's to play with her. There too, they said, "You did fine!" So I thought I had done a fine job and was proud of myself.

112 Japanese syllabary comparable to A, B, C.

35

After a few days I could stay by myself though my aunt had to accompany me to and from school. Every day she would put my favorite cookies in clam shells, seal them with red pieces of paper, and take them out for me from the altar drawer the moment I returned from school and got rid of my satchel. I liked to choose a few from among them, unable to easily decide which to take.

Soon I was transferred to Class A. The pupils in the class surrounded this newcomer promoted from Class C and whispered among themselves, apparently sizing me up. Soon one of them saw the German letters my brother had written on my satchel and approached.

"Look, he's got English on his bag."

The others edged in, exclaiming, thrusting their faces up close to me. When one of them asked me what the writing meant, I said it was my name, as I'd been told at home. For a while they looked at it enviously.

"Damn it!" said one. "He's Japanese, right? But he has a darn foreigner's name!"

Then another found my amulet bag with its tiny bell and began fingering it with his grubby hands. I didn't like that but I was afraid and didn't dare stop him. The bag was woven with aquamarine and white Nanjing beads to make a checkered pattern, and on the bell was embossed a bell insect. A glass gourd was attached to the other end of the purple string. What the hell do you have to carry a bell around for? the same kid asked. I said it was for my aunt to hear and come to get me when I was lost. They looked at each other with obvious contempt. Soon their fumbling proved too much for the bag; the weak threads stringing the beads together broke and the beads scattered on the floor. I began to snivel. At once the children drew back, looking as though they had done something terrible.

"I didn't do it! A third-year crow did it!" they chorused while watching me worriedly from a distance. I didn't know what to do, with no one coming to my rescue, unable to cry even if I had wanted to. I was just staring at the scattered beads, sniffling, when fortunately my sister arrived. All at once my sorrow overcame me and I burst into tears. The kids feared my sister might scold them. Keeping time with their feet and calling, "Weeping worm, hairy worm! Pinch him up and throw him away!" they hurried out of the room.

My sister consoled me with a promise that she would make me another bag. Spoiled as I was, I insisted on going home at once. Eventually she calmed me down and was helping me wipe the tears and blow my nose, when the bell rang. She left, saying she'd come again during the next recess. In came the evil kids who were watching the whole scene secretly from outside the room.

"Weeping a minute ago! Now laughing like a crow!" they chanted and danced around me.

The teacher in charge of the new class was a bearded man called Mr. Mizoguchi. Like Mr. Furukawa, Mr. Mizoguchi was a good person born to take care of children. He saw that I was withdrawn, and treated me with special kindness.

The kid who shared the double desk with me was called Iwahashi; the son of a roof-tile vendor, he was reputed to be a bully. He drew a line with a pencil at the middle of the desk and if my elbow intruded into his territory he elbowed me sharply or smeared his snot on me. He talked to me during one lesson, and though I didn't like it I responded without paying much attention. When Mr. Mizoguchi spotted this, he wrote our family names on the blackboard side by side and drew large black marks above them. The moment he saw this, Iwahashi leaned forward onto his slate and began to cry. But I didn't know what it was all about and just kept looking at the teacher, puzzled.

When the lesson was over and my sister came, she said with a smile that I must have talked during the lesson. Who had already told her, I wondered, but sensing I'd done something wrong, I said I hadn't. She said I didn't have to hide it because my name was marked with a black mark on the blackboard. When I learned that the circle was put there when you misbehaved, I was suddenly overcome with sadness.

36

Iwahashi's books were smeared with red pencil. In an illustration that showed a patrolman coming away from a house on fire, leading a lost child by the hand, shafts of light ran wildly in all directions from the child's head, and the patrolman's eyeballs bulged as if about to burst. Once he drew things like a One-eyed Boy and a Three-eyed Boy on his slate and showed them to me:

"Look! Look!"

Remembering the black mark from the other day, I ignored him. This prompted him to make a fist under the desk and, flexing it, he glared at me sideways. As soon as the lesson was over and our teacher went away, he breathed on his fist and came toward me, so I went out into the hall and stood alone in a spot where he was unlikely to find me. An older member of the same class, a red-faced, dirty kid came by.

"I'll give you something nice." He had something in his hand and asked me to hold out mine. I was afraid he'd trick me, but I also feared him, so I held out my hand without fuss. He dropped a couple of red berries into it. I didn't want anything like that but, happy that somebody was being kind to me, I smiled.

"Thank you."

It was only five or six years later that I learned they were the berries of "handsome-man's vine"[113] at the back of the school. Because of his red face, the student was nicknamed Monkey-faced Footman; also because his name was Chōhei, he was called Choppei as well. He was the son of a fishmonger in front of the Denpō-in.[114]

After this Choppei became my only companion and, though I wouldn't have even spoken to him if that had been possible, he must have found something in me, for he often talked to me. One day he said to me:

113 *Binan-kazura (Kadsura japonica):* a shrub that bears glossy red berries. The sap from its stalks used to be used as hair oil, hence the name. Also called *sanekazura.* It is a popular plant in classical Japanese verse.

114 This probably refers to a sub-temple or temple.

"During the next lesson let's go and piss together."

"I don't want to. The teacher will scold us," I said. At once he chanted, making a fearsome face.

If you don't want to,

Don't even try to,

Who's that in the reeds!

"I will, I will." I hastened to say. He at once recovered his good humor and said, "It'll be all right if you do what I do."

Soon after the lesson started, he raised his hand. "Mr. Mizoguchi, may I go to do number one?"

"Do you really need to? I'll find out soon enough if you've lied to me," the teacher said. This didn't deter Choppei. "Yes, I really need to."

Mr. Mizoguchi had to be concerned about a pupil losing control in the classroom. "All right then, go. Come back as soon as you're done. Dawdle on the way, and I'll give you a black mark."

Several others raised their hands, asking to be allowed to go to the bathroom in a group. As he was leaving the room with them, Choppei gave me a quick glance. Startled, I fearfully raised my hand and, copying what the others had done, said, "Mr. Mizoguchi, may I go to do number two?"

Mr. Mizoguchi, not knowing that Choppei had instigated it, gave permission on the spot.

The bathroom was some way off from the classrooms, located as it was right under a thicket of bear bamboo[115] belonging to the next-door building, the Lord Hachiman's. Choppei was waiting for me there.

"Let's wrestle," he said.

I looked around. The other kids had climbed over the railings of the passage-way and were digging for sweet-roots[116] on the embankment or making balls out of

115 *Sasa (Sasa nipponica)*: a variety of bamboo, though, unlike regular bamboo, *sasa* is a low-growth plant with a profusion of leaves.

116 *Amane: chigusa (Phalaris canariensis)?*

crumbly mud and throwing them at one another. For them, number one was an excuse to have a break. Choppei pressed me: "Come, come on."

I, who until that very moment had done only the Shiōten versus Kiyomasa's combat scene with my aunt as my opponent, didn't know what to do, but there was no getting out of it.

"It's dangerous. Please be gentle," I said plaintively and unthinkingly grappled Choppei. Choppei, who was strong, pulled me round and round while calling out lustily, "Fight! Fight!"

Alas, this was too much for the reputable Kiyomasa; stepping on the hem of his own hakama, he fell right on his haunch.

"You're weak. We'll do it again," Choppei snottily said, and started back. I adjusted my twisted kimono and followed him.

As he entered the classroom, he gave a quick bow with an innocent air.

"Sir, I'm back."

I bowed without saying anything. The others also returned, one after another. The kid who'd dug sweet roots kept chewing on one for so long that he was made to stand in a corner. Worse, the sweet root he had in the chest of his kimono edged out and was spotted, eliciting a fine rebuke. I decided not to go to the bathroom again.

37

Among the subjects for study the one that pleased everyone the most was ethics. This was because our teacher hung a scroll of pretty pictures on the wall and told us interesting stories. One picture showed a mother bear who had been shot with a bullet and had died while still holding up a rock to enable her cub to keep looking for crabs underneath it; another showed a general watching a spider make a cobweb, chin in hand. Enchanted by the beautiful pictures and fascinated by the stories, the pupils always asked for more. Mr. Mizoguchi would turn the pictures one by one and say:

"As long as you behave, I'll tell you any number of stories."

Most times he would end up going through the whole scroll of pictures. Strangely, though, he always skipped the picture that was at the very beginning, which showed a foreign woman fallen in the snow with a child in her arms. The pupils, though they saw that it was there, never asked to be told its story, either. But I, especially attracted by that picture, each time waited expectantly, in vain.

When the bell rang, the pupils would noisily surround the teacher in his chair, one climbing on his knees, another holding on to his shoulder, and so forth, crying, "Tell us that story again! Tell us that story again!" forcing him to tell the same stories over and over again. Unable to be as bold as they were, I would stand a little apart, vaguely looking at the pictures. But once, Mr. Mizoguchi turned toward me and asked, "Naka-san, shall I tell you a story, too? Which is your favorite?"

I merely blushed, so he urged, "You must tell me."

Feeling as if my life were about to end, I finally mumbled, "This one," pointing at the picture in question. No one seemed pleased, for they all said, "It's no good."

"That's not interesting," Mr. Mizoguchi said, adding, "Is that all right?" I nodded in silence.

Mr. Mizoguchi realized that I didn't know the story yet. So, persuading the other pupils who complained, he told the story for the newcomer. It concerned a mother who, lost in the snow, kept taking her clothes off to cover her child until she finally froze to death. The picture was not colorful enough to delight children, and that was all there was to the story, so they weren't excited by it, which was why Mr. Mizoguchi had skipped it. But to me, it was more than interesting. I listened to it with as much pity as I felt when my aunt told me the story of Lady Tokiwa.[117]

117 Tokiwa Gozen (1138–90?): concubine of Minamoto no Yoshitomo (1123–60). After Yoshitomo was defeated during the Heiji Disturbance in 1160 and killed, Taira no Kiyomori

When the story was over, Mr. Mizoguchi asked, "It wasn't interesting, was it?" In all honesty, I nodded yes. The teacher looked surprised, and the pupils giggled contemptuously.

38

It was around that time that I often felt the desire to escape people's eyes and be alone and hid myself under a desk, in a closet, wherever it might be. While withdrawn into such a place and thinking about various things, I would feel an indescribable peace and sense of satisfaction. Among the hiding places I liked most was the space by a chest of drawers. It was in our gloomiest room, illuminated only by the light that shone in through the north window facing the storehouse. Between that window and the cabinet there was just enough space for me to install myself, knees tucked up. Squatting there, I looked at the radiating cracks on a windowpane, the *kaya* tree[118] right next to it, the "handsome-man's vine" entwining a dead tree, its red vines, and the aphids sucking the sap at their tips.

There I would spend half a day, even a whole day, mumbling to myself, acquiring, I know not when, the habit of writing with a pencil the hiragana representing the sound *wo* on the side of the cabinet; in the end

(1118–81), who emerged victorious, ordered that Tokiwa's three sons— Imawaka (later, Ano Zensei, 1153–1203), Otowaka (later, Gien, 1155–81), and Ushiwaka (later, Yoshitsune, 1159–89)—be captured and killed. Told of this, Tokiwa fled Kyoto, taking her three sons along with her. As the military tale *Heiji monogatari* tells it: "It was the 10th of Second Month. The persisting cold was severe, and it snowed ceaselessly. She made Imawaka walk ahead, led Otowaka by the hand, and carried Ushiwaka hugging him, with the two boys not even wearing footwear as they walked barefoot on ice. 'It's cold, it's freezing, Mother,' the young ones cried and wept. She took her robes off and had them wear them, making sure that they were on the quiet downwind side, she on the severe upwind side."

118 *Torreya nucifera*: a large evergreen tree.

countless *wo,* large and small, formed lines. Becoming suspicious about my proclivity to get into that corner, my father eventually looked in and in no time discovered those lines. But he just thought they were no more than idle graffiti and did not scold me much, merely saying that if I was doing writing exercises, I ought to do so in a notebook. But for me they were not, heavens, mere graffiti. The hiragana *wo* somehow resembles a seated woman. With my tiny heart, with my feeble body, whenever something happened, I sought consolation in that character, these characters surmised my thoughts well and consoled me with kindness.

Even after moving to the new place, I was assaulted by frightening dreams as often as once every three days and would run about the house in the dead of night. One such dream was that of a black swirl hanging in midair, about a foot in diameter, which pulsated like the spring of a clock. That was spooky enough, but even as I tried to hold myself in check, a monstrous crane would fly in from somewhere and hold the swirl in its beak. Another was something like intestines pushing against one another making a splat-splat noise. Then these would turn into a woman's face that kept its mouth wide open like a fool, suddenly opened its eyes and made a long, long face. Or else it would close its mouth, extend it sideways, crimping and shrinking its eyes and nose, turning itself into an extraordinarily flat face. It would go on extending and shrinking until I burst out crying.

The suspicion arose that I was assaulted only by such dreams because of my aunt's fairy tales. Also, the suggestion was made that I try a new bedroom, so it was decided that I ought to sleep by my father. Yet the tales of military exploits of such men as Miyamoto Musashi[119] and Yoshitsune[120] with his Benkei[121] that he told me every

119 A swordsman famous for simultaneously using the two swords that a samurai carried (1584?–1645). The best-known among his tracts on swordsmanship is *Book of Five Elements (Gorin no sho)*.

120 Minamoto no Yoshitsune (1159–89): a warrior-commander who helped his clan, the Miyamoto, win the war against the rival clan, the Taira. See note 117 on Tokiwa Gozen in Episode 1.37.

121 A legendary warrior-monk who remained steadfastly loyal to Yoshitsune.

night proved to be of no use, with the ghouls thinking nothing of a mere father and still visiting me as in the past. In the previous bedroom there was a demon in the ceiling of the alcove; in the new room the octagonal clock on the pillar turned into a One-eyed Boy and the four sliding doors scared me by becoming gigantic mouths.

39

Following our doctor's recommendation, my father decided to take me and my mother, both of us prone to being sickly, to a certain seashore for our health. On our way I was extremely happy to see nature unfold before my eyes exactly as I had longed to see it, child though I was, having only seen it in the pictures on poem cards and in picture copybooks. I saw the mysterious sea, which I could not possibly ladle into my small vat of imagination. It was transparent indigo, with sailboats running on it, their sails gleaming like silver. When we passed between steep cliffs, I felt an unbearable loneliness and pitied the straggly grasses that grew on them.

At a shrine for Chinese people that looked like the Dragon Palace,[122] an old Chinese woman was praying for something, dropping a pebble on the pavement for each of her prayers. And a doll-like child with her hair parted with pomade, walking unsteadily on her lovely legs, was, I thought, pretty. A store selling trinkets made from

122 Ryūgū(jō): the undersea palace where the Watatsumi (Sea God) lives. It is famous for the Urashima legend. A young fisherman, Urashima Tarō, out fishing in his boat, meets and marries the Watatsumi's daughter, Princess Oto, and spends three glorious years in the palace. When he returns to his fishing village, he discovers three hundred years have passed. The best account appears in the Tango *Fudoki*, one of the regional reports compiled in 713. The large verse anthology *Collection of Ten Thousand Leaves (Man'yōshū)* has a poem on the legend, no. 1740. In both accounts the palace is said to be Paradise (*tokoyo*), but in neither is it called Ryūgū.

seashells was packed with displays of treasures from the bottom of the sea. Father bought several hairpins as souvenirs for my older sisters and a bag of "vinegar shells"[123] for me, but I wondered why he didn't buy all of them, everything being so beautiful. As we rode a carriage through a seashore pine grove, the pines were endless. Pines were in the hanging scroll of Takasago[124] that we hung during the New Year and, because my aunt had often told me that the pine is a divine tree, I was superstitiously fond of pine trees.

In a while we arrived at our inn. I had just enjoyed a quiet pine grove, but here there was the hubbub of people, so I started crying, saying, "I want to go home." At once the manager and maids rushed to me and, calling me "Little Master," coaxed me into feeling that I was an old acquaintance of theirs. So, I was relieved and soon stopped crying. And for the rest of the day, smelling the fragrance of the salt wind, I remained entranced, watching the waves crashing noisily beyond the low pine trees, oblivious to everything else.

At night the lamp was lit. Its shade was a tubular bamboo basket with paper pasted on it, and it sat on a black-lacquered, elegant box. Longing for light, "side-crawlers"[125] flew in and perched on it. Of a beautiful green and with a wide space between their eyes, they were terribly cute. When you tried to press on one with your finger, it suddenly crawled sidewise, escaping to the next segment of the basket. "Dove insects"[126] also came.

One night I was out on the verandah

123 *Sugai (Turbo [Lunella] coreensis)*: a species of marine snail.
124 Harbor at the estuary of the Kako River, in Harima (today's Hyōgo), once famous for its picturesque scenery. Takasago is also the name of a celebratory nō play by Zeami (1363–1443?), which is based on the legend that the pine of Takasago and the pine of Sumiyoshi, in Settsu (today's Osaka), are husband and wife, and on the belief in the pine tree as a symbol of peaceful coexistence and longevity. The protagonist of the play is a benign-looking, handsome old man with white hair and white eyebrows, and he holds a rake.
125 *Yokobai (Japanagallia pteridis)*: an insect that looks like a tiny version of a cicada.
126 *Hato-mushi* or, more commonly, *hato* or *aobahagoromo (Geisha distinctissima)*: a light-green insect one third of an inch long. *Aobahagoromo* means "blue (green) wing feathery cloth."

watching the fireworks shooting up, when a beautiful woman came by with candies wrapped in paper.

"This is for you," she said.

I'd heard that she was a "geisha," that geisha are scary people who deceive you. The "geisha" came very close to me and said, "What a lovely child! How old are you?" She put her hands on my shoulders and looked into my face, her cheek almost touching mine. Enveloped in her fragrant sleeves I was unable even to respond, ears burning, as I clung to the rail, when I suddenly realized she'd come to deceive me. Terrified, I forced myself out from under her sleeves and ran back to my mother. When, my chest thumping, I told her about it, she chided me, with a little smile, on my bad manners. After that, each time I saw the fireworks, I would tell myself that the next time the geisha asked me something I'd reply to her, that if she gave me candies I'd thank her. But she must have been offended, for she wouldn't even come near me after that. I was truly sorry I did not have a chance to tell her of my regrets.

One day I went into the depths of a deep pine grove with father. There was the scent of pine, and pine cones lay everywhere. Father walked slowly, but since I was picking up pine cones, from time to time I had to rush to catch up with him. As I scurried after him while talking intimately in my mind with the gathered pine cones that filled my chest and sleeves, we came upon a gazebo and an old man with snow-white eyebrows raking pine needles. I was overjoyed, taking him to be the old man of Takasago—I really did—and, unusually for me, said various things to father. Back at the inn, father said to mother, with a laugh: "Today our Octopus Boy babbled quite a bit."

40

Back from the trip I felt a loneliness resembling betrayal when I found out that while we were away O-Kuni-san and her family had moved to a distant place because of her father's assignment. From then on I ceased to be assaulted by terrible dreams and, besides, my body began to grow visibly. But my innate slow-wittedness and neglect of school remained unchanged. This was not only because of my feebleness, but also because school life, too complicated and filled with too much pain for an innocent child, made me dislike it. Except, happily, Mr. Nakazawa, who was in charge of our class at the time, was a good teacher whom I liked a great deal and, on top of that, my seat was right in front of his desk. No matter how often I failed to show up, he did not say anything and no matter how poorly I did in the class he merely giggled.

Still, he scolded me once, and that was when I had a fight with the kid seated with me, Andō Shigeta. For some reason we hated each other's guts and were always at odds. One day, during an hour on arithmetic, he insisted that I look at his slate on which he'd drawn a face with one of its eyes blinded and my name scribbled by it. So I drew a large wooden clog, attached eyes and a nose to it, wrote "Wall-eyed" next to it, and showed it to him. He suddenly kicked me on the shin. Not about to accept submission, I elbowed his side. We were engaged in this private fight for some time before our teacher noticed; when school was over, he made us stay behind. Looking angry as he seldom had, he asked, Why did you have a fight? I told the whole story, insisting that I wasn't to blame, but Shigeta lied by saying that I made fun of him first, so our teacher refused to let us go home, saying, It's a case of "the two parties in a fight are equally punishable."[127] All the others were happily going home holding their belongings wrapped up in cloths. Some of the more curious kids were looking in the door, laughing.

When all the pupils of the school were gone, everything turned quiet, which I didn't like. What would I do if it went on like this and night fell? I wouldn't be able to eat, and I wouldn't be able to sleep. When will aunt

127 *Kenka ryōseibai*: an old adjudicatory principle. One reason the famous Forty-seven Samurai carried out their vendetta for their lord, in 1703, was the shogunate's failure to uphold this principle in punishing both their lord and the man he tried to kill.

come to get me and apologize? Such thoughts swirled in my head, and tears slowly began to well up in my eyes. Our teacher from time to time looked at us, from one to the other, now both almost whimpering, while he pretended to read, giggling. This kid Shigeta, who'd been fingering the strings of his satchel hanging from his shoulder, obviously eager to go home, finally burst into tears and said, "I'm sorry, sir."

"So you apologized. That's fine. I forgive you," Mr. Nakazawa said, and let him go home.

I myself would have rather gone home too, but deeply offended as I was that I was made to stay though I wasn't to blame, I persisted, holding back the tears each time I started to sob. In the end, though, I had no choice but to sob. And once I started sobbing, I whimpered helplessly, for that was my habit, rubbing my eyes with my fists, even while slowly reflecting on the right and wrong, the fairness and the unfairness of it all. And whenever I decided that I was to blame, I would stop sobbing at once, while when I did not, I would sob audibly, bitter that I was unreasonably oppressed just because I was small and weak, and thinking, Wait until I get back at you all. There is also the fact that, after you've sobbed to your heart's content, you feel as if your chest were aired, a sort of unbearably pleasant sensation down in your windpipe.

Mr. Nakazawa in the meantime was at a loss.

"If you apologize, I'll let you go," he would repeat, but I wouldn't, insisting that I wasn't to blame. As I slowly began to listen to what he had to say, however, I could finally see that, even though it was Shigeta's fault to start a fight, it was wrong for me to have responded to it during a lesson, so I bowed to him and said, "I am sorry, sir," and he let me go.

Back home, on hearing that their timid Octopus Boy had had a fight, my family all laughed, as if it were a miracle.

41

128 Toyotomi Hideyoshi sent an invading army to Korea twice: the first time, in 1592, for the purpose of conquering China—the Ming Dynasty at the time—and the second time, in 1597, for a punitive purpose, Hideyoshi claiming that China had violated the terms of the ceasefire agreement concluded a year earlier. In the first expedition, Hideyoshi's army of 160,000 soldiers won a series of victories but had to abandon the idea of reaching China. During the second expedition, the Japanese army of 140,000 soldiers again won quick victories but decided to withdraw because of Hideyoshi's death. Katō Kiyomasa, who had served as a top commander in the first expedition as well, had to defend the fort he had built in Ulsan—actually the outermost one of a network of eight forts— from the combined Ming-Korean forces twice, the first time from the end of 1597 to early 1598, the second time, in the summer of 1598, and beat them back both times. For Kiyomasa, see note 19 in Episode 1.8.

The penalty for neglecting to study was direct: when the time for tests came I knew almost nothing. To be left alone in the classroom when everyone else quickly does the tests and leaves, it would be as uncomfortable as an octopus being boiled, even in a dream. Most painful of all was the reader. I was finally summoned to the teacher's desk. In question was the chapter called "Defending the Ulsan Castle." I had never seen anything like "Ulsan" before. I just stood there without saying a word, so my teacher, thinking of nothing better to do, made me read, teaching me one or two characters at a time, but I was simply entranced by the illustration showing Katō Kiyomasa surrounded by Ming forces,[128] while comprehending nothing of the book. My teacher, running out of patience, tossed the reader down in front of me and said, "Well then, read any part you can."

"I can't read any part of it," I said, as if nothing was wrong.

Even after the tests were over, I stayed on in the same seat. I had assumed that because I was in the very first row I was number one. That my name plate hung at the very end, that I was called last in the roll call, or that I was in fact the worst learner, did not raise the least suspicion in my mind. To be placed next to my favorite teacher and not to be scolded at all—if this didn't show I was number one, what else could? Besides, I had never been called to accept my diploma, and when I went home from school and boasted that I was number one, everyone would laugh, saying, You're fine! You're fine! So, as far as I was concerned, everything was all right.

Around the time that this semester was coming to a close, a new family moved in next-door. Between that house and ours, beyond the vegetable garden in our backyard, there was only a cedar hedge, allowing free passage between us. When I was out in the back spying on what was going on, a young lady about my age came out to the hedge, then suddenly hid herself behind it, evidently stealthily spying on our side from between two cedars. After a while she came out again and gave me a glance, so I gave her a glance back, too, then both of us looked away. While we were repeating such things over and over, I noticed she was skinny, with an air of sickliness, and I somehow came to like her. The next time our eyes met she showed the suggestion of a smile. So, I gave a smile, too. She, as if to avert her face, turned round on one foot. I did the same. She jumped. So did I. She jumped and I jumped. While we were jumping like that, I gradually moved away from the shadow of an almond tree, she away from the hedge, the two of us coming close enough to talk. But just then there was a call: "Missy, it's mealtime." With "Yes!" she quickly ran away.

I went regretfully inside, finished my meal in a hurry, and went out again. She was already there waiting.

"Let's play," she said, walking toward me in a friendly manner. Because I was all prepared to jump several more times before becoming more familiar, this unexpected turn of events made me blush, but I said, "Let's," and walked up to her. She was no longer bashful and asked clearly, "How old are you?"

"Nine," I replied.

"I'm nine, too," she said, smiled a little, and said something you might have expected from a grown-up: "But because I was born in the New Year I am old for my age."[129]

129 In the old way of counting one's age, a person was one year old at the time of birth. Someone

"What is your name?" I asked.

"Kei," she said clearly.

Having declared our names to each other as formality required and exchanged the greetings of a first meeting, O-Kei-chan said, "I'm going to school soon. Let's go to the same school."

I was happy to hear that. So I wracked my tiny brain enumerating how nice my school was, how wonderful the stories for ethics were, how gentle the teacher of my class was, and so forth, in my attempt to attract O-Kei-chan to my school. O-Kei-chan was spirited and not at all shy, and had clear, round eyes and jet-black hair. In her pale, smooth cheeks I could see a beautiful color of blood. And with her strong temperament and precocious mind she had the tendency, I sensed, to behave like a queen toward me, timid, slow-witted, and young for his age. But I decided with satisfaction to yield myself to the beck and call of this queen, who had newly appeared to reign over me.

42

One day, when I saw O-Kei-chan come into the school accompanied by her grandmother, my heart pulsed as if anew. From the next day on she came to the one classroom holding her wrapping cloth and, being a newcomer, was seated in the front row, right next to me. I couldn't devote myself to the lesson under way and gave her a sidelong glance. She kept her eyes down steadily, in modesty. During playtime she, still with no one to be friendly with, looked absentminded. I wanted to talk to her but kept my mouth shut, afraid that everyone would make fun of me. She must have known how I felt but, feigning ignorance, looked unconcerned. It was with a

born in an earlier part of the year, as in the New Year, had advantage over someone born later in the year in growth and other respects, even though they were the same age.

chaotic feeling that I finally waded through the day's lessons. On my way home I thought, I'll talk about this, I'll ask her about that. As soon as I returned home I went around to the back where I found her playing with a ball, all alone.

"O-Kei-chan!" I called out and ran up to her, as if ready to pounce on her. O-Kei-chan, however, said, with obvious contempt, "I'm not playing with the class dummy," and quickly went inside her house. Expectations thwarted, I went back into my house crestfallen and told my aunt about it.

That evening, when my family gathered as usual in the dining room, I was told for the first time, in no uncertain terms, that I was indeed truly the class dummy. At first I insisted, stubbornly, that I was number one. But when I heard that my teacher had recently warned my family that, even though he didn't want to be unreasonable to me, their feeble-brained child, the way I'd been doing so far he wouldn't be able to promote me, so he hoped I'd pay a little more attention to the next tests—when I heard this, I burst out crying. All at once I felt the indignity of having been the class dummy all this time. So my teacher, believing that I had a feeble brain, had allowed me to take the day off as often as I wanted, and didn't scold me no matter how little I seemed to learn. I had been regarded as an idiot after all. Even I knew it was shameful to be the class dummy. But I hadn't worked because I knew I was number one however lazy I was. Had they told me all this earlier, I would have reviewed my lessons, I wouldn't have played hooky. As I thought about it, I resented everybody. My thoughts excited to boiling point, I remembered this and cried, remembered that and cried, until my aunt, now crying herself in sympathy, took me to the bedroom saying, "You don't have to cry, you don't have to cry."

From then on, I was given a small desk and was made to review each day's lessons precisely, prepare for the next day, and periodically recapitulate what I'd learned. My aunt took care of the abacus, calligraphy, and whatever else she could do for me, and my older sisters took care of the rest. It was both painful and infuriating to come face to face with O-Kei-chan in class every day. But from that time on I never took a day off from school. O-Kei-chan was utterly unconcerned about all this as she played with her friends. Nervous among my classmates, I tended to be withdrawn, but the pain of going home and being forced to sit in front of my desk was something else. I'm ashamed to say this but I had not comprehended any of the things I'd learned up to then. So, disheartened, I was tempted to give up on all of it often enough, but I was deceived with cookies and other rewards until finally I began to see, as though peeling away one onion skin after another. As I learned one character, then two, in the reader, as I solved one arithmetic problem, then two, my knowledge made a geometrical progression, in the end enabling me to gain self-confidence. And with my own curiosity added to it, I started to take out my desk upon coming home before anyone told me to. Needless to say, the motive was to be complimented. Even though the tests were coming up soon, thanks to my studying, I came second in the class in the next semester. O-Kei-chan was fifth among the girls.

43

As I suddenly gained knowledge and the world became fresh and bright as if it had sloughed off one layer of its skin, my feeble body visibly grew capable. I soon began to find myself among the two or three strongest in everything—wrestling, "flag-taking," what have you. By the time I became class leader, succeeding the kid named Shōda, who was tops in the class but left, my regret and fury about O-Kei-chan had long disappeared. As a result, I hoped that the young herb of friendship that had sprouted the very first day, ready to open its leaves, but had begun to wither at its roots even before coming into flower, would sweetly revive again in the spring sunshine. And I could see that O-Kei-chan felt the same way. But for some reason there was no proper graft and both of us waited for an appropriate opportunity.

In children's society, as among dogs, the single strong one beats the rest into submission. With Shōda gone, the whole world became mine alone, and I took advantage of everyone's obedience and to some extent wielded willful power, although I'd like to allow that I was the most understanding among the "generals of brats" of my own age.

Once, Choppei, ostracized for some incident and being taunted with his sobriquet Monkey-faced Footman, dashed back and forth, his face red hot, scratching at everybody—until finally, overwhelmed, he started to cry, putting his face down on his desk. Having watched this, I suddenly plunged into the middle of the noisy crowd and issued a stern injunction against calling Choppei Monkey-faced Footman. After that he was freed from that dirty name. By this I returned a small part of the favor he'd done in giving me red berries when I first came to school, which I had never forgotten.

Iwahashi remained the leading bully, playing dirty tricks on the girls. One day, when our teacher led us all to the sorrel hill for exercise, as he often did, I saw Iwahashi in a bush, alone, intently collecting "dog lice."[130] I guessed he was going to play some trick again. Sure enough, he emerged clutching lots of dog lice in each hand, his eyes glinting as if he were playing Takechi Mitsuhide.[131] The girls were always frightened of him and none of them was around. Unfortunately, O-Kei-chan happened to come his way. Iwahashi wasn't about to let this chance go by: he at once blocked her way and threw a couple of dog lice at her.

"No, don't do that!" O-Kei-chan ran,

130 *Inu-jirami*: Naka probably refers to a plant in the *Oenanthe* family commonly known as *kusa-jirami*, "grass lice," or *yabu-jirami*, "bush lice" (*Torilis japonica*). Its tiny seedpods are burs that stick readily to clothes and hair.

131 A figure in the kabuki *Taikō ki*, modeled after Akechi Mitsuhide. See note 19 in Episode 1.8. In historical plays and other accounts written during the Edo period, changing the real names, often in palpably obvious fashion, was routine because the Tokugawa government frowned upon descriptions of actual historical figures, current and in the recent past.

shielding herself with her sleeves, but Iwahashi chased her and persisted in throwing dog lice at her. Trying to dodge, she fell on her knees and burst out crying. I dashed forward, knocked the victorious Iwahashi down, and, watching his furious face over my shoulder, walked up to O-Kei-chan. She had gotten up on her feet but was hiding her face in her sleeve, without even dusting herself off. I walked up to her and removed, one by one, all the dog lice that clung to her hair and kimono. At first O-Kei-chan continued to sob in frustration, not knowing who it was that was being nice to her even while abandoning herself to their care. Finally, though, she peeked out from her sleeve, as if to find out who that person was, and when our eyes met, she smiled a pleased smile. Her long eyelashes all wet, her large eyes shone beautifully. After that the friendship between us unfurled and thrived, just like the swollen bud of a peony that, pregnant with fragrance and ready to bloom, begins to open up at the tickling breeze stirred by a butterfly's wings.

44

Coming home from school we could hardly wait to finish reviewing the day's lesson and preparing for the next day before running out into the memory-filled backyard. When I was out first, I would play hopscotch or jump rope, alone, impatiently waiting for her. When she was the first out, she would bounce a *temari* ball as if she wanted me to hear the sound. The ball was prettily wrapped in stripes of red and blue woolen yarn. The moment we saw each other, we would do "rock, paper, scissors" before anything else. O-Kei-chan had the habit of shaking her shoulders as if exasperated when she lost.

Miss Start-of-Year, O-Yone's ten,
Miss Start-of-Year, O-Yone's twenty

MARITSUKI: TEMARI-BALL PLAYING

I was good at playing ball and seldom let it get away. O-Kei-chan, scarcely able to wait for her turn, would throw a piece of rope at the ball or thrust a stick out to make me drop it.

Onenjo sāma, oyonejo tō yo.
Onenjo sāma, oyonejo hatachi yo.[132]

O-Kei-chan, her face hot with excitement, would nod along with her bouncing ball, turning round and round as best she could. Each time she turned, her long hair would play around her shoulders, her feet twirling after each other like mice. Trying not to lose her turn, she would sometimes hold the ball with her chin or hold it up against her chest, until she would begin to totter.

Hō-hokekyo,[133] *bush-warbler,*
bush-warbler,
as she happened to go up to the Capital,
go up to the Capital,
she took a nap on a little plum twig,
dreamed of an Akasaka footman,
and a letter came out
from under her pillow,
a letter came out
asking O-Chiyo to come. . . .

At times she would be so carried away she wouldn't notice that the lower hems of her kimono were dragging on the ground. Like playful rabbits, her hands, left and right, jumped around above the ball even as her peeping voice tumbled out from inside her round, open lips. Those innocent songs sung in her beautiful voice still remain in my

132 One of the *kazoeuta,* "counting rhymes," in playing *temari.* In a collection of his essays on customs and the like toward the end of the Edo period, *Kiyū shōran* (1830), Kitamura Nobuyo (1784–1856) quoted a version of these counting rhymes, saying, "The meaning is hard to get." See Horibe, p. 163. The tentative translation given here is based on Kyoko Selden's suggestion that *nenjo* may mean "start of year." *Jo* of *oyonejo* is a suffix meaning "girl" or "woman."

133 The onomatopoeic reproduction of the warbler's warbling. It is thought to be particularly auspicious because it also means "The Law, the Lotus Sutra." What follows is one of the *temari* songs current in those days.

ear as a fond echo. As the evening sun set beyond the field and in its place the moon began to rise somewhat unsteadily, small moths that had been hiding in the leaves of the flower garden danced up, tremulously beating their gray wings. In the black pines of the Shōrin temple crows flocked, vying for branches, and in the "coral tree" in my garden sparrows chirped, chirped, chirped. Then we would look up at our dear moon, whose yellow was finally fading, and sing the "Rabbit Song":

> *Rabbit, rabbit,*
> *what do you see, you jump so?*
> *I see our dear fifteenth-night moon*
> *and I jump,*
> *leap, leap, leap!* [134]

Hands on our closed knees, the two of us, bent over, would jump about. Our legs, by then tired out, would utterly lose their spring after a couple of jumps, and we would fall on our bottoms. We would find that hilarious, too, and laugh and laugh. We would be so engrossed in our games as to be oblivious of everything else, until someone from one of our houses called us in. No matter what we were doing, O-Kei-chan, ever obedient, would respond with a simple "Yes!" when there was the call, "Missy, time to come home." And though her face showed reluctance, she would quickly go home.

At such partings we would hook our small fingers in pledge to play the next day and shake them so hard that they felt like they'd drop off our hands. We'd say that if we'd told a lie, our fingers would rot. I knew no such thing would really happen but would still feel slightly afraid.

134 *Usagi, usagi:* one of the more popular children's songs in praise of the moon. It dates from the Edo period.

OTEDAMA: PLAYING WITH HAND BALLS

45

As days passed and whatever reserve we may have had faded, trivial quarrels would sometimes occur between us—I, who was loath to lose in anything we did, and O-Kei-chan, who'd easily become exasperated when she did. One day, when we were playing with the ball as usual, the longer we played, unfortunately, the bigger the "debts" that O-Kei-chan accumulated, until in the end she claimed I was cheating and, weeping, buffeted me with both her sleeves. As she did so, the *o-tedama*[135] in her sleeves fell on the ground. She wouldn't even try to pick them up.

"I don't want to play with you any more," she said, still covering her face. And without listening to my profuse apologies, she went away.

Left alone, I could think of nothing but to pick up her *o-tedama* and take them home. But then this very act became a seed of worry. What would I do if O-Kei-chan became exasperated enough to say I took them? Should I quietly take them back and leave them where they were? Or should I take them to school and put them in her desk? Such scheming and plotting came and went, worried as I was that I had in my drawer someone else's possessions. Thus passed an uneasy night.

The next morning, half afraid of seeing her and half worried about not seeing her, I went to school before everyone else and, sitting at my desk crestfallen, I thought about what had happened yesterday, and before then, and so on, as the classroom gradually filled up with pupils coming in ones and twos, and grew noisy. But O-Kei-chan didn't show up: Is she so angry she's decided to take the day off? Well, but I can't say that because it's not yet time for her to come. I was growing frustrated, when Choppei, one of the group who were pretty late, arrived and the time was finally almost up. No longer able to stop myself, I went to the gateway and peered out around the doors and at last, to my great relief—at least for now—saw her come down the slope holding her wrapped

135 Literally "hand-balls": small palm-sized bean-bags decoratively made and used for a table game.

belongings. O-Kei-chan, unaware of anything, came through the gateway. I stepped out of the door casually, and we looked at each other. She put on a little embarrassed smile but without saying a word, went on in. So she's all right. She doesn't seem that angry.

O-Kei-chan spent that whole frustrating day playing lustily with her friends. Back home at my desk I was wondering if I should or should not go out into the backyard, when the latticed-door at the foyer quietly opened and a small voice said, "May I come in?"

I jumped up and out and from behind the partition said, "O-Kei-chan!" and stood on the step-up space.[136] Perhaps because this was her first visit, she looked a little shy, but she flashed such a radiant smile nonetheless that the burden I'd been carrying was lifted at once. I invited this rare guest into my study, which was right by the side of the foyer.

O-Kei-chan was restless for a while, looking around the room, leaning on the elbow-high window to gaze at the stone lantern in the "light-stick azalea"[137] shrubs, but when she had calmed down a bit, she placed both hands on the tatami and apologized with evident regret: "I am sorry I behaved so poorly yesterday."

Faced with such an adult-like, formal apology I felt a little confused and as I thought about all the trouble she'd given me I even resented the fact that I had apologized to her myself. O-Kei-chan said that when she had gone home yesterday she was scolded. And she begged to have her *o-tedama* back. So after tantalizing her for quite a bit, I finally brought them out of the drawer for her. The *yūzen* silk crepe[138] of the

136 *Shikidai.* In the old-style Japanese house, the foyer *(genkan)* consisted of sliding entrance doors, a ground-level space where footwear was taken off, a step-up space (usually made of wooden boards), followed by a small tatami room. A *tsuitate,* "a partition," was placed in the room, near the step-up space.

137 *Dōdan(-tsutsuji) (Enkianthus perulatus):* a species of azalea with clusters of small, white pot-shaped flowers.

138 *Yūzen chirimen.* "A new technique of silk dyeing called *yūzen* [which came into being during the Genroku era, 1688–1704] allowed freeform drawing of fine white lines in resist that when dyed created crisp outlines between sharply defined small areas of color. Yūzen

sacks originally came from a kimono for special occasions, she said, and you could see fragments of paulownia blossoms and phoenix wings on them. This was the story of the *o-tedama* that the two of us played with. As they flew up and down like butterflies, O-Kei-chan's face likewise nodded up and down, making the tufts of her hairpin dyed in red and white stripes flutter around her temples.

> *I'm switching horses,*
> *I'm switching palanquins,*
> *I'm switching horses,*
> *I'm switching palanquins. . . .*

Trying not to drop the *o-tedama* from the back of her hand, O-Kei-chan kept pulling mean tricks.

> *Pass under the small bridge,*
> *Pass under the small bridge. . . .*

With her slender fingers she formed a bridge on the tatami and let the *o-tedama* pass under it effortlessly. Her earlobes were beautiful, hot with excitement. The more exasperated the more stubborn she became and each time she made an error at a crucial point, she would throw the *o-tedama* at me or bite into my sleeve. Still, from then on she brought them to my house every day to play with me.

46

When we completed a reader our teacher would make us do "seize-and-read" on the pretext of review. The class was divided into

was a more painterly technique than earlier methods of dyeing, and it provided the technical means to create wonderfully detailed pictorial themes." Dalby, p. 40.

AYATORI: CAT'S CRADLE

boys and girls, and if someone in one group made a mistake in reading aloud, someone in the other group would quickly take over; this was continued until the book was finished, and the group with a greater number of pages read would be the winner. Boys were usually very boastful about various things, but when it came to competitive reading they became such weaklings and were always beaten. Also, when your turn came, you got nervous and stumbled, the turn seized.

On this occasion, chosen to start the reading, I was mindful of this and began to read very slowly. Seeing that I was unusually hesitant, everyone was sneering with contempt, but unfortunately for them I didn't make a single reading error, droning on and on in a most boring fashion. The passage where Prince Yamato Takeru sweeps down the grass sideways,[139] the passage where there appear many horses and stories about a roan, a bay, and a dapple gray are told, the passage where a Negro crosses the desert on a camel, and so on and on—I kept reading one page after another, until I reached the chapter on the Mongolian invasion of Japan, which was near the end of the book. There was a picture of messily destroyed Chinese warships with Japanese skiffs rowing toward them, and on the night of the 30th of the intercalary Seventh Month, the writing said, a divine wind blew, reducing the 100,000-man strong military force to a mere three men.[140]

139 A semi-mythological figure in the *Record of Ancient Matters (Kojiki)*, compiled in 712. The story here probably retells the following passage: "To see the deity, the Prince went into the field. Then the Governor set the field afire. Realizing that he had been deceived, the Prince opened the bag his aunt had given him, and found flint stones in it. So he first mowed away the grass with his sword. Then he struck the flints and set a counter-fire which burned away from him."

140 The second of the two invasions of Japan that Kublai Khan attempted, the first one, in 1274, and the second, in 1281. In 1274 Kublai sent an armada of 25,000 troops in boats across the Tsushima Strait. After overwhelming initial victories in land battles, the Mongolian troops regrouped in the boats on the 20th of Tenth Month—a fateful decision: that night a violent storm struck and an estimated 13,500 troops were drowned, forcing a general withdrawal of invading forces. In 1281 Kublai sent another invading force—this time a combined total of 140,000 troops—but even while various armies were engaged in skirmishes, a typhoon struck and drowned more than one third of the invaders,

Sorely regretting that they'd been off guard, the girls would raise their hands even when I paused to take a breath, eager to take over. Amused by their bewilderment, I became even more composed and went on to the chapter called "Ceramics," which, to my chagrin, made me falter. Because I wasn't much interested in ceramics manufacturing methods, I'd skipped that section in my routine reviews. I was readily taken over. Yielding my turn to the girls with great reluctance, I looked to see who my hateful enemy was and unexpectedly saw it was O-Kei-chan. I felt at once half happy and half resentful. It appeared she had been weeping out of exasperation, for her eyes were red at the rims. And though she rose to her feet holding her book, she sobbed so badly she couldn't read a single character. In a while the bell rang and the day ended with the boys' total victory, a rare event.

After school was over, when O-Kei-chan came to play with me as usual, her eyelids still looked a little swollen, and she was embarrassed.

"But I was truly bitter," she said. She then took a plaited string out of her sleeve and said, "Let's play cat's cradle." Above our little knees, touching as we knelt together, she draped the beautiful string around her pale wrists, and the string, taut between her slender, arched fingers, turned into many shapes.

"Water," she said, transferring the string to me. I took it carefully.

"Lozenge."

Manipulating her ten fingers through the string one by one, she made a koto. "Pluck, pluck, here's a koto."

"Mr. Monkey."

"Hand-drum."

As if our mutual friendship were woven on our fingers and transferred back and forth, we would spend days intimately playing in this way.

again forcing a general withdrawal. The two fortuitous storms reinforced the notion that Japan is protected by *kamikaze*, "the divine wind."

SHŌ, TSUZUMI: MUSICAL INSTRUMENTS

47

One day, during the hour on ethics, our teacher said, "Today instead of me telling you stories, each of you will tell us a story."

Pulling up his chair to the brazier and warming his hands over it, he called on some of the more brash or humorous ones to tell stories. Even someone who normally serves excellently as the general of brats on one side or loves to be a comic figure tends to stiffen or become tongue-tied when standing on the platform, with his face exposed to stares from all directions.

The first to be called on was a tall, skinny boy named Tokoro who always served as a "horse."[141]

"I'll tell a story about socks, sir," he said, his knees trembling.

"A story about socks? Sounds very interesting," the teacher said encouragingly.

"One sock floated by from over there," Tokoro stammered, "another floated on from over here, and when they bumped into each other in the middle, they cried out, 'Sock it to me!'" Thereupon he stepped down in a hurry.

The next one was Yoshizawa, a totally honest fellow whose lower front teeth almost covered his upper front teeth. Giggling for no reason, he said, "I'll tell a story about spears."

"This time a story about spears. Sounds interesting, too," the teacher said.

"One spear floated by from over there, another floated by from over here, and when they clattered into each other in the middle, they cried out, 'Spare me, sir!'" Yoshizawa said, and stepped down.

All such convenient stories were being exhausted and I was inwardly cringing when, unluckily, my name was called at the very end. I knew any number of stories because of my aunt, but I couldn't think of a single one that was short and easy to tell. In the end I told a story

141 The game leapfrog: *uma-tobi*, "jumping horse."

"about a *kappa* whose plate dried up."[142] Once I started on it I gained courage and, glancing in O-Kei-chan's direction from time to time, I finished my story, though in a somewhat halting way. As I bowed to the teacher before returning to my seat, he smiled and gave me a light rap on the head.

"I didn't expect you to be so cheeky."

Now it was the girls' turn, but none of them was willing to step forward, clinging as they did to their desks. So the teacher decided to name them in the order of seating, beginning with the first. Still, no one was willing, some even bursting into tears. Finally he came to the fifth seat, O-Kei-chan, who had evidently made up her mind and obediently stepped up on the platform. Even so, understandably, she was blushing to the nape of her neck and kept looking down.

After a while, though, moving her hands as if she were swimming in a dream, she began to speak, pausing with each phrase. Overcome with anxiety and sympathy, I was so agitated I could barely look her in the face. Nevertheless, as her story progressed her large, clear eyes became steady and alert, her posture adult-like and sharp, and in her incomparably limpid voice she went on telling a story briskly, neatly—the story about the Hatsune Drum,[143] one that I had told her. Enchanted by the unexpected poise of the narrator and drawn by the strange, fascinating story, the pupils became unusually quiet.

When her story was finished, the teacher said, "Today all the boys told stories well, while it was expected that none of the girls would come out, so they were supposed to lose, but with Kei-san's[144] single story just now, they won. I was impressed."

The girls broke into smiles. O-Kei-chan blushed and walked back to her seat, eyes modestly lowered. I watched her with a strange feeling, half happy, half jealous. I hadn't intended *her* to tell that story.

142 For *kappa*, see note 13 in Episode 1.6.

143 See note 15 on *The Thousand Cherry Trees* in Episode 1.6.

144 Actually, the teacher most likely referred to her by her surname as was and is customary in teacher-pupil relations, but O-Kei-chan's surname is not known.

48

Games on winter nights are deeply felt and enjoyable. O-Kei-chan would arrive, hands frozen, and, upon coming into the room, cling to the brazier. For this lovely guest my aunt made a large charcoal fire every night. Her shoulders hunched from the cold, she would remain almost bent over the brazier for a while. Waiting impatiently, I would tug at her bangs or poke my fingers in the rings of her *ochigo*-style hair.[145] She, being as temperamental as I was, would at times overreact and start crying. When she did I would immediately surrender without a moment's hesitation and apologize unconditionally. Sometimes I would put my mouth close to her ear as she lay face down on the floor and repeat, "Forgive me, forgive me," but she would continue shaking her head. After crying a while, though, she would abruptly change her mood and say, "That's enough," and give me a reproachful, forlorn smile. At such times I might wipe the tears off her slightly flushed eyelids.

She was good at faking crying. After exchanging a few trivial words she would suddenly pout, put her face on my lap, and cry ostentatiously. Feeling her heavy warmth, I would try various tricks to restore her good spirits, pulling out her hairpin, tickling her, and so forth. But if she continued to cry I could only apologize as best I could, even though I knew I'd done nothing wrong. After giving me a lot of trouble, though, she would abruptly raise her face, stick her tongue out at me, and, as if to say, "Serves you right," triumphantly laugh and laugh. Hers was a slippery, slender tongue. I had this trick played on me so often that I finally learned to distinguish real crying from fake by seeing whether or not the veins on her forehead were bulging with tension.

She was also skilled at the glaring contest and always beat me at it. She could change her face freely, making any expression at

145 A hairdo for girls started by aristocrats. The hair was turned up in such a way as to make two erect rings at the top of the head. *Ochigo* means "respectable child."

will. Saying, "Eyes slanting up, eyes slanting down," she would extend or shrink her eyes with her fingers as if they were made of rubber. I really hated the staring game. This was not because I was bound to lose, but because I was, to tell the truth, horrified to see her neatly arranged facial features brutally disfigured as she showed only the whites of her eyes or turned her mouth into an alligator's.

In a while I came to regard O-Kei-chan as one of my possessions, along with the Divine Dog and the Rouge Ox, and to feel keenly any praise or disparagement, any happy or unhappy incident, that befell her. I began to think she was a pretty girl. How proud I was of this! But at the same time my own face became a painful burden in a way I had never expected it to be. I wanted to be a prettier boy to attract her. I wanted only the two of us to be friends and play with each other forever. That was the kind of thing I began to think.

One evening we were sitting by the elbow-high window side by side, singing, bathed in the moonlight shining through the leaves of the crepe myrtle. I happened to look down at my arm hanging outside the window and was enchanted to see it was so beautiful, so pale as to be transparent. It was a momentary trick our dear moon played, but tempted by the thought that I could be more confident about myself if it were true, I put my arm before O-Kei-chan.

"Oh, it looks so beautiful."

"It does," my lover said and, rolling up her sleeve, she showed her arm.

"Mine, too."

Her pliant arm looked like alabaster. Mystified by it all, we exposed our flesh to the chilly night air—the upper arms, then the legs, from the legs to the chests, oblivious of time in wonderment.

49

Around that time a family whose second job was brocade stitching moved to the house next door, to the west of us, and their son Tomi-kō[146] became my new classmate. He was no good at class work but he spoke well and he was two years older and strong besides, so in no time he became the boss of my class rascals. Naturally I ceased to be able to wield my authority and as I couldn't just go to him and bow because of my own dignity, I ended up being left out of his circle. Because he didn't have any friend in the neighborhood, he would come to take me out to play in the backyard after coming home from school. Not liking him much and eager to play with O-Kei-chan, I was not at all willing, but I feared arousing his antagonism and, unable to think of anything better, I kept him company.

A born tomboy, O-Kei-chan at first watched us play from her side of the fence with an amused look on her face, but soon she came out and learned to do jump rope and hoop trundling just by watching us. Tomi-kō, who was a real smoothy, humored her by calling her Missy and showing her various tricks, standing on his hands, somersaulting. O-Kei-chan liked such things very much and followed him everywhere, calling him Tomi-chan. Having been brought up by my aunt alone and having played only with O-Kuni-san before then, I was in no way trained in such fabulous tricks and could only watch helplessly as Tomi-kō, who wasn't good-looking, monopolized the happy attention of the little queen.

O-Kei-chan continued to visit in the evening, but now only talked about Tomi-kō and paid no attention to the picture books and story books I'd take out to humor her. And when the three of us played together, if Tomi-kō in a triumphant mood called me clumsy or a weakling, she would join him in making fun of me. Belatedly I resented my aunt for bringing me up to be someone with no skills, standing on hands

146 *Kō,* "duke," was originally a suffix reserved for a certain class of nobility, hence a title of respect; later, when applied to an ordinary male, an adult or a boy, it came to express friendliness or a mild contempt.

or somersaulting. All this made me dislike Tomi-kō intensely but I controlled myself, trying not to go against his wishes, until one day what he said was too much to take, my self-control snapped, and I talked back at him resentfully. Thereupon he threw a barrage of foul curses at me, capping them with a whisper into O-Kei-chan's ear; then, eyeing me knowingly, he called out, "See you soon, you big baboon!" and started to go back home.

O-Kei-chan copied him and went away after him, repeating, "See you soon, you big baboon!" Tomi-kō must have taken her to his home.

After this O-Kei-chan stopped coming to see me. When on the rare occasion she spotted me she would hide herself without showing me a smile. Tomi-kō gave her that willfulness, I thought, and in my small heart I couldn't help feeling a boiling jealousy and fury. At school, too, he incited everybody to get on my back in prickly ways. Not just in that ability but in brawn as well, I certainly had to defer to him. The only consolation was that I was the number-one pupil. Nonetheless, without O-Kei-chan, that was an empty position to occupy, wasn't it?

50

Maddening days continued. One day, when I had confined myself in my study again, suffering, I suddenly heard "plonk-clogs"[147] going plonk-plonk, jingle-jingle. I was taken aback but, calming myself down, refused to open the window. In no time that lovely voice that I hadn't had time to forget was saying at the latticed door:

"May I come in?"

"May I ask who you are?" my aunt went out pretending not to know. In a while I

147 *Pokkuri*: festive clogs for girls, each one made of a single piece of wood with its sole hollowed, so it may make a plonking sound when used. The ones described here apparently are also decorated with small bells.

could tell she was helping her up, saying, "Oh, oh, I was just wondering what kind of guest would visit us, and lo and behold, we have this lovely miss!" And she, apparently helping the girl up, went on to ask if she had had a cold or been away visiting someone because she didn't know the reasons behind her recent absence. O-Kei-chan came in obediently through the sliding paper-door that my aunt opened and put her hands on the floor elegantly.

"I'm sorry I've neglected to come and visit," she said.

That did it. All the tensions I'd held under control till then broke, and as soon as I involuntarily called out "O-Kei-chan!" tears of mortification gushed down. O-Kei-chan, though, didn't seem troubled much by that and began to take her *o-tedama* out of her sleeve.

"Why didn't you come?" I asked.

She was unexpectedly unperturbed. "I was visiting Tomi-chan."

I shot back accusingly, "Why didn't you go today?"

She was quite untroubled as she replied, "Mother scolded me saying I shouldn't be going to a place like Tomi-chan's."

Flabbergasted though I was, I managed to express some of my resentment for what had happened some days ago.

"I'm sorry." With this preface she offered an excuse by saying Tomi-chan had said she didn't need to play with someone like me because he had a lot of interesting things in his house.

"After mother scolded me," she added, "I've come to hate Tomi-chan very much. Let's be friendly again."

How could I express my feelings then? O-Kei-chan was mine after all. Not knowing this, Tomi-kō must have kept waiting for her the whole day. The following day, unaware that I was watching out for her, he stealthily went up to her and started to say something, but she peremptorily turned him down, declaring she no longer liked him. It appeared that she'd become truly contemptuous of him after she was scolded by her mother.

51

The cunning Tomi-kō, finding himself neglected, came up to me with a palpably fraudulent air of friendliness and, after humoring me in various ways, slandered O-Kei-chan and said that since he'd no longer play with her, I shouldn't either. I laughed to myself and gave him nothing more than vague responses.

Nevertheless, as soon as he perceived that O-Kei-chan and I had gone back to being as good friends, he plotted a horrible reprisal. Every day during recess he incited everyone to taunt us. When they got tired and slackened their taunting, he went around whispering into each one's ear outrageous things he had concocted to provoke them. Shunned by our friends and surrounded by knowing eyes we fell into a miserable circumstance. This made us even more intimate, however, and when, with the day's unpleasant school work done, we went home and played, we felt an indescribable joy and consolation overflow our hearts.

Tomi-kō's retaliatory acts grew nastier day by day, and my hostility intensified proportionately. I didn't think anything of his foot soldiers, and I guessed he himself couldn't be that strong. The evidence was that each time I got upset and started toward him, he ran away to avoid one-on-one combat and tried to torment me from a distance. In the end I made light of him even as I made a stirring decision to retaliate some day to my heart's content.

One day, just when school was over, Choppei stealthily came to me and said, "He says he's going to waylay you tomorrow," and rushed away, fearful he might be spotted. I was happy with Choppei for his thoughtfulness. The following morning I hid a two-foot length of particularly knobby Hotei bamboo[148] under my *haori* and went to school determined to take on anyone and anything.

148 A species of bamboo *(Phyllostachys aurea)*, which, toward its base, grows "monstrous" protuberances. The name Hotei derives from the Chinese Zen monk Futai (d. 917) who is said to have had constant smiles and a

When the last hour was over, Tomi-kō was the first to run out of the classroom, signaling for the others to follow. Three or four who were among his worst apple-polishers did so, scampering. Resolutely prepared, I chose to be the last to leave for home. As expected, they were waiting for me at a deserted spot near the bamboo-grass bush in the Lord Hachiman's, with the apple-polishers noisily clearing their throats for derisive effect. Not showing my determination to finally take him on, pretending not to notice, I tried to walk past them, when Tomi-kō issued a command.

"Now, get him!"

Most of them had nothing particular against me and were, besides, no match for me, so they just encircled me, babbling, except one, the bleary-eyed son of a priest who, out of what kind of loyalty he felt for Tomi-kō I don't know, suddenly grabbed me by the neck from behind. Tomi-kō, inwardly afraid, gained courage from this dependable ally's action and walked up to me.

"Hey, you snot!"

Suddenly I struck him smack on the forehead with the Hotei bamboo. To my surprise, this took all the air out of Tomi-kō.

"Nooo, you are too violent," he said and started sobbing feebly, his hands on his forehead. Watching their general's sorry defeat, their faces saying they had sided with a terrible one, his foot soldiers sensed danger might soon fall on themselves and separately slunk away, mumbling things like "It's none of my business."

What alarmed me, though, was the bleary-eyed bonze who wouldn't let go. Eyes shut, he heavily hung on to me as if resolved to be killed in battle along with his commander. However tough-minded I may have been, this was too much for me; when I finally managed to tear myself apart from this clinging bastard and made it home, I myself was on the verge of tears, to tell you the truth.

large belly. He is reputed to have made the rounds carrying a large bag for alms. In Japan Hotei is counted among the Seven Deities of Good Luck.

52

As we broke icicles and fished snow with hard charcoal,[149] the Peach Festival[150] came around. My family had a set of ancient dolls that was said to have mysteriously survived the Great Fire of Kanda;[151] it was in a terrible state with the five musicians reduced to three, the arrows of the arrow carrier mostly broken, and so forth. Nonetheless every year it was set out to soothe the children. My aunt would gather together all the junk from all over the house to make up for missing furniture and such, putting up a folding screen decorated with seashells here and piling roasted barley on origami paper on the ceremonial trays there, skillfully making the whole set appear wonderfully beautiful to a child's eyes. Nothing made me happier than when the beautiful people were lined up on the daises covered with scarlet rugs, with the uppermost dais designated to be mine, the next one to be my younger sister's, and the third one to be my youngest sister's. Then we were allowed to offer lozenge cakes and popped rice. I remember provoking mirth by expressing my fear that the turban shells might crawl away while I was asleep.

For each festival we made a point of inviting O-Kei-chan. She would come in a very fancy kimono, complete with an overcoat adorned with red tufts. When we sat cute and neat in front of the dolls' daises eating popped beans like the good friends that we were, my aunt would give the smallest of the set of three cups to our dear guest

149 *Yukitsuri*, "snow-fishing." A simple game of throwing a piece of hard charcoal tied to a string into the snow and pulling it in as the charcoal collects snow around it.

150 See note 102 in Episode 1.30.

151 It appears that during the period Naka describes, "the Great Fire of Kanda" usually referred to the one in March 1892, when Naka was seven years old. It reduced the entire district to ashes and spread to the neighboring districts, burning down 4,200 houses. The novelist Tayama Katai (1872–1930) has a brief description of the fire in his account *The Thirty Years in Tokyo (Tokyo no sanjūnen)*, originally published in 1917. However, from Naka's manner of reference, the fire may refer to the one that struck the district a few months before he was born, in May 1885.

and the middle-sized one to me and pour gruelly white sake[152] for us. The sake would dangle out of the spout of the dispenser like a stick, making a rising mound in the cup, and we would chew on it with our front teeth, our noses side by side like minnows, before swallowing it. My aunt, who doted on children, enjoyed nothing better than to delight small ones in this fashion and, all happiness, she would rub us on the back with her hands.

"Both of you are so lovely, so lovely."

Our wet nurse would say, as she always did, "You are a husband and wife like the dolls," which we didn't like.

Very fancily dressed as she was, O-Kei-chan remained all prim and proper and, even though she had brought the ball and the *o-tedama*, she would merely fiddle with them, not offering to play with them. When she became a little excited after we played Backgammon, "Water-flower,"[153] "Sixteen by Six,"[154] and competed in stringing together Nanjing beads, I finally succeeded in luring her out into the backyard, taking with us the battledore[155] featuring Narita-ya's *Kanjinchō*[156] and Otowa-ya's *Sukeroku*,[157] which my older sisters had passed down to me about that time. But overdecorated like goldfish as we were, and with the battledores too large for us, we would drop the shuttlecock after hitting it a couple of times. And so, just for the fun of it, we took turns slapping each other's behinds.

Oil vendor's O-Some,
Hisamatsu is ten.[158]

152 *Shirozake*, which is made for the Peach (Doll) Festival. Unlike *amazake*, "sweet sake," it contains a considerable amount of alcohol. Today it is classed as a liqueur.

153 *Suichūka*: artificial flowers that are put in the water for them to "bloom." Marcel Proust describes them in *À la recherche du temps perdu*: "And just as the Japanese amuse themselves by filling a porcelain bowl with water and steeping in it little crumbs of paper which until then are without character or form, but, the moment they become wet, stretch themselves and bend, take on colour and distinctive shape, become flowers or houses or people, permanent and recognisable," etc. Tr. C. K. Scott Moncrief.

154 *Jūroku-musashi*: originally a gambling board game, later adopted as a children's game.

155 *Hagoita*. Casal: "a stemmed quadrangle of light wood. . . . For centuries the *hagoita* have been used as a medium for showy

HAGOITA: BATTLEDORES

53

extravagance, so much so that the feudal government time and again intervened and restricted their luxury. Formerly painted with appropriate designs, often lacquered in gold, they were later embellished with figures of heroes and, chiefly, of famous actors and courtesans, in raised silk-crêpe and with jet-black silk hair."

156 A fancy portrait of Benkei. *Subscription List (Kanjinchō)* is a kabuki play written by Namiki Gohei III and first staged in 1840 with Ichikawa Danjūrō VII playing Benkei. Narita-ya is the "house name" for Ichikawa Danjūrō and his troupes. For Benkei, see note 121 in Episode 1.38.

157 A kabuki play whose author remains unknown. Its Edo version was staged first in 1713 with Ichikawa Danjūrō II playing the lead role of the dandy Sukeroku. Otowa-ya is the "house name" of Onoe Kikugorō and his troupes.

158 There are a number of plays and songs based on the double suicide committed, in 1708, by O-Some, an Osaka oil-vendor's daughter, and Hisamatsu, one of his young store clerks.

Soon after the festival O-Kei-chan's father passed away and she did not come for the time being. But one evening she came to play, making the plonk-plonk jingle-jingle of her plonk-clogs. Yet, perhaps because we were being oversensitive about it, she seemed terribly depressed, which made me jittery and anxious, and members of my family, feeling sorry for her, tried to console her in various ways. Then she said, We are moving tomorrow. Her grandmother and her mother were going back to their home province.

"I am happy about moving," O-Kei-chan said disconsolately, "but I don't like it because, if we go far away, I'll be unable to come here to play."

This made me so helpless I didn't know what to do with myself, and the two of us were downcast. Saying that this was the last chance for parting, everyone joined in our play that evening. Our wet nurse, too, kept gazing at O-Kei-chan's face repeating, "You are such an unlucky child."

The next day, her grandmother holding her hand, O-Kei-chan came to our foyer to say good-bye. Hearing her voice as she elegantly said her piece with her usual mature turns of phrase, I wanted to run out to see her, but overcome by a sudden, inexplicable shyness I remained hidden indecisively behind the sliding screens. O-Kei-chan was gone. Later every one in my family who'd seen her off said, "What a pretty young lady she is." They said she was wearing the kimono she wore for the Dolls' Festival. Sitting by myself in front of my desk, I was in useless tears, wondering why I hadn't gone out to see her. My aunt, quickly spotting this, said, "I'm sorry for you, too."

The following day I went to school before everyone else. As I quietly sat on O-Kei-chan's seat my longing for her enveloped me anew and I remained holding her desk in my arms. O-Kei-chan was a prankster. All over her desk were her pencil-drawings of mountain-water goblins[159] and adder-monsters.[160]

This is a story that is already twenty years old. For some reason I can't help feeling that O-Kei-chan has died since. On the other hand, from time to time I also feel that she is still alive, occasionally remembering things from those days too.

159 *Sansui tengu*: A goblin's face drawn by writing the simple Chinese characters for "mountain" and "water" in the fluid style.

160 *Hemamushi nyūdō*: A human figure drawn by writing the four katakana, *he, ma, mu, shi*, and two Chinese characters for the word for the tonsured lay priest in the fluid style.

PART TWO

I

Our teacher Mr. Nakazawa was a gentle soul but had a very bad temper; when enraged for some reason, he could lash you on the head with his whip until the ground beneath you started to quake. Despite this I was very fond of him and sometimes took the trouble of taking a stem from the Chusan palm in our garden to provide him with a new whip to experience more pain. Each time I did this, he would give an ironic smirk.

"Thank you very much. This is the best thing to hit a head with," he would say and pretend to hit me with it.

I never followed his instructions, doing what I wanted, so he seemed not to know what to do with me. But I had convinced myself that he had a soft spot for me. When his pupils' bad conduct made his temper flare and his face turned into a ball of fire, they would all cringe and fall silent. Even at such times, I was completely unperturbed, surveying the scene with a smile. So one day when the principal came by on his round of inspection, Mr. Nakazawa complained to him about me, saying that I was utterly unfeeling. I was standing by them, looking amused to hear them talk about me.

"Aren't you afraid of your teacher?" the principal asked.

"No, not at all," I replied.

"Why aren't you afraid?"

"Because I think my teacher is also a human being after all."

The principal and Mr. Nakazawa looked at each other with sour smiles but didn't say anything. From around that time I had begun to see a comic child inside a grownup's stern exterior, and I was unable to have the kind of special respect for adults that ordinary children have.

At about this time, the Sino-Japanese War[1] began. I came down with a bad case of measles and had to take days off from

1   The war between Japan and China—the Qing or Manchu Dynasty at the time—over Korea's sovereignty that began in July 1894 and ended in May 1895.

school. When I finally made it back our class teacher had unexpectedly changed. I was told that Mr. Nakazawa had been drafted. They said he was a former naval officer but had been put on the reserve list because of illness. No wonder he had often talked about warships. Sadness filled my heart when I thought of how he had told us those mysterious stories from the *Saiyūki*,[2] how he used to lick his paintbrush and paint neat pictures, how I had liked everything about him except his hitting a head with a Chusan palm whip, and how I could no longer see him. So, after school, I gathered together my friends and tried to learn in detail at least how he had looked when he came to say farewell. But, distracted as they were by their daily games, they just sat there as if they'd completely forgotten all about it even though barely half a month had passed since they parted with him. And they fidgeted, pouting, apparently dissatisfied that they'd been prevented from their games. Finally, though, after struggling to remember something, one of them blurted out: "He was wearing an overcoat with lion hair."

"Lion hair! Lion hair!" several others echoed him.

These fools had been so entranced by the lion hair they saw for the first time—though that, too, was probably a mistake—they didn't remember anything else. Even so I tried to find out everything I could. After exasperating me no end, one of them spoke up.

"I am going to war now and may not be able to see you again," the teacher had said. "You must listen carefully to the new teacher, study hard, and grow up to be great men."

At these words tears suddenly welled up and rolled down my cheeks. Taken aback, my friends stared at me, some even sneering contemptuously, eyeing each other, tugging

2 *Xiyouji* or *The Record of a Westward Journey*, or as Anthony Yu who made the first complete English translation calls it, *The Journey to the West* (Chicago: University of Chicago Press, 1980). As Yu explains, it is a story "loosely based on the famous pilgrimage of Xuanzhuang (602–64), the monk who went from China to India in quest of Buddhist scriptures." A collection of wondrous tales put together probably by Wu Cheng'en (ca. 1500–82), it features a monkey, a pig, a *kappa*, and a horse, all with magical powers as guardians of the traveling monk. Arthur Waley's *Monkey: Folk Novel of China* (Grove Press, 1994) is an abbreviated translation.

at each other's sleeves. They still didn't know one could cry like that, as they simply believed that the code our teacher taught us, that a man is allowed to cry only once every three years,[3] could not be violated.

2

An even more unhappy thing was that I did not at all get along with the new teacher, Mr. Ushida. He was known to be good at jūjutsu, so the pupils were afraid of him, and he was evidently proud of it himself, at times flipping backward all by himself to impress us. Indeed, there was nothing admirable about him, except that once, during a drawing class, he praised the gourd I'd painted, saying, You are better than me, and gave it three circles. Just as I disliked him, he must have disliked me. I couldn't tell from when, but in time we became enemies, more or less.

Aside from that, after the war started my friends' talk, from morning to evening, was all filled with the Yamato Spirit[4] and chinks.[5] Worse, our teacher joined in, repeating the Yamato Spirit and chinks at every turn as if he were inciting dogs to fight. I found it all so distasteful and unpleasant. He wouldn't make any reference whatsoever to the stories of Yojō and Hikan.[6] Instead, he only talked

3 A proverbial saying. A variation: "A man is allowed to cry only when he is born and when his parents die." Another: "A man is allowed to cry only three times in his lifetime: at birth, at his parent's death, and when his shin's hit." A similar variation: "A man is allowed to laugh only once every three years," because to laugh is to lose male dignity.

4 *Yamato damashii.* Yamato, originally a small area in today's Nara, finally came to designate all of Japan. Ueda Akinari (1734–1809) characterized something like *Yamato damashii*— that which the people of one country regard as the spiritual essence of their being—as the "stink" of that country. In Part 6 of *I Am a Cat*, Natsume Sōseki makes fun of this indomitable Japanese spirit by having the main character announce mockingly that every Japanese, from the victor at the Battle of Tsushima, Admiral Tōgō Heihachirō, on down, has it: a pickpocket, a fishmonger, confidence man, a mountebank, a murderer.

5 *Chanchan bōzu.* During the Edo period the term referred to a boy with a Chinese-style hairdo and was not derogatory.

6 Yojō (Yurang in Chinese): a character that Sima Qian (145–86? B.C.) describes in "The

Biographies of Assassins" of his *The Records of the Grand Historian (Shiji)*. In trying to avenge the lord who treated him well, Yurang changed his voice and appearance by swallowing charcoal and painting lacquer on his body in order to approach his enemy. When he failed to achieve his aim the second time, he stabbed himself to death. Hikan (Bi Gan) is a character mentioned several times in *The Records* as an example of someone whose proper advice to his master was rewarded with death—in this instance the tearing out of his heart.

7   See note 140 in Episode 1.46.

8   See note 128 in Episode 1.41.

9   *Fugutaiten* (Chinese: *bujudaitian*) is an expression that appears in the Chinese classic *Book of Rites*. Lit. "Not sharing Heaven together," i.e., "Cannot live under the same sky," "mortal" as in "mortal enemy."

10 *Setta*, "snow footwear": slippers of bamboo bark with soles of leather. Said to have been invented by the tea master Sen Rikyū (1522–91) for use in the snow, although the origin of the name is obscure.

11 Hōjō Tokimune (1251–84), regent of the Kamakura shogun and de facto ruler of Japan during the Mongolian invasions. Known

interminably about the Mongolian invasions[7] and the Korean conquests.[8] And when it came to songs, he had us sing bleak war-related things while making us dance utterly uninteresting calisthenic-like dances. Even worse, as though those chinks with whom we "couldn't live under Heaven"[9] had actually swarmed toward them, everyone, shoulders raised and elbows spread out, stomped their snow-slippers[10] with such abandon as to almost tear apart the leather pieces as they bellowed songs out of tune, out of rhythm, in the suffocating dust that swirled up. Almost ashamed to stand in line with these wretches, I deliberately sang even more out of tune. Also, now in the school yard, which was small in the first place, only Katō Kiyomasas and Hōjō Tokimunes[11] snottily went about, all the wimps having turned into chinks to be beheaded.

If you walked in the town, you saw in every store for picture-books and children's books that all the origami paper and "older-sister dolls"[12] had been hidden away, replaced by dirty-looking pictures of bullets exploding now displayed everywhere. Whatever I heard or saw annoyed me. Once, when a number of boys gathered together somewhere were yet again cooking up outrageous war stories out of the rumors they'd heard here and there, I ventured an opinion opposite to theirs and said Japan would be defeated by China in the end. This unexpected, bold prediction left them eyeing each other for a while, but their laughable but admirable antagonism had heightened to such a point as to ignore the class-leader's authority.

"Wow, that's bad, that's bad!" one of them blurted out exaggeratedly.

Another lightly brushed the tip of his nose with his fist. Yet another mimicked our teacher.

"Sorry about that, sir, but the Japanese have the Yamato Spirit."

With much greater antipathy and confidence than I'd ever had before, I took on their attacks all by myself.

"We are sure to lose, sure to lose!" I insisted.

And sitting in the midst of these clamorous boys I wracked my brains and defeated their groundless arguments. Many of them hadn't even perused the newspapers or looked at a map of the world. They hadn't heard the stories from *Shiki* and *Jūhachishiryaku*.[13] As a result, they were all argued down by me alone and with visible reluctance fell silent. But that didn't mean their indignation was quelled, for the first thing they did in the next hour was to tell the teacher.

"Sir, Naka-san says Japan will lose."

Mr. Ushida, with his usual knowing face, declared, "The Japanese have the Yamato Spirit," and then, as always, heaped various dirty curses upon the Chinese. I was incensed as if those words were personally directed against myself.

for his "resolute, energetic character," according to Papinot. He is also known for turning to Zen because of his inability to control his fear as a samurai. Daisetz Suzuki, *Zen and Japanese Culture* (Princeton University Press, 1959), pp. 65-66. At the time the role of Tokimune's fear may have been downplayed.

12   *Anesama-zukushi* or simply *anesama*: Bride-dolls made of origami paper.

13   *Shiji* and *Shibashilu* in Chinese. The latter, *Eighteen Summary Histories*, was compiled toward the end of the 13th century. It is said to have been read more in Japan than in China.

14   Kan'u (Guan'yu in Chinese, d. 219) was a great warrior-commander during China's Three Kingdom period (184–280). His reputation was such that his enemies are said to have run away from him without battle. He was entrapped and killed. After his death shrines were built for him as a deity of war. Chōhi (Zhangfei in Chinese, 166–221) was another great warrior-commander of the same era. The two became sworn brothers of Ryūbi (Liubei in Chinese, 161–223) and

"Sir, if you say the Japanese have the Yamato Spirit, the Chinese must also have the Chinese Spirit," I said. "If we have Katō Kiyomasa and Hōjō Tokimune in Japan, they have Kan'u and Chōhi[14] in China, don't they? Besides, sir, you once told us the story of Kenshin sending salt to Shingen[15] to teach us that being compassionate to the enemy is the Way of the Warrior. If that is the case, you can't badmouth the Chinese like that, can you, sir?"

With that said, I had poured out all my accumulated frustrations. Mr. Ushida made a grimace.

"Naka-san has no Yamato Spirit," he said after a brief while.

I felt my temper quickly swell the veins of my temples but, unable to take out the Yamato Spirit and show it to them, I could only redden and keep quiet.

The Japanese soldiers, being "incomparable in loyalty and bravery," smashed my clever prediction to bits. That, however, hardly changed my distrust of our teacher and my contempt for my peers.

All this made me feel that it was silly to spend time with the other kids, and I gradually began to distance myself from them and just stand by and watch their absurd carryings-on derisively. One day, standing alone in the corridor, my elbows on the railing rubbed shiny by the hands of brats over the years, I was laughing as I watched them romping about under the wisteria trellis, when a teacher happened to pass behind me.

helped him become emperor. The stories of these men are famously told in *Romance of the Three Kingdoms (Sanguozhi)*. Its first edition appeared in 1522.

15 Uesugi Kenshin (1530–78) and Takeda Shingen (1521–73) are warlords famous for their rivalry. As the historian Rai San'yō (1780–1832) tells it in *An Unofficial History of Japan (Nihon gaishi)*, the salt episode goes like this: "Shingen's province [Kai] did not have any coastline. He obtained salt from the Tōkai. Ujizane conspired with Hōjō Ujiyasu and secretly closed the supply routes for salt. Kai suffered greatly. When Kenshin heard this he sent a letter to Shingen and said, 'I hear, sir, that Ujiyasu and Ujizane torment you by means of salt. This is cowardly and unjust. I fight you, but I fight with bow and arrow, not with rice and salt. I beg you, sir, that henceforth you obtain salt from my land. The quantity may be large or small, depending on your need.' He then ordered merchants to supply Shingen with salt at an equitable price."

"What are you laughing about?" he suddenly said to me.

"The way those children play is funny," I replied.

The teacher burst out laughing. "Naka-san, you are a child, too, aren't you?"

"I may be a child, but I am not as silly as they," I said seriously.

"That's troublesome," he said. Then he went into the teachers' room where I saw him talking to other people. I guessed I was troublesome to the teachers.

3

Even though I regarded every one of the pupils of my class as a hopeless Santarō,[16] holding them in utter contempt, I nonetheless had a heartfelt, precocious sympathy for Kanimoto-san, who could be described as captain of all such Santarōs. He was almost an idiot, though judging from his height he was probably sixteen or seventeen already. What I had heard was that he had remained in each grade for two or three years and, as he was gradually pushed upward he had ended up with us latecomers. Naturally he didn't know his own age and because he had an infantile face common among morons, no one knew how old he was. His happily fat round face had a mole as big as a horse bean on one cheek, a kind of billboard for him that endeared him throughout the school.

If someone half-jokingly said, "Kani-

16 A personal name origi-
nally used as a general
term for a shop boy that
then came to mean "fool"
or "simpleton." In his 1960
translation of *Shanks'
Mare (Tōkaidōchū hiza-
kurige)*, Thomas Satchell
translates the term as
"country bumpkin." Jip-
pensha Ikku (1765–1831)
wrote the picaresque
novel from 1802 to
1822. Naka's friend, the
philosopher and literary
critic Abe Jirō (1883–1959),
called his book of medita-
tions on youthful angst
in confessional style
*Santarō's Diary (Santarō no
nikki)*. Published in 1914, it
was for a long time known
as "an eternal book of
philosophy for youth."

moto-san, you have ink on your cheek," he would respond with a slow giggle, saying indulgently, "It—is—no—i—nk. It—is—a—m—o—le."

Carrying across his back an abacus that had not a single bead left on it and was disproportionately small for his body, he would saunter in whenever he liked and when bored would go home abruptly even if it was during a lesson. Human beings in general pity and love only those who are far inferior to themselves, and the sympathy so felt is despicably selfish. Attracting such sympathy, though, there was no one under heaven who enjoyed a world as free as Kanimoto-san's. Still, because he was alive, there were days he felt good and days he felt bad. When he felt bad, he seldom showed up, but when he did show up, as he occasionally did, he wouldn't even crack a smile, sitting at his desk, head bowed. Then, no one knows what thoughts prompted him, he would suddenly begin to weep loudly and wouldn't stop until he had wept his heart out. And when he had exhausted in loud unrestrained weeping the sorrows that had welled up unknown to anyone and accumulated in his dark unhappy heart, he would put his abacus on his shoulder and go home as though nothing had happened. On such days, even if someone happened to speak to him, he wouldn't even show his good-natured smile—one virtue in such a misfortune—but would invariably utter a guttural scream like a parrot and drive the person away.

If for some reason he was in an elegant frame of mind, though, he would offer, unasked, "I'll be your horse."

He was tall, strong, and corpulent, so made a fine horse to ride. But he was also an untamable wild horse, because the moment he lost interest he would stand up straight even in the midst of a grappling combat between two commanders.[17]

17 *Kibasen,* "mounted combat": A game in which four youths in a team form a horse with one of them as rider. The combat, which entails one rider grappling another down to the ground, may be fought one-on-one, as here, or as a group. In the latter case the rider who remains on horseback to the end is the victor.

I decided to grasp, in whatever way I could, the true nature of his unfathomable silence, the tears that overflowed from the bottom of that silence, and, ignoring everyone's sneers, I tried hard to befriend him. Every time I saw him in a good mood, I said brief words of greeting such as "Good morning" and "Good-bye." But he was to me what an emperor would be to his subject, and wouldn't even respond with a smile. I did not mind this and persevered tirelessly, diligently, until one day he left the desk to which he had clung like a louse and shuffled over to me.

"Na—ka—sa—n—is—a—g—o—o—d—per—son," he said, with his usual lisp. He then went away with a low, happy laugh.

I almost jumped for joy at that one remark. Whatever he said didn't have an iota of falsity. By then I knew more than I wanted that people's words contained lies, so I was deeply touched by that casual, arbitrary remark and was overjoyed as though I had finally gotten hold of the key to the door to that darkness, thinking I was sure to make friends with him and would be able to console this unfortunate person. So, deciding that I'll finally make it today, I went to a desk next to his and spoke to him in various ways; but he merely smiled his pointless smile, leaving me frustrated. In a while he even stopped doing that, and bent his head low over his desk. Soon he dealt me his decisive card, assaulting me with his guttural scream. At that one parrot call, all the trouble I'd taken came to nothing. It was not that Kanimoto-san was forced to be alone because he, like me, didn't have any desirable companions; it was that he simply, truly, did not need any.

4

My older brother—out of a curiosity and kindness heavily laden with the odor of self-aggrandizement that everyone at his age is bound to have at least once—took pains to twist me, a human being born to be shaped differently from him and destined to go in opposite ways as to the east and to the west, into his direction, against my will, through the power of a truly thoroughgoing, harsh education. And, because he liked fishing to the point, people said, of madness, it must have occurred to him that in order to save me, his poor younger brother, from falling further into evil ways every day, every month—to make me like him—he had, above all, to teach me fishing.

Every day when there was no school, he would forcibly take me out, reluctant though I was, and make me carry the fishing gear, even though I was following him only because it was painful to ruin his mood—and because I had no choice. Then I had to plod after him all the way to Honjo where there were a great many fishponds that, in my brother's theory, were the ideal ones but, in my opinion, were exceptionally revolting. On our way I'd be the butt of his pettifogging criticisms—that my hat was crooked, that I held my head too low, that I was distracted far too long by the lanterns just put out for sale, that my arms weren't swinging back and forth evenly—in short, from the tip of my head to the ends of my toes, so that all the mental strain, coupled with the great distance, would completely exhaust me by the time we finally reached a fishpond. But no sooner had I ducked in under its flag and felt a whiff of relief than I would be made to sit on the dampish edge of the moat and forced to realize I'd have to spend the whole day there once again, and I'd feel as fed up as if all my energy and bones had deserted me.

The pilings driven into the muddy, bad-smelling moat were loaded with growths of green moss. In a stagnant pool in one corner, with red rust floating on it, water scorpions[18] caught water striders and giant water bugs[19] bobbed up and down. Watching such things alone made me sick, but there also were the uninterrupted banging, clanging noises of someone beating sheets of iron at a factory nearby that gave me a splitting headache. My brother might say to me, You've gotten

18 Mizukamakiri, "water-praying-mantis" *(Ranatra chinensis)*. A predaceous water insect that grows to be 1.5 inches long. Its front legs are shaped like pantographs (raptorial). It has two hairs at its tail.

19 Tagame, "paddy-turtle" *(Lethocerus deyrollei)*. The largest water insect, it grows to be more than 2 inches in length. Its front legs, shaped like a pair of sickles, can grab a fish or a frog in a single sweep. During the night it flies to lights.

better at cutting earthworms, I like that, but this wouldn't please me at all. Though I didn't even know what to do with the single rod given me, I nonetheless made the pretense of alertly watching my float while thinking one unpleasant thought after another, such as, Why do I have to learn to like fishing? Meanwhile, my brother, who was supposed to suffer from myopia, suddenly seemed to acquire several sharp eyeballs the moment he arrived at a fishpond. He would set up five to seven rods and before I knew it would be watching out for my float, too.

"Look, the fish is taking your bait!"

If I pulled the fish out of the water, he would bark at me for one reason or another—that I was too clumsy scooping it up or that I was no good unhooking it. So, hoping that the fish would get away quickly, I would lazily pull the thing in. Then, a muddy yellow belly and parts would show, and I'd just watch, thinking, That's a dirty carp. This would make my brother lose his temper and throw it at me. By then the fish would unhook itself and get away.

When the day's ordeal was finally over and the time came to go home the raw-smelling creel became a new burden. And, again for my education, my brother would deliberately make a detour, taking the route I didn't like—the road that had antique shops, warehouses, carts, and ditches, the road where power lines whined in the wind, the road lined with food stalls. I would trot after him, my feet deadly fatigued, all the while being scolded for this thing or that. And because we took a longer way, the sun would have set before we neared home. The unpleasantness and the complaints I had at such a time. . . . Once, as one star, then another, began to shine in the evening sky, I was so enchanted gazing at them—gaining strength from what my aunt had taught me, that stars are where gods and buddhas are—when my brother became angry that I had fallen way behind.

"Why are you being so damned slow?"

Startled, I said, "I was looking at our dear stars."

Hardly understanding what I said, he barked, "Stupid, just say 'stars'!"

Pitiful person! What was wrong with my calling the cold stones

20 Vaisravana in Sanskrit:
One of the Four Heavenly
Kings and commander of
the north side of Mount
Sumeru where the True
Law or Darma is kept.
In Japan he is counted
among the Seven Deities
of Good Luck.

21 *Shō-kokumin.* A popular
magazine for boys that
started publication in
1889, at first monthly,
from the second year
twice-monthly, under
the able editorship of
Ishii Kendō (1865–1943). It
carried articles on ethics,
history, literature, and
entertainment, all written
in plain language. It was
discontinued in Septem-
ber 1895, suggesting that
the issue Naka's brother
bought him was one of
the last.

22 One of the Seven Big
Festivals in Japan, held on
the 7th of Seventh Month.
Casal: "If you go into the
country on that day, you
may still find rows of
freshly cut bamboo stuck
into the ground in front
of the houses, or affixed
to doors and eaves. They
will be adorned with
numerous pieces of gaily
coloured paper: neat
strips which twirl on a
thread, and which, close
inspection will show, are
covered with inscriptions,
poems in fact. They are
all in praise of Tanabata,
the Weaver Princess. On
the eve of the festival
the children sat around a
table and with the help

circling the sky "our dear stars" out of a
child's longings, just as I called this person,
who by some chance had become my companion in Hell, my dear brother?

5

Once, again in the name of education, I was
taken to a certain seashore. Not knowing
that my unusually good response to the idea
of going there was on account of my memories of a trip some time back that I had
enjoyed, and of a friend—my brother's—
who had gone on ahead and was waiting
for us, my brother was in very high spirits
the night before we left, and took me to the
fair of Lord Bishamon[20] and bought me the
magazine *Little Citizen.*[21] The next morning,
accompanied by an unusually kind brother
and relieved that things might work out all
right, I left home with only *Little Citizen* for
me to carry.

It happened to fall on Tanabata Day,[22]
and the peasants' houses everywhere had
bear bamboo[23] adorned with poem cards of
five colors aloft, hare's ears[24] coolly blooming on their thatched roofs. Enchanted
and distracted by them, I wondered aloud,
Why don't they do the same in towns?, and
drew the first angry word from my brother.

TANABATA: BAMBOO WITH POEM CARDS

Buoyed by the green paddies, the sky, the sea, and white sails, I had many things I wanted to say and wanted to ask about, but because it was painful to be scolded, I just thought this or that, wondering if it wasn't a mistake after all to have come along, when I drew another, fresh angry word for not saying anything. Why did he get upset for no reason? As it turned out, he was in a foul mood because I didn't put to him the question, How does the train move?

The place we arrived at was a thatched hut in a fishing village surrounded by gloomy brushwood fences that had seashells and things strewn about, where, other than our friend who eagerly welcomed us, lived a very dark old couple and their daughter with the same coloring. It was just lunch time, and the mother and daughter, who looked like black cats, brought two grubby raised trays for the three of us. But, told to hurry because the tableware was what the family used themselves and they couldn't eat until we had finished our meal, I felt harassed and put down the chopsticks after finishing half my food.

The house being so small, it was decided that my brother and I would move to a cape about two miles away. Our friend, who offered to accompany us by way of taking a walk, and my brother said they'd catch up with me, so I was put in a rickety cart and went on ahead. The cart puller was a corpulent man who appeared to be simple and honest, and I didn't dislike him at all. But as we passed round and round those gloomy brushwood fences, loneliness welled up in me and before long I couldn't bear it any longer. I did my best to distract myself but only such things as the cedar hedge of our house and the way our dining room looked kept coming to my mind's eye. Thinking, I

of their elders tried to compose them, as fine ones as possible; and where the poetical vein was insufficient they had recourse to well-known anthologies. Provided with India-ink and brush, they then laboriously traced the characters in their best hand on the *goshiki no kami*, the 'papers of five colours'—green and yellow, red and white, and dark blue as a substitute for the primary black."

23 *Sasa*: a low-growth variety in the grass family whose leaves resemble those of bamboo. As Casal says, the use of regular bamboo is more common.

24 *Hotaru-sō*, "firefly grass" *(Bupleurum sachalinense)*.

won't be going back there tonight or tomorrow night, my face turned weepy despite myself and tears dropped on my lap. Fishermen's children noticed this.

"Hey, look at that! He's crying! He's crying!" they called out and laughed among themselves.

The cart man turned to look from time to time and said something soothing, but his words were different and I couldn't understand him at all. As we went along, out of the corner of my eye, I caught sight of beautiful Benkei crabs[25] coming out of the cracks of roadside fences and then, startled by the noise of the cart, dashing back into them, and I wanted the crabs. But before long we came out on the shore. The path meandered between a hillside and the water's edge. I was agitated that at any moment the tide might come in to block our way, but the cart man was unperturbed, apparently thinking about something else as he trudged along. When we reached a point where the path cut through a hill I happened to turn back to look and caught a glimpse of my brother and our friend. Just when I'd managed to suppress a sob struggling to rise in my throat, my brother hurriedly caught up and took me down from the cart.

Here and there formations of boulders serrated like dorsal fins jutted out of the rocky shore into the sea, and the waves, their paths blocked, rose up round-shaped like the shaven head of a sea monster and quickly crashed, splashes flying. Every time our path turned, the shore became smaller and narrower as it closed in into a cove, and the low waves at certain intervals rolled in, kaboom, kaboom. Hearing the sound, a lump formed in my chest for some reason and, though I had managed to stop sobbing, tears rolled out again. A wave crashed kaboom, its foam swished away, but even before I was relieved to think, That's gone, the next wave crashed kaboom. When we'd finally passed that cove, the next cove came along with more kaboom. Even

25 *Sesarmops intermedium.* A species of crab that inhabits seashores and marshy places. It has a scarlet-red-brown square carapace well over an inch long. The crab's name comes from the tough appearance of its carapace, said to resemble Benkei's fierce-looking face. For Benkei, see note 121 in Episode 1.38.

though I was getting hungry and my feet were growing tired, the cape seemed to remain just as far away and the sound of waves never ceased, no matter how far we went. When we caught up with a string of several mares clop-clopping along being led, our friend noticed the tears filling my eyes and pointed this out to my brother in a whisper.

"Leave him alone, leave him alone," he said, walking briskly ahead.

Our friend kept turning back to see, until finally he stopped and kindly asked, Are you tired? Are you feeling ill?

"I am sad about the sound of waves," I said honestly.

My brother glared at me.

"Go back by yourself," he said and quickened his pace. Our friend, surprised as he was by my unexpected response, nonetheless, tried to calm my brother down.

"A boy has to be a little tougher," he said to me.

6

By the time we arrived at the quiet inn standing in isolation near the foot of the rocky cape, the sun was already setting, the flaming clouds wrapping it turning like a wheel. These gradually turned red, purple, then indigo, in the end becoming one with the color of the sky and fading. As I held on to the post on the porch and watched the waves crashing at the cape, radiating phosphorescence, my windpipe felt irritated and tears ceaselessly rolled down my cheeks. I kept rubbing the tears on the post, my only thought being, May tomorrow come as soon as possible.

Winds pregnant with rain began to make the pines sough, and insects started to cry as though they had crawled out of nowhere. A maid came to close the outer sliding doors. I had no choice but to go into my room and, trying to hide my teary face, took out *Little Citizen* and began reading it. One illustration showed Kidōmaru, his forehead pierced with an arrow, lifting the hide of the bull with one hand, holding his sword close to himself, aiming to kill Raikō.[26] As I turned the pages one by one, I caught sight of the title, "The Boy Drummer,"[27] and started to read it. The illustration showed the protagonist, the boy drummer, beating the drum hung on his chest, sticks held high, and advancing, paying no attention to the soldiers on his side being left behind. As I read on, the drummer—who had a large head, was clumsy, and was always made fun of by people—became me, and my tears pattered down on the book until I finally drew a bark from my brother.

The next morning the sea was entirely enclosed in fog. And the noise of a scull rowing through it pleased me terribly. The boat was invisible, only the noise sounding like some bird calling or the cry of some baby beast looking for milk.

Our friend came by, and we went out on the shore together. The sand, stones, and seaweed thrown up in the shapes of waves were all soaked with morning dew, and the insects, though so many of them had been crying last night, now remained only here and there chirping, chirping, in a lovely manner. The dune between the flatland and the sloping beach had weeds and black pines bent by the blowing winds clinging to it. There were a simply shaped fishing boat pulled up on it, the frames for sliding the boat, a creel like a bird nest, a bilge scoop, ropes, sea urchins, dead starfish, and other things.

After a while the fog cleared. About the time the morning sun, which rose red above a sea that gleamed indigo-blue deeply, was beginning to make me itchy, my sweat seeping out, fishermen, women, and children noisily came down the narrow paths on the dunes and began drawing in a dragnet. As they pulled it step by step with quiet

26 Kidōmaru, "Demon Boy," is a fiendish rogue who figures in the stories about the warrior-commander Minamoto no Raikō (Yorimitsu: 948–1021). In this scene he tries to waylay Raikō by hiding himself in the stomach of a dead bull or a bull he killed.

27 *Shōnen taikouchi*. A story of a boy drummer for the Ninth Regiment of Napoleon's Army invading Russia that appeared in the August 1895 issue of *Shō-kokumin*. The boy was described as "exceedingly skinny, with only his head bigger than anyone's." See Horibe, pp. 184–46.

yo-heave-ho's, the Ceylon moss, heaped up in many places and ignited, belched sputtering white smoke. Meanwhile my brother had swum away all by himself to a boulder beyond it all, so I waded into a pool that turned into a rivulet only when it rained and began picking up stones and seashells. There were a great many baby hermit crabs there, which, though at a glance they looked like ordinary seashells, would put out their hands if you left them alone for a while and crawl about in a wobbly fashion. They lived in whatever shells they found, pointed ones and round ones. The funny thing was they were all baby hermit crabs.

Our friend found a conch shell about two inches long and brought it over to me. It had two holes that could take a thin string. So I was thinking things like, Back home I'll attach to it the tuft of a Western umbrella my older sister gave me, when my brother came out of the water and told me to throw away all the seashells and stones I had in my hands. I had no choice but to throw them away, one at a time, with evident pain, in the end all of them, except the conch shell. Unable to part with it, I squirmed. My brother became angry at this and raised his fist, but our friend stopped him and persuaded him, extremely reluctant though he was, to allow me to take at least that one home. That conch shell, with the tuft attached to it, is still in my old toy box.

7

My brother tried to educate me intently, exactly, and sternly, but one unexpected incident severed with complete finality the relationship that was hard on both of us.

I don't know when but at some point my brother ceased to be satisfied only with the carp in the fishpond and began to practice net-casting; making me carry the creel as he'd done before, he would take me again and again to a river nearby. If you walked just four or five hundred yards and crossed a bridge, there was a field that sloped into the river where frames for *mizuhiki*, dyed red and white,[28] were lined up like shields. Soon there was a water-wheel. Looking at the water coming down the trough pushing and shoving madly, I almost thought it was alive and got goose flesh. The large water-wheel exhaled breaths of spray, dripping splatters of sweat, as it clattered round and round terrifyingly. In the pounding place inside, which was filled with bran dust, countless pounders, like one-legged dancers, pounded rice, making dull, thud-thud noises. Going there, I didn't know why, I would taste bitterness at the root of my tongue and feel oppressed.

Walking lazily upriver from there, you came to a dam, beyond which the blue, stagnant water parted in three directions: one down the trough, one into the forest on the other bank, and the rest tumbling out of the mouth of the dam with earth-shaking boom-booms. Splashes of water dancing upward, boiling foam, the flow crawling up the bank, the water skittering away—looking at all this, I was invariably assailed by an unbearable loneliness and terror, my only thought being, I must go home as soon as possible.

The master of the basin at the waterfall, some said, was a kappa. He was, others said, a carp six feet long. And everyone said he'd heard it from someone who had actually seen one or the other. Every year, singled out by the master, one or two children lost their lives. So, for those pitiful ones a single memorial marker had been erected, I don't know when, on the meager pebbly beach. How are those children doing? Looking at the great expanse of green paddies making wavy motions in the wind, I would get a sudden lump in my chest, tears quickly forming under my eyelids. These tears having welled up from a deep, deep part of my heart, I had no way of stopping them. To hide my weepy face I would desperately glue my eyes to my feet until we walked into one of the four or five thatched huts that stood in a row, set apart from one another. This was where they rented nets and sold fishing gear, and on the tatami

28 *Mizuhiki* or *mizubiki*: special paper cut into strips to be turned into decorative strings used on gift envelopes and boxes. The paper is dyed red and white. Here the dyed paper is being dried on wooden boards.

discolored by the sun floats shaped like sake bottles, acorns, and round plates, and fishing poles were on display. At the end of the yard flowed a ditch in which minnows and shrimp swam, the paddy ridge was lined by scrawny young oak trees,[29] and at the far end of the green paddies rose a mountain covered by a black forest that seemed to continue forever.

My brother with his net, I with the creel, both now barefoot, would climb down the bank by the side of the waterfall and walk about the dented area below the other bank, fishing. My brother was all happiness because he, who until only recently used to tangle his net into the shape of clustered gourds, could now spread it into a round shape. But to me that wasn't at all interesting. Listening to cicadas, thinking of the milk vetch in the paddies, I would stand in the dark shadow that the forest cast into the river. My brother would occasionally come along with one or two *gebachi*[30] and dace he'd caught, and saying, "I've gotten so much better at it now," he would put them into the creel that I was holding.

I'd dunk the creel in the water so the fish might breathe. Then, feeling they'd become my friends, I would peer into it. They were so timid, the slightest noise would startle them into bumping their snouts against the side of the creel. In the meantime my brother would complain aloud that I wasn't looking at the way he cast his net.

One day, while all this was going on, I was standing in the river when I happened to bend down to pick up a snow-white stone I'd spotted near my feet. My brother noticed this at once.

"What are you doing?"

"I'm picking up a stone."

"Don't be so stupid!"

But I was no longer afraid. I had thought about this for some time now.

"May I ask you a question?" I quietly addressed him from behind. "What's wrong with my picking up a stone while you're catching fish?"

"Don't be so fresh," he barked.

I smiled coldly and, looking him right in the face, said, "Tell me if I'm wrong in what I said."

29 *Kunugi (Quercus acutissima).*
30 A catfish-like fish.

"I'll hit you," he said and raised his hand.

Without saying a word, I hung the creel at the end of a drooping branch and climbed up the bank to go home. But then I saw him squatting in the dark shadow of a tree, as if cringing, and I suddenly felt sorry for him. He says things like that but he must be lonesome, I thought, and from the top of the bank called to him with all the energy I could muster.

"Shall I stay with you?"

My brother ignored this, now arranging his net.

"Goodbye," I politely raised my hat and went home alone. After this we never went out together again.

8

Because there were some mulberry trees left uncut around our house, we once had some silkworm "seeds" from someone in our neighborhood and raised them, following father's idea that it would be a diversion as well as a practical education for the children. Mother and my aunt protested, and kept protesting, that it was too much trouble, even as they enjoyed themselves, happily slicing up mulberry leaves. In truth, they were somewhat proud, remembering the one hardship of the past that would not, no, never come back again, they trusted.[31]

At first, the silkworms simply hid themselves under the leaves, but every day they grew larger as they nibbled and chewed the leaves from the edges, flipping back their monk-heads. I, too, was given several of them, in a small *yōkan*[32] box. And because my aunt told me that silkworms were originally princesses, I made it a rule to say "Be well and happy" to them before going to

31 During its last, "five-sleep" period before making a cocoon, the silkworm requires 24-hour-a-day attention for about ten days.

32 Sweet bean paste. Regarded as an expensive gift item until not long ago, it came in a sizable rectangular box.

bed, "Good morning" when I got up and, when I left for school, earnestly asked that good care be taken of them. And when I came home, my older sister would wrap her head in a towel, tuck up the two ends of her apron into her sash, and go to pick mulberry leaves, with me carrying a basket. And turning our fingers black, we would compete in picking the most delicious-looking leaves as far up as our hands could reach.

These worms, which, on account of the beautiful luster of the thread they spin out of their cold lips, have been raised by humans over a long time, do not seek food on their own, but with their heads laid on a straw mat, obediently wait for mulberry leaves to be scattered over them.

"They were once princesses, they say, and look how well-behaved they are," my aunt would say as though it was all true.

Their greenish smell, and their cold bodies, were creepy at first. But once I decided they were princesses, I didn't mind any of that, and I came to think that the crescent-shaped marks on their backs were their lovely eyes.

These princesses, after coming out of the fourth round of Zen meditation, become so clean and clear that their bodies grow almost transparent and, not even eating the mulberry leaves, looking around here and there, they seek a place for nirvana. You then gently transfer them to cocoon shelves where they settle down in a spot of their choice and, moving their heads quietly, begin weaving white curtains to hide themselves. At first they seem merely to be shaking their heads, but before you know it they cease to move. The only thing you see are rolls of curtains like tube-shaped bags hanging from the cocoon shelves that they've woven with a divine power, without even a shuttle. Feeling left behind, I insist on keeping them forever, but mother and aunt quickly pick them up and boil them in a pot. And as the wet, yellowish threads are wound around a frame, the curtains cruelly unravel, in the end producing corpses shaped like which-way-is-wests.[33] My brother puts them in his bait box and dashes to his fishpond. Thus

33 *Nishidotchi*—the pupa of a butterfly or moth is so called because if you squeeze its lower half, asking, "Which way is west?" it moves its upper body in one direction as if in reply.

was I awakened from my dreams of princesses, while the threads, sent off to a weaver, were woven into a cloth with odd-looking "country-stripes."

Some of the cocoons that formed in the *yōkan* box were left as "seeds." But perhaps because my heart reached into the depths of their curtains, or perhaps because those princesses were unable to abandon the world of the shining summer, they soon revealed lovely figures suggestive of what they had once been in the past—with beautiful eyebrows raised above their black eyes, wings trembling with fresh joy. Then, they walked about to the right, to the left, as if drawing circles, looking for their spouses to mate with. I watched them with greater fascination than I would have felt for the person born from a bamboo.[34] Silkworms grew old and became cocoons, the cocoons unraveled and turned into butterflies, and when I saw the butterflies lay eggs, my knowledge was complete. It was a truly mysterious cycle of puzzles.

I want always to look at my surroundings with such childlike wonder. With many things, people stop really seeing them simply because they are used to seeing them. When you think of it, though, the tree buds that flare out every spring should astonish us afresh each year. If you say you do not know this, that is because we do not even know as little as what is wrapped up in this tiny silkworm cocoon.

By the time those "seeds" hatched, the number of mulberry trees had been further reduced and we did not have enough people to raise so many silkworms. So, with the silly notion that sparrows would eat them up in no time, my family secretly threw out half of them in the backyard while I, who had become the brother of those princesses, was not home. Startled to find them there when I went out to pick mulberry leaves, I rushed back and asked the reason why. But everyone evaded my question, refusing to deal with me directly. I finally sensed the reason myself and almost groveled before them, pleading

34 The heroine of Japan's oldest extant full-length tale, *Taketori monogatari*. She is found as a doll-like figure in a bamboo, grows to be the most beautiful woman in the land, and, after giving fabulously difficult assignments to five suitors, ascends to the lunar world where she was originally from.

with them to pick them up and feed them. But they wouldn't listen. Still, seeing that their wily sophistry could not deflect an innocent child's compassion, they in the end tried to scare me by the conventional means of raising their voices. Overwhelmed by chagrin and hate, I glared at them, madly cursed at them, dashed out back, and wept. If at that moment I'd had strength enough to grab and crush those people, I would have chainganged them and fed them to sparrows. After this, I would leave school early every day with the excuse of a headache and pick mulberry leaves for my sisters who were shaking their heads to show their hunger. But those were weak ones who could not bear the cold of the night or the heat of the day, and every day some of them succumbed to the mud.

It happened one evening when it had begun to rain. I would not come in no matter how many times I was called, so my aunt came out only to find me standing with an umbrella held over the abandoned silkworms. And the moment I saw her face I burst out crying and clung to her apron. A true Buddhist by nature, my aunt wanted to do something about it but there was nothing she could do. In the end, repeating prayers, she managed to take me inside by coaxing and humoring me. Later my family found a small tablet of tuffaceous sandstone erected at the spot with "The Grave for Oh Loyal Subject Kusunoki"[35] written in my hand.

35 *Aa Chūshin Nanshi no haka*: the words that "Deputy Shogun" Tokugawa Mitsukuni (1628–1700) wrote on the tomb he built for Kusunoki Masashige (1294–1336) at the Minato River where he fought and was killed. Until Japan's defeat in the Second World War, Masashige was Japan's greatest national hero because he willingly threw himself into a hopeless battle out of loyalty to the emperor. As a boy Naka knew the words and the history that had inspired them. Here he used them to express grief for the silkworms.

9

Partly because of circumstance, partly because of my character, I tended to suffer a lot. But I had one incomparable consolation, painting. I had a scroll of model paintings given me by my father. He said he'd received it from his lord, who was skilled in the Shijō School of painting.[36] It was at once what I treasured the most and, for my aunt, the panacea which, like the Divine Dog and the Rouge Ox, she could bring out hastily to calm my temper and suppress my demon. This scroll—a scroll that beautifully assembled only beautiful things, presented in beautiful figures, in beautiful nature, such as egrets, cranes, pine trees, and the sunrise—would readily fill my heart that was, after all, still empty and clear with the intoxication of inexpressible dreams and longings.

By that time, however, I was no longer content to merely look at the pictures. Knowing full well that it would destroy the mood of my brother, who disliked such things above all else, I managed to have my family buy me a cheap painting set—a dark-blue, shoddy cardboard box, which had only about eight paints and a single brush, with a trademark of a leaping lion attached to the upper end. With these, and the brush-washer that my older sister handed down to me, as my friends, I began to paint, first tracing directly from picture books and then copying easy pictures from the model scroll. Still, having no one to teach me, confining myself in my own room, I had all sorts of trouble, making mistakes repeatedly because I had to figure out on my own how to draw a line, how to produce a particular color. Nonetheless, it was for me all a process of free creation. Was the Jewish God, in creating all those myriad things, able to savor as much satisfaction as I did in being able to paint a single bird, a single flower? Simply obtaining orange from red and yellow made me leap with joy.

As expected, my brother was unhappy about all this. At times when I put up on my desk a painting particularly well made and was admiring it he would come by and dump horribly on it. But that did not quash the courage of this small creator as he was filled with joy and power. I would add my preferences in various ways, such as by changing the colors of

36 The Japanese-style school of painting founded by Matsumura Goshun (1752-1811), so named because when Goshun started it he lived on Shijō Street, Kyoto.

the kimono of a courtesan or a princess in a picture book or by putting a line under her chin or drawing a different eyebrow and, like a god of the past, I would turn my creations into my lovers, storing them carefully in my drawers. Still, in the meantime, I was irritated by the thought that I would never be able to find in the real world those beautiful things I created on paper.

I was also fond of school songs. Again I was not allowed to sing while my brother was around, so I would snatch bits of time in his absence. On clear nights especially, when I sang a quiet, quiet song while gazing at the translucent face of the moon, tears would form under my eyelids and the moon would begin to sparkle with a halo. A friend of my older sister's who had a good voice came to visit from time to time and taught me. Though I may have been the best at school, I would simply feel cowed by her mellifluous voice and could only follow her in a small voice. It was at the elbow-high window where I used to play with O-Kei-chan. Many a night the leaves of a sultan's parasol would rustle in the wind, insects cry, and a flock of night herons fly by, guacking. . . .

10

The school subject I hated above all else was ethics. In the senior classes they gave up the hanging scrolls and used a textbook instead. But for some reason it had a grubby cover, clumsy illustrations, and both its paper and the printing were coarse and bad. It was such a shoddy book, it made you feel creepy just picking it up in your hands. The stories it carried were worse, all about such things as a son full of filial piety given an award by the lord of his domain or an honest man becoming rich, every one of them told with no taste or flair. On top of this, the teacher had no ability beyond adding utilitarian explanations in the basest sense of the word. In consequence, ethics not only utterly failed to make me good-natured in any way but even created exactly the opposite result. Even in view of what meager things a mere eleven- or twelve-year-old child had seen and heard or experienced on his own, I could not believe these stories as they were. I thought ethics books were there to deceive people. So, during this fearful hour in which bad manners were said to deserve reduced marks for conduct, I deliberately behaved as poorly as I could to let my irrepressible resentment be known—propping up my chin with a hand, looking around distractedly, yawning, or humming.

After I started school, I must have been taught the phrase "filial piety"[37] a million times. However, their "Way of Filial Piety," when all was said and done, was based on gratitude, that it was our supreme happiness to be given life in this particular fashion and to continue that life in this particular fashion. How could that have any authority for a child like me who had begun to feel the pain of life early on? Wanting to know clearly what the reason was, I once asked the following question on filial piety, which everyone had swallowed whole and been afraid of touching as though it were a malignant abscess.

"Sir, why should anyone show filial piety?"

The teacher rounded his eyes in astonishment. "Because you are able to eat when you are hungry, take medicine when you are ill, thanks to your father and mother," he said.

37 *Kōkō* (Chinese: *xiaoxing*): The Chinese scholar-writer Zhou Zuoren (see the introduction) translated this section, along with the one on the Sino-Japanese War, into Chinese because he, like Naka, had a strong aversion to "filial piety." In writing an essay on this subject, he agreed with the philosopher Watsuji Tetsurō (see the introduction) and the historian of Asia Naitō Torajirō (also Konan: 1866–1934) that the idea of "filial piety," along with that of "loyalty" (*chū*; Chinese: *zhong*), was not indigenous to Japan but the deleterious result of Confucianism. In the essay on "the humane beauty of Japan" (*Nihon no ninjōbi*), Zhou observed: "The relentless advocacy of loyalty and filial piety have not just generated various tragedies among individual [Japanese]; it is also the principal reason for their being turned into a target of hatred." See Ryū, *Tōyōjin no hiai*, pp. 150–51.

"But I do not want to live all that much."

His displeasure became pronounced. "Because it's higher than the mountain and deeper than the sea."[38]

"But my filial piety was much greater before I knew any such thing."

The teacher flared up. "Those of you who understand filial piety, raise your hands."

All the buffoons raised their hands at once and stared rudely at me even while I, almost bursting with fury at this unreasonable, treacherous ruse, was unable to raise my hand, blushing with embarrassment that I was the only one who couldn't. Chagrined though I was, I could not say anything further and fell silent. After this the teacher always used this effective means to shut off my questions. On my part, to avoid this humiliation, I began to not go to school whenever there was an ethics class.

II

One night someone suddenly suggested we go to the Shōrin temple to play, so we did. In the temple lived a boy called Sada-chan who was one year below me both in age and grade, and even though I had seen him and knew him, time had passed with no opportunity for me to make friends with him or to hope to do so. Because it was my first time like this, I passed through the doorless main gate with considerable anxiety and curiosity. We went to a spot under the magnolia tree near a well I remembered seeing before and took turns calling his name until Sada-chan opened the door into the inner foyer with a clatter and guided us into the dining room.

For me, an unexpected guest, Sada-chan's

38 A saying dating from a textbook for children published in 1658. More fully: "Your indebtedness to your father is higher than the mountain; your mother's virtues are deeper than the sea."

family had taken out a hanging lamp that they saved for just such an occasion. An old model one seldom saw even in those days, the lamp was in a square glass box. Under the bright light that it cast dazzlingly above and below, to the left and right, we became absorbed in games such as Dominos[39] and Traveling with Dice.[40] I remember how the latter had a picture of a bonito-seller at the Nihon Bridge[41] that was the game's starting point and how Sada-chan's family laughed when I read the two characters for Goyu[42] as "*o-abura.*" It was the first night game I had ever played in my life, and I was also happy that Sada-chan's family, merry and apparently fond of children, played with us. Even though it was the first time I'd met them, I became quite excited playing with them.

True, with my sickliness as an excuse, I was, among my siblings, treated the most generously and had indeed behaved in a very spoiled manner. Nevertheless, worried as I was about all the restrictions posted up in every direction, no matter what I did— whether I walked, breathed, sat, or lay down to sleep—I had never played in the way a child should and did not have a place to play, either. As a result, that space inside the doorless main gate, which seemed liberated for the sort of child I was, became, to me, a place of freedom that I cannot possibly forget. With this first visit as impetus, I began going there to play every three days or even oftener. Indeed, as a place where an unchild-like child, who for a variety of reasons had

39   *Shōgi-daoshi.* So called because the game is played with the pieces for the game *shōgi.*

40   *Dōchū sugoroku:* A board game played with dice that resembles Monopoly, except here, as the name suggests, the purpose is to complete a journey first.

41   Nihonbashi, "the Japan Bridge." Originally built in 1602 as a wooden structure, it was considered the center of Japan from which all distances were measured. Nihonbashi is also the name of the district that includes the bridge. It had a large fish market. Hiroshige's famous painting series of "The 53 Stations along the Tōkaidō Road"— between Nihonbashi and Kyoto—begins with a picture of the bridge with a few fishmongers in the foreground, though the tubs they carry appear empty.

42   The 35th of the fifty-three stations along the Tōkaidō Road. It's in today's Aichi. As every Japanese knows, the kind of misreading of kanji described here is common.

lost many of the happy characteristics that an ordinary child is supposed to have, such as innocence and cheerfulness, was able to spend joyful, unselfconscious moments like a truly childlike child; as a place where a withdrawn, melancholy child could store childlike knowledge about nature that could be endowed only out in the sunshine; and as a place where I was able to nurture and develop a certain innate character—a character that to my brother was quite disreputable—that shaped what I would later become, the precincts of the Shōrin temple have a special meaning for me.

The temple once counted shogunate aides-de-camp among its chief parishioners and was famous enough to be in a pictorial guide to Edo. But after the Restoration most of those people scattered away, and even the few who happened to stay on had declined in fortune. Naturally, the temple had fallen into worse difficulties than had been expected and was deteriorating every year. Even so, it retained most of the features it had when I used to visit it on my aunt's back: The peacock on the screen in the foyer still proudly drooped his gorgeous tail and, around the peony flowers variously blooming, butterflies continued to dance as if intoxicated with the dreams of the past.

Beyond a tall hedge covered with Chinese hawthorns and to the left was the kitchen. And if you went there and turned right, there was a courtyard with flowerbeds and strawberry patches and old trees left uncut, casting large dark shadows here and there. If you turned right there again to make an L shape, in one corner of the garden of the main hall facing west stood a large black pine with its rock-knob-like roots rioting into the middle of the garden and its branches extending every which way, forming, for hundreds of pilgrim monks, a green heavenly cover and, for us, a shelter from evening showers and cool shade from the summer sun. Daikon radishes and rape would flower in the bluff-side vegetable patch further down. And in a thicket all jumbled up with snake-gourds and sorrel vines was an old well from the bottom of which mosquitoes sometimes would glide up toward you. If, from behind the black pine, you took the dog's path on the embankment covered with bear grass,[43] you popped out suddenly on the north side, into an open space, which was a cemetery with chestnut trees growing all over the place, everything buried under chestnut flowers, leaves, and burrs, and on the brownish stained grave stones you could often see land planarians[44] crawling about.

Sada-chan was a good-natured boy and a clown and he happily complied with whatever wishes I made, while I hadn't done much playing outdoors before and totally lacked the knowledge it needed. So he served as my teacher in such things, and the two of us became good playmates.

12

In spring we would go to the spacious field over a hill and fly kites. Sada-chan's was a bearded Dharma, and mine a Kintarō on a square-latticed frame. At first a kite, with its string held down, utterly submits itself to your whims, but as it rises, it begins to behave haughtily, in the end controlling you the flyer who, via a single string, is gazing up at the sky rapturously. Humming, swaying its tail languorously, the kite looks as if it is swimming in the ocean of the big sky. When the tautness becomes strong enough to start pulling you, or when the kite, annoyed by something, begins to turn round and round, you become scared and, calling out, Forgive me! Forgive me!, give out more string from the spool until it regains its good mood.

What was terrifying was the

43 *Kumazasa (Sasa veitchii)*: a variety of bear bamboo (see note 115 in Episode 1.36), though with much larger leaves.

44 *Kōgaibiru*, "hairpin leech" *(Bipalium fuscatum)*. The Japanese name comes from the fact that it looks like a certain type of Edo-period hairpin *and* like a leech, but it is not a true leech. Usually 2 to 5 inches long, this animal grows to be as long as 32 inches. It has a velvety black back and grayish-white belly and is very slimy. It feeds on slugs, earthworms, and snails.

TAKOAGE: KITE-FLYING

Boy's-Lattice[45] with eight parts that the son of the head of a construction crew[46] flew. Its jutting-whistle made of rattan let out a thrilling sound while the end of the kite's long tail leapt powerfully up and the rasp attached to the balancing strings glistened, glistened. Everyone disliked the two-part kite with a Hangya[47] that a bully from a lower part of town flew. This fellow's intention was to fight others from the start, for his was a *motten*[48] without even a tail and he raised it jerkily, threateningly, as it made a disgusting peeping noise with its paper-whistle. The Hangya, frowning even more horribly than usual with its central balancing strings drawn tight, madly snapped at her neighboring kites, in no time chewing apart their threads with a newly invented anchor-rasp.

Before setting off, we would check to see that there weren't any fighting kites. As you walk with the heavy spool in one hand, the other hand holding the balancing strings as if on to a bit, your kite, jumpy as a racehorse, tries to leap out and away. Among the kites up in the windy spring sky with self-assured vigor, my Kintarō on its shoji frame, perhaps because of my own conceit, looks particularly conspicuous. While flying kites, you become oblivious to everything else. The other children all go home, leaving only the two of you in the darkening field. Noticing this, you're suddenly scared and start pulling the strings, but it is just at such times that the strings seem particularly taut and the more pressed you feel, the less able you are to bring your kite down. The sun continues to sink, and all you see in a sky that is growing darker minute by minute are the Kintarō and the Dharma's glaring eyes. Each of you

45 *Dōji-gōshi*, a design with alternating fat and thin stripes; so called because it is said to have been the design of the robe that Shuten Dōji, "Drunken Boy," wore. For Shuten Dōji, see note 64 in Episode 1.18.

46 *Tobi-gashira*. Though here given as "a construction crew," *tobi* originally referred to members of fire companies set up in Edo, in 1720. Later, firemen often doubled as construction workers and mostly formed mini-monopolies in their localities.

47 Also, *hannya*: a nō mask representing a woman's face distorted with grief, jealousy, and anger. Contradictorily, *prajñā*, the original Sanskrit for the word in a Buddhist text, means "wisdom."

48 A kite made to "fight" by tightening the balancing strings at the center so that it may rock as it flies. It moves swiftly.

knows how the other is feeling but, hating to give in, you maintain your careless miens even while worrying, What'll I do if I can't bring my kite down until after nightfall, I shouldn't have let out all the string, and so on. When you bring down your kites at long last and finish winding up the strings, you feel what's been filling up your chests dissipate suddenly and, looking at each other, you burst out laughing, Ha-ha-ha-ha. Still, one of you will admit the truth: "A minute ago I didn't know what to do."

"Let's not tell anybody," you promise firmly before going home.

13

In summer we frittered away our carefree lives catching cicadas. Saying, You spoil their wings if you catch them with birdlime, we would attach a sugar-cube bag to the end of a pole and walk from the garden to the cemetery looking for them. With so many trees, we caught a disgustingly large number of them just by going through the place once. The "oily cicadas"[49] are merely noisy and don't look nice, so catching them doesn't particularly elate you. The "*minmin* cicadas"[50] are roly-poly fat and their chirps are clownish. The "monk cicadas"[51] have an interesting song; besides, they're so swift you chase them as if they were your mortal enemies. You can't do anything with "darkening cicadas."[52] The "mute cicada"[53] struggling in your bag without uttering a sound breaks your heart.

Also, in each season we would move

49 *Abura-zemi (Graptopsaltria nigrofuscata)*: a species of cicada—the only one with non-transparent wings. The name "oily cicada" comes from its shirring that resembles the sound of frying something in oil.

50 *Minmin-zemi (Oncotympana maculaticollis)*: a species of cicada. Its name is onomatopoeic.

51 *Hōshi-zemi*, also called *tsukutsukubōshi (Meimuna opalifera)*: a species of cicada. The name *hōshi-zemi*, "monk cicada," comes from China. *Tsukutsuku*, in Japanese, is onomatopoeic.

52 *Higurashi (Tanna japonensis)*: a species of cicada whose limpid shirring early in the morning and late in the afternoon is prized. Sometimes translated as "clear-tone cicada."

53 *Oshizemi*: a female cicada. It does not sing.

from one fruiting tree to another like birds looking for food. After a Japanese plum[54] scatters its flowers, pale-blue, you impatiently watch its bean-sized fruit swell from day to day, until they grow to the size of a sparrow egg, then to that of a pigeon egg, acquiring a yellow tint, then a reddish one like your cheeks, branches finally bending to touch the ground. Then, though you know you'll get permission "as long as you don't get a bellyache," you secretly, and continuously, pluck and eat them until you have a plum belch. Even then you can't eat them all, and those that turn purple, overripe, splotch down. Crows come over for them and peck at them swaying their tails hatefully.

What we looked forward to were the chestnuts in their prime. One of us holding a bamboo pole, the other carrying a basket, we would walk in the cemetery "with a cormorant eye, a hawk eye."[55] What a joy it was to find ripened ones as if ready to drop like dew. Rap it lightly with the tip of your pole and the burr shakes its head giving a truly delicious response. So you give it a hard knock. The chestnuts patter down. You rush to them and pick them up. And eat at least one of the three just to see. Strawberries. Persimmons.

The *yusura* plum[56] and jujube fruit aren't that good but you are shamelessly greedy and don't leave a single fruit on the branches. The quince put on flowers that, unlike the tree, are gentle and bear fruit that, unlike the flowers, are rugged. But the fruit merely drop thud, thud, and though their smell is nice, they are puckery and, besides, they are like stones: your teeth are no match for them.

The flowerbeds in many parts of the spacious garden and the trees standing everywhere had no end of flowers, each according to its season. Lilies, sunflowers, yellow ox-eyes, globe amaranths, amaranths. The flowers of the hemp palm that resemble fish roe.

In early summer the nature of this garden delighted my heart the most. Late spring makes you feel almost suffocated with haze, and restless—south winds and north winds

54 *Botan-kyō: Prunus salicina.*
55 *U no me taka no me*: an old expression whose meaning is comparable to "hawk-eyed."
56 *Yusura (Prunus tomentosa).*

blowing alternately, no cold, no warmth, no clear day, and no rain ever lasting. When that season passes, heaven and earth become the domain of an utterly young, sparkling early summer. The sky becomes transparent, like water, the sunlight overflows, a cool wind blows down, purple shadows sway, and even that gloomy black pine looks unusually brightened up, if only because that's the way you feel. The ants build their towers here, there, and everywhere, winged insects come out of their holes and fly about as if the whole world were theirs, lovely baby spiders begin to dance under branches, under the eaves. We fish out grubworms with candle wicks, we bury the holes of wasps and listen to their piercing noises, we look for cicada shells, we walk around poking at caterpillars. Everything is young, joyful, alive. There is nothing to be hated.

At such times I liked to stand under the semi-dark shadow of the black pine and gaze toward the hues of distant mountains that were beginning to darken quietly, quietly. I could see the green rice paddies, I could see the forests, I could hear the sound of the waterwheel and the voices of frogs that the wind carried to me. And from within a stand of trees on the hill way beyond, the sound of a bell reached me clearly, brightly.

The two of us would watch a flock of night herons pliantly winging in the evening sun that still remained in the sky and sing "Evening glow, lovely glow." From time to time a white heron went away with its legs outstretched.

14

In the silvery heat haze that envelops the flowers of the earth in its warm dreams and makes them smile meltingly, and, like the queens of this dream country, peonies bloom in many parts of the flowerbeds: white, scarlet, purple. Also, as in dreams, butterflies clad in various feathery wings flutter about playing with the flowers, and spotted beetles, all covered with pollen, become hopelessly intoxicated with honey. It was about this time that the sliding doors of the detached quarters, which mostly remained firmly shut and without a sound, would open to reveal an old monk leaning on his armrest. In front of those quarters was an old peony tree that the monk treasured, and on it light-pink single flowers amply bloomed, their petals laden with fragrant breath. From the main hall, the detached quarters lay beyond an arched bridge spanning a narrow courtyard. Under their sunlit porch thrived naturalized hardy begonias. At the edge to the left stood a blue paulownia and at the edge to the right a "white-cloud-tree,"[57] both casting cool shadows. The old monk, who had turned seventy-seven, confined himself there and made no sound except in the morning and evening when he read sutras. All we knew, by way of the scent of the incense that occasionally leaked out of some crack, was that there was a man in there who was as quiet as a stone. At times he rang a bell for his tea that sounded like the song of a "darkening cicada." If no one heard him, he would hold a tea cup as he might a small begging bowl and cross the bridge awkwardly to get the tea himself.

At other times the monk, summoned to a Buddhist service, would walk out forlornly, his hood slightly pulled up, a rosary in one hand, a stick in the other. Anyone who saw him so shabbily dressed would not imagine that this same person, when occasion required, wore a vermilion robe. Indeed, he lived separated from this world beyond a single bridge, quiet and unconcerned as if he knew nothing but that, come summer, peonies bloomed. Before long, child though I was, I developed reverence for the monk and began thinking of turning to him for succor. By that time I had become quite familiar with the people of the temple, and whether Sada-chan was there or not, I would go almost every day to play and

57 *Haku'unboku (Styrax obassia): Flora of Japan* (Smithsonian Institution, 1966): "Small tree with horizontally spreading stellate-pubescent branches while young, becoming dark brown ...; leaves membranous ... vivid green and usually glabrous above, densely white stellate-hairy beneath ...; the flowers stellate-pubescent; ... fruit white." The name "white-cloud-tree" comes from the clusters of white delicate flowers the tree puts on that resemble puffs of white clouds.

walk in the garden with hands on my hips like an old man or tour the cold cemetery—from time to time with tears in my eyes as I thought of the fate of other people or the fate of myself. . . . It was my habit to walk, face down, staring at my feet, thinking, feeling like a chain-dragging convict who is ashamed of his appearance.

15

One day when Sada-chan wasn't home and I was playing by myself, the usual "darkening cicada" bell rang in the detached quarters. But it was bad timing; there was no one in the dining room. So I mustered some courage and went myself. In the dim room that you reached immediately after crossing the bridge was a robe-hanger holding things like a surplice and a dangling rosary, and there was a thin waft of incense seeping in. There I suddenly became a little unnerved and hesitated. Hard of hearing, the old monk must not have heard my footsteps, for he clunked his bell again. Finally, I opened the fusuma door and placed my hands on the tatami. Without thinking, he held out a large saucer, but then he saw my face and said, "Oh, my, oh my."

Eyelids trembling, I bowed, received the saucer, and, feeling embarrassed or happy or as if some big wish had been fulfilled, went over to the dining room, poured the *bancha*[58] that was there, as I had seen it done, and took it back. The bridge was rotten and swayed, making me almost spill the tea. When I lowered my head and offered it to him, he said, again, "Oh, my, oh my."

I quietly closed the fusuma and, relieved, returned across the bridge. From then on I sometimes went to the monk in place of his

58 Chamberlain: "the tea of the lower classes . . . made out of chopped leaves, stalks, and bits of wood taken from the trimmings of the tea-plant; for this beverage is tea, after all, little as its flavour has in common with that of Bohea or [the choicest] Uji."

family but, even though my only hope was to have a chance to speak to him, once I found myself in front of him I was unable to say anything. I would simply receive his cup silently, offer it back to him silently, and come away. He, too, would merely repeat "Oh, my" as if he were an owl or something and would not try to speak to me. Once while I was crossing the bridge holding the black-lacquered saucer, a bulbul that had come to eat nandina[59] berries hastily flapped up, making me spill the tea. At other times, on moonlit nights, white flowers fluttered down to the bridge. And so I crossed the bridge often enough, but there was no way of breaking the ice with this hermit who was like a dead tree. However, once, when the bell had clunked yet again, I placed the tea cup before him, as always, and was leaving, when unexpectedly he called to me from behind.

"I'll do some painting for you. Buy some paper and bring it here."

Feeling as if tricked by a fox, I bought Chinese paper[60] and put it before him. He rose from the spot by the armrest where he usually sat as if rooted, and took me to the next room, which was sunlit. Everything in the room had turned sooty-brown and there hung a small framed calligraphy with Camellia Age[61] written on it.

Made to sit a lot closer to him than I was used to, I became drenched with sweat even while watching closely, as if it were something mysterious, every move made by a person who till then I had assumed would ring a bell until his death as stiffly as a stone buddha.

The old monk brought out a large inkstone, made me rub an ink stick, took up a brush, and drew a picture of a dishcloth gourd with casual ease: one leaf, one vine, and one dishcloth gourd. On it he wrote:

Yo no naka o nanno hechima to omoedomo
burari to shitewa kurasaremo sezu[62]

59 Nanten (Nandina domestica): a shrub with white flowers that turn into red berries.

60 Tōshi (Tangzhi in Chinese): thick paper with designs printed into it. So called because it originated in China.

61 Chinju (chunshou in Chinese): a metaphor for longevity. In Chuang Tzu: "In very ancient times there was a tree called Great Camellia. It had 8,000 years worth of springs and 8,000 years worth of autumns."

62 A tanka attributed to the famous Zen monk Ikkyū (1394–1481).

Regarding this world as no more than a dishcloth gourd,
  I still can't make a daily living just hanging out

He then drew a cipher that looked like a kettle, examined the whole thing from this way and that, and suddenly laughed a bright, dry laugh.

"Now, I give this to you. Take it someplace."

He then put the inkstone on a shelf, washed his brush, and quickly went back to his diamond seat[63] to turn himself into the stone buddha that he was. Like a monkey who has fallen from a tree,[64] I was crestfallen as I went home with the picture of the dishcloth gourd.

It was about three years afterward that the old monk passed away. I had gone up to middle school, Sada-chan had left home to become a live-in servant, and so my link to the temple had been gradually severed. But suddenly one night a messenger came to tell us the monk had passed away, so I went with father to offer condolences. The monk had had no special illness and had run his life span, so to speak, we were told. During his last days his past disciples, now resident monks in various places, had taken turns caring for him. For the first time in a long while I crossed the bridge, of which I had many memories. The detached quarters were thick with the smoke from incense, with many monks I remembered from Dai-Hannya rites[65] gathered there talking. In a ritual chair placed in the room where he had once drawn a dishcloth gourd for me, the old monk was seated in utter quietness, legs

---

63   *Kongōza,* in which the Lord Buddha entered nirvana.

64   *Saru mo ki kara ochiru,* "Even a monkey can fall from a tree." A proverbial saying cited in the haikai treatise-cum-anthology *Kefukigusa,* published in 1638, it normally means "even those most accomplished can make mistakes." Naka uses it here in a somewhat different sense.

65   Rites in which a few passages from each of the 600 "volumes" that make up the Dai-Hannya (Great Wisdom) Sutra are recited. These rites used to be held frequently— the first and fifteenth days of each month, the first three days of the first month, and so on—and also to offer prayers for national security, for a good harvest, or for fire prevention. The sutra expounds the doctrine of emptiness.

ritually bent, clad in a surplice of gold brocade, a *hossu*[66] in hand, like the stone buddha he had been in the past. As in the past I went before him, bowed, and offered incense. The bumpy-headed priest whom we had nicknamed Abbot Henjō[67] was munching a wheat cake, saying, "That was a great rebirth, that was a great rebirth." I felt even more like a monkey who has fallen out of a tree.

16

By then it must have been many years since my aunt, having luckily found a good traveling companion, had left our place to visit her ancestral grave, moved by old memories of her native place, thinking she'd be away only for a brief while. Soon after arriving there, though, she fell gravely ill and for a time she was certain to die, they said. But she must have had some more years left to live: she finally managed to make a full recovery. Still, because of her age she'd grown too weak to travel back to us. She herself had given up on the idea and became, by request, a house-sitter for a distant relative.

Following my father's old-fashioned notion, "Send the child you love on travels,"[68] I was made to travel, during the spring vacation of my sixteenth year, to the Kyoto and Osaka region to cure my inborn melancholy. It must have cured my illness for I remained away, doing as I liked, until I was called back home. On my way back I decided to visit my aunt, thinking it would be my last farewell. The place she lived in

66 A Buddhist utensil used by the leading monk in a service. A brush of long animal hair, it was originally used, in India, to flick away mosquitoes and horseflies.

67 See note 65 in Episode 1.18.

68 *Kawaii ko ni wa tabi o saseyo*: a proverbial saying born in the days when travels were difficult. A related saying went, *Tabi wa ui mono tsurai mono*, "Travels are depressing and painful." The idea is that if you love your child, you must make him experience hardship in the outside world and not spoil him in the comforts of home.

was a section crowded with small houses by a riverbank called Boat Crew, where during the shogunate the boat-crew unit of the fiefdom is said to have lived. I couldn't find her house easily, continuing to make inquiries until the sun set, when I happened to walk in the gate to a temple-like place facing a hardware store. I couldn't tell whether people lived there or not; it was all ancient and empty, with neither a single stalk of grass nor a tree, all denuded and parched. I stood at the open entrance and called out a couple of times, but there was no reply. I was in a strange town, it was night, and I felt diffident as I looked around. Then I noticed a small wooden door next to an empty plot on the left the size of four tatami, which didn't exactly look like a garden. I quietly opened it and looked in and saw a grubby old woman crumpled up like a shrimp alone sewing at the end of the porch, with no lights on though it was dark. Feeling guilty that I'd walked into a stranger's garden without permission, I stepped back and, bending forward over the wooden door, said, "Excuse me."

The old woman, unconcerned, went on moving her needle.

"Excuse me."

Was she deaf? For some time now my hand holding the luggage had felt ready to drop off. I couldn't take it any longer.

"I wish to ask a question, ma'am," I said and strode in. The old woman, finally noticing me, raised her face. I couldn't see well in the dark, but terribly aged and harrowingly gaunt though she had grown, she was, unmistakably, my aunt. I was too startled to do anything but to stare at her face. She hurriedly put her work aside and placed her hands on the porch in a show of formal respect.

"May I ask who you are, sir? Lately I can hardly see. . . . I've also become very hard of hearing. . . . And I always end up giving people trouble."

I remained silent. She leaned her upper body forward a little.

"May I ask who you are, sir?" she repeated.

Struggling with the lump in my chest, I finally managed: "It's me."

Even then she continued: "Who are you, sir, if I may ask?" After closely looking me up and down awhile, she must have decided I was, in any event, someone she knew well. She rose to her feet, picked up a cushion as thin as a rice-cracker that was by a brazier in the inner part of the room, and laid it by the Buddhist altar.

"Now please come in," she said, stooping as someone inviting a guest inside. In the meantime I finally calmed myself down and laughed.

"Aunt, can't you tell? It's me, Kansuke."

"Yes?" She hurried out to the edge of the porch, looked into my face for a while without blinking, and then, tears flooding and repeating, "It's you, Kan-sa. Oh, oh, it's you, Kan-sa," she caressed me, who had grown much taller than her, from head to shoulder, like the Lord Pindola.[69] And as though afraid I might fade away, she kept her eyes on me even while taking me in to sit me down next to the hand-warmer.

"My, you've grown so big but you haven't changed a bit." And hardly finishing the routine greetings, evidently wanting to touch me more, and prayerful, she wiped away her tears.

"I'm so glad you came. I had thought I might not see you again before I die."

17

My aunt lit an ancient *andon*.[70]

"Would you please wait here for a moment? I must run out for a moment." Mumbling something about her unsteady feet, she awkwardly lifted herself down from the porch and went off someplace. Left alone by myself I thought, This is the last time I'll see her. And I was thinking about her decline that was much worse than I'd expected, how I'd grown big while not realizing it myself, and about things of the past, when there

69 See note 31 in Episode 1.12.
70 See note 50 in Episode 1.17.

was a light clattering of footsteps and she came back with a couple of strangers. They were her old, still surviving friends, they all lived in the neighborhood and talked with each other about this and that, I was told. My aunt was so happy she'd impulsively called them together.

"Kan-sa has come to visit me from Tokyo. Come meet him at once."

These people, who had nothing to do and were easy-going and good-natured, had come with some curiosity to see what kind of a boy the Kan-sa they had heard so much about was like but, finding that the Kan-sa of such great reputation was an ordinary boy after all, they kindly went back home, only to return and roast for me a great deal of corn crackers loaded with sugar that, when held over the fire, became hopelessly twisted. Realizing that I hadn't eaten supper, my aunt, stubbornly turning down the offers from her friends to do it for her and, as if it was her happy privilege, went out to buy some food, holding an Odawara lantern[71] with the family crest drawn on it.

After she left, I learned that the mistress of the household had been away helping her daughter's family for a long time now, that my aunt was there all alone, and that she said she felt bad about giving trouble to people and did the household chores herself even though she could hardly see. In a while she came back breathlessly, turned on the miniature lamp in the kitchen, and, while preparing supper with a quiet rhythm, asked me about this or that person in Tokyo. Seizing an appropriate moment, her friends went away.

"Living in a place like this I can't make much of anything for you. You must forgive me," she said apologetically even as she put a large sushi plate right next to my tray. Then she brought over flatfish that were were raising puffs of steam from the pot on the heater, carrying each one, as it was cooked, with chopsticks. I said I had had enough, but she ended up lining them all across the plate.

"Don't say any such thing. You must eat a lot."

In utter agitation and with no time to

71 The tubular foldable lantern with a wooden bottom and a wooden lid invented in Odawara, Kanagawa. It was convenient for travelers.

think how to show her welcome, my aunt had gone to a fish store nearby and bought all the flatfish on offer. Truly happy and grateful, I gazed at the twenty-odd flatfish as I filled my stomach with them.

My aunt twirled about so fast I was worried it might affect her later. When everything was done, she sat primly, so close to me as to make our knees almost touch each other, and talked about various things, intently gazing at me as if to store my figure in her tiny eyes so as to take it with her beyond the Ten-Thousand Billion Lands.[72] I tried my best to tell her not to work if her eyes were so bad, but she wouldn't listen.

"I feel bad if I do nothing and give people trouble," she'd say.

Remembering the days when she was with us, I took a cotton needle[73] from the grubby pin-cushion and threaded it ready for her work next day. Then, because I was tired and also because I was concerned about her health, I soon went to bed. But my aunt, saying, I must offer gratitude to the Lord Amida, reverently sat before the Buddhist altar and, fingering her crystal rosary, began to recite a sutra. Illuminated in the flickering candle light, her body, emaciated from illness, seemed to waver. My aunt who had staged for me those Shiōten/Kiyomasa fights, aunt who used to take out a cinnamon stick from my pillow drawer for me to wake up with, that same aunt had now become like a shadow. She finished her sutra at long last, closed the doors of the Buddhist altar, and came to the bed laid out next to mine.

"Some time back when I became badly ill, I thought that was the last time I'd see the world, but it seems I had some more years left to live, and I've again been occupying a spot in this world. But I've lived to this age, I think I can take leave anytime. Before going to bed I plead with the Lord to summon me to be near him and I go to bed, but . . ."

She saw me put a bedspread over myself.

"You're not cold, are you? I wouldn't know what to do if you came down with

72 *Jūman-oku-do*: the number of Buddhist lands between this world and Paradise presided over by the Amida Buddha, thus indicating the great distance you must traverse before reaching Paradise. It also means Paradise.

73 *Momenbari*: May correspond to the "darning needle" or "finishing needle."

a cold. . . . Every morning I wake up, I say to myself, Oh, oh, I'm still alive. . . ."

Our talk seemed interminable, but I put it to an end at some point to go to sleep. Both of us, trying not to disturb each other, feigned sleep but neither slept well. The next morning I left while it was still not quite light. My aunt remained standing in front of the gate dispirited to see me off, for ever and ever.

She passed away soon afterward. She must be sitting before the Lord Amida as she had dreamed of doing for such a long time, I imagine, and offering her gratitude to him reverently just as she did that night.

18

I spent the summer of my seventeenth year by myself at the country house of a friend with whom I was on good terms in those days. It was a thatched building on the beautiful, lonesome peninsula to which my older brother had taken me previously, and it stood shyly ensconced at the foot of a small mountain rising from its shore. A flower vendor, an old woman who lived by herself in the neighborhood, was to do all the chores for me. This old granny was from the same province as my deceased aunt and because for me, she, with her age and accent, was like my aunt, and for her, I understood the language of her province well and remembered what I'd heard about the way it used to be in the past, we soon found ourselves talking at ease with each other.

Her older brother, who was her surrogate father, had ordered her to marry a certain gambling boss but she refused, so he gave her about thirteen ounces of raw cotton, telling her to do whatever she could with it to make a living. So she turned it into thread, took the thread to a wholesaler, and exchanged it for more cotton; then she turned that into thread again and exchanged it, and with the money she got for it being this much, the price of rice at the time being that much, she eventually managed to save some money from the difference. And so she bought some fabric and was sewing it into a kimono when her brother found out and scolded her terribly, saying, Why did you buy something like that without even speaking to your brother who's like a father to you. And she carelessly walked out of her home thinking to go to the Zenkō temple[74] to pay her respects, perhaps earning her way as a weaver or something.

She was then seventeen. And once on the road she was followed by a fellow who looked like a pimp and she was spooked so decided, in Tsumago Station, Shinshū,[75] to put up at an inn while the sun was still out. But then she saw the same guy arrive at the same inn and slink inside before her. She decided not to stay there, after all, and was about to leave when the owner, saying this and that, tried to force her to stay. Puzzled, she said to him, I've just sat down here and haven't even talked about the inn's rate yet; besides, the sun is still high, so why are you being so unreasonable trying to stop me? The guest you saw a minute ago asked me not to let you go until he leaves, the owner said, and he refused to listen to her. A man from the same province happened by and she had no choice but to explain to him what had happened and had him speak to the owner. And the owner, agreeing on the spot, said, I'll let her go at once. But the minute the helpful man went away, the owner tried to stop her with a menacing face.

So this time she spoke to an old man who happened to pass by, and he casually agreed to take care of her, saying, For now just come to my house and I'll let you go to the Zenkō temple with a postal runner.

74 A popular place for believers that is in the city of Nagano. Papinot: "Established in 670, it at first belonged to the Tendai sect, then passed to the Shingon. Towards 1630, it returned to the Tendai-shū and became a dependency of the great temple Tōei-zan of Ueno (Edo). It is dedicated to Amida, Kwannon and Daiseishi, whose statues according to legend have been miraculously carried there from Korea in the 7th century." The saying, *Ushi ni hikarete Zenkō-ji mairi,* "Led by an ox you go to the Zenkō temple to pay respects," means accomplishing something nice by sheer luck or unintentionally.

75 The province of Shinano (today's Nagano Prefecture).

She simply accepted what the old man said and followed him, but for as long as a month he just made her help with his peasant work, apparently with no intention of letting her go. Finally she found work as a live-in maid, managed to get hold of a travel companion, and left for the Zenkō temple. On her way there, at an inn, "by some mysterious karma," and with the bearers of a palanquin she'd taken, an inn owner, and a station official serving as go-betweens, she married a sheriff's assistant. But for some reason she couldn't stand the man and she meant to run away from him but ended up living with him for years before she finally fulfilled her wish and went with him to the Zenkō temple to pay her respects. But by bad luck both came down with terrible measles and had to take to bed.

Later, when she finally regained her ability to move about, she turned umbrella-making, which she knew a little, into a business. She was repaying the debts in many places when she happened to make some decorative hats[76] for a certain temple, so she thought to go back to her province making decorative hats in places on the way. But when she managed to reach a certain place she wasn't allowed to pass the check-point and she drifted and drifted until she settled down in a town not far from here and started another umbrella business. Luckily it prospered and turned into a substantial store, and she even kept several apprentices. But because her old man's eyes deteriorated, she gave up the business and started to plant the flowers she liked. With her old man's death nine years earlier at age sixty-nine, her luck had begun gradually to decline until she became what she was now.

On odd-numbered days she would get up early in the morning and, carrying a basket on her back, walk about selling flowers. Because everyone loved her, giving her cookies and dishes to eat, all she needed was five *sen* to buy a pint of rice a day. Besides, with an oracle saying she'd die in one and a half years, she had already arranged for eternal sutra reading,[77] and because she could get her funeral expenses by selling the house she was in now, rundown

76 *Daigasa*: A hat or an umbrella put in a bag and carried at the top of a pole in a procession.

77 *Eitai-kyō*: Arrangement with a temple to have a sutra read on the anniversary of one's death.

house though it was, she had nothing to worry about now, she said. She brought out a grubby notebook wrapped in a purple wrapping cloth.

"Everything is written here."

I opened it and saw dreams and other things from about the twenty-second year of Meiji jotted down messily by various hands. The cover said, "Record of Dream Moxa Treatments," but it contained nothing about them. Since she couldn't even read the *i* of the *i-ro-ha* syllabary, she didn't know of the writers' unkindness and thought they had written down everything she told them. Furthermore, she even had a carefully folded drug ad in the notebook that had happened to slip in. And though she couldn't read, she looked into it by my side.

"I have also met the Lord Kōbō,"[78] she said. "I have met the Lady Kannon,[79] too."

After some days had passed I learned that she'd behaved so confidingly toward me not just because of the reasons I had thought and because I listened seriously to her stories, which, by today's standards, were so superstitious as to invite mockery. The first time she saw me, she said, she'd thought, "Here's a gentleman so deeply devoted to the Buddha he should have become a monk!"

What other things did you think, I asked. She wrinkled up her face and said, "No, sir, nothing else." But she was by nature unable to lie or keep anything to herself and she followed her denial with, "You see, sir, you'll never be able to have a good bride."

She explained that, though I was deeply devout, I was also unable to become a monk because people had put up obstacles against me and would continue to do so from now on, too.

78　*Kōbō Daishi* ("Great Master for Propagating the Law"), the title given to Kūkai (774–835) who established the Shingon (True Word) school of Buddhism in Japan. Counted among Japan's three greatest calligraphers. Hence the saying, *Kōbō mo fude no ayamari*, "Even a Kōbō makes mistakes with his brush," and, conversely, another saying, *Kōbō fude o erabazu*, "A Kōbō doesn't select his brush"—meaning that someone accomplished can work with any instrument, regardless of its quality.

79　The feminine aspect of the Bodhisattva Avalokiteśvara, the "Goddess of Mercy." She is often depicted with a child in her arms.

"You mean being deeply devoted to the Buddha won't do me any good?" I said as if aggrieved.

She instantly made a serious face. "No, sir, not if you keep your single-minded faith. You see, the Lord Buddha's powers are vast!" she emphasized as if she'd forgotten everything.

"Unlike me you can read, so read the sutras," so saying, she read my palm. "You see, all the lines for interference have disappeared. Yes, I have already had True Pledge[80] for you but you haven't abandoned Self-Reliance[81] at all. You are a bad person," she said and let my hand go.

19

One afternoon, while I was climbing the mountain behind us aiming for the large pine tree at its top, I lost my way and wandered into a pathless valley. Blindly pushing aside the bushes that were taller than I, cheeks whipped by the branches from bumpy shrubs, feet roughened by vine leaves like military fans,[82] I barely managed to pull myself out of the suffocating depths onto a peak. The peak was shaped like a bull heaving itself out of the center of a deep valley that opened toward the sea. I followed a meandering trail along its back to its shoulder that rose up like a hump. Wizened short pines clung to reddish-brown fragments of granite that had coalesced into surfaces like shark skin, and droppings of birds who'd eaten tree seeds lay everywhere. Trying to prevent myself from sliding down toward the valley at any moment and holding onto

80 *Hongan:* Originally the pledge of Amida or Amitābha, "the Buddha of Infinite Light," to provide salvation to all people.

81 *Jiriki:* salvation through one's own efforts. In certain schools of Buddhism, especially in the Pure Land School. The opposite is *tariki,* Other Reliance, which refers to the salvation through reliance on the Amitābha.

82 *Gunpai:* "Military fan," a fan carried by the commanding officer in a battlefield. Today it is used by the *sumō* referees.

the gritty rocks with my strength concentrated in the tips of my hands and feet, I finally managed to climb up on the hump that was the shoulder. In a sky brimming with glaring light the sun flew with waves of heat.

From there it was a languid downward slope along the neck for about a hundred yards, with the cliffs on both sides becoming steeper, the valley deeper, until I reached a tiny flat space that corresponded to the snout, a dead-end atop a precipice. There, along the coast for about seven miles, an odd range of mountains, each one to two thousand feet high, branched out everywhere into the sea, forming countless coves. One of the three main branches was eroded by the water at its base, creating a formation that looked as if a wedge had been driven into it. With a peak behind, a series of higher rocky walls lined up like panels of folding screens beyond the valley; the blue sky serving as a ceiling, the place formed a monstrous cathedral. A falcon above my head, with its rising calls, made a quick descent from time to time, cutting the air before my eyes to rise up high again into the sky.

Looking down into the valley to the right, I spotted a single trail meandering through the black luxuriating forests as if sewing the range of mountains together while it descended toward a village beyond. And in a crack that afforded only a glimpse, I could see mountain after mountain, each one folded upon the next, layer upon layer of them endlessly, red, light-red, purple, light-purple, all leading up to the clouds. Filled with admiration and bliss mixed with a kind of terror, I started to sing in a high-pitched voice. Echo! It repeated me, as if someone were hiding behind the mountains, following me. Incited by the song of the singer who did not reveal himself, I sang with the highest voice I could manage. He similarly sang with the highest voice he could manage. As always I felt a primitive joy about something that was all so understandable when you thought about it. And after spending a happy half day singing, around the time the summer sun sank into the sea, I finally returned to the place within the fence of "yielding leaf" trees.[83]

83   See note 28 in Episode 1.11.

20

To wash my feet I went around to the backyard and, deciding that by now the bath had to be ready, opened the bathroom door and got in. And completely immersing myself in the bathtub with water that had cooled down just so, I stretched out my tired legs, relaxed, comfortable. The water crept up to my nipples and gave me a sensation as if I'd tied them up lightly with a thread. With both hands holding down my body as it tended to float up, I rested my head, face up, on the rim of the bathtub and, occasionally blowing on my warmed body, relived the happiness of the day. I named the place Echo's Peak. That it was found because I happened to take a wrong path, that therefore there was no one other than me who knew about it, that to get there you had to rush over that dangerous cliff—all this gave me an even greater joy.

After a while, somehow I found myself eyeing the stagnant surface of the water. And I noticed that though almost imperceptible, it had a thin, white sheen of body oil that I hadn't seen before. Had someone taken a bath already? When I thought that, it seemed to explain everything. Someone else must have come. I began to feel a sudden, profound anxiety. To me, someone I didn't know was someone I disliked. So, utterly sobered up, I was in a funk when my maid, noticing, came in to help me wash.[84] And apologizing for not having changed the water, she said the young wife from the Tokyo house had come. There shouldn't have been anyone like that in my friend's household. He'd told me his older sister who was in Kyoto would be coming to Tokyo this summer, so perhaps this was her. If so, there was nothing I could do, and I resigned myself to it, but I thought it was trouble nonetheless. Before leaving me, the maid lowered her voice in an exaggerated fashion and said, "She's such a beautiful, beautiful person."

I stealthily went to my room like

84 In the old days public bathhouses had men whose job was to help customers, male or female, wash; in private houses maids and members of the family did the same work.

someone with something to be ashamed of and sat lost, leaning back against the post. Nothing is more bothersome than meeting someone for the first time and saying something appropriate. And the pain of sitting stiffly in front of some unfamiliar person is like being tied up with an invisible rope, in the end making me feel as if the space between my eyebrows is being squeezed, the area around my shoulders becoming hot as if scorched. She seems to be in the detached room beyond. If she's my friend's older sister that I've heard about, I wouldn't mind much, but what am I expected to do? I was chasing one such thought after another when quiet footsteps approached on the porch and suddenly stopped beyond the shoji. Even as I was removing myself from the post to reposition myself before my desk, a calm, soft voice said, "Excuse me," and as if the voice itself opened it, the shoji slid open.

"Oh my, I haven't even given you a lamp yet," I heard her say as if to herself, and in the dim rectangle of the doorway, a white face was clearly embossed.

"How do you do? I am so-and-so's older sister. I am taking the liberty of staying here for a few days."

"Yes." That was all I could say, and I simply awaited the sentence for my crime. But she gracefully placed before me a plate with fragrant Western cookies on it.

"I have nothing special to offer . . . I don't even know if you like these," she said. At that moment the solemn, cold statue abruptly turned into a beautiful person and smiled somewhat bashfully. But then, as she said, "I'll fetch a lamp now," she turned back into a statue, and disappeared into the darkness.

I breathed a sigh of relief. Even while embarrassed that I was so pitiful, I tried to remember the figure that had disappeared, but it was all dream-like and amorphous. However, as I kept still, eyes closed, things gradually began to take shape as when you suddenly walk out into the light. Her hair was done in a large "round-knot" style. It was jet-black hair. Beneath distinct eyebrows shone jet-black eyes. The outline of everything about her was so clear that I felt it would be difficult to get used to her or close to her, and I thought even her lovely lips—the lower one pro-truding a little from the upper one—looked as if chiseled from cold coral from the bottom of the sea. But when both ends of that mouth pleasantly pulled up and pretty teeth appeared, a zephyr-like smile softened all, her white cheeks blushing, turning the statue into a beautiful person.

21

From then on, I do not know why, but in my attempt to avoid coming face to face with her, I would go to Echo's Peak the first thing in the morning and, in returning, deliberately shun mealtimes. Even so, living in the same house, at times we had to be together during the day. Up on the peak I would not sing. Like a bird out of season. And I would spend the whole time vaguely looking at the deep hues of the mountains visible between the rocky walls.

One night, very late, I was standing among the flowerbeds, looking at the moon rising from the mountain behind us. Thousands of insects were tinkling their bells, and the briny winds, coming over the fields, were carrying the fragrance of the sea and the sounds of waves. The round window of the detached room showed the light was on inside, and in the lotus vat in front of it I could see several leaves and white folded flowers with the coolness of the evening shower that had just passed turned into dewdrops on them. Sunk in the nameless thoughts that are the deepest of all thoughts, I was oblivious to everything as I gazed at the moon that was growing more and more crippled[85] night by night. . . . Suddenly I noticed the older sister standing in the same flowerbeds. Both moon and flowers disappeared. Just as when a water bird swoops down on the surface of the pond reflecting picturesque shadows, all

85 *Fugu ni*: Naka here uses an expression that is rarely, if ever, used as applied to the moon.

the shadows disappear at once, leaving only the white figure that casually floats on it.

Agitated, I began, "The moon . . ." but just then, unfortunately, she, out of consideration for me, started to turn away, startling me, making me blush, ears burning. Such trivial things, a little mistake with a word or a confusion, would embarrass me terribly. Older sister continued her quiet walk, making a small turn around the flowers and returning to where she had been and, as she did so, said, ". . . is truly wonderful."

The way she rescued me so skillfully made me both truly happy and grateful.

22

The next day I went to the detached room to return the newspaper and found her combing her hair, her back turned toward me. Her long hair, softly uncoiling, slid down her shoulders over her back in abundant waves. I was about to close the shoji and leave when she stopped, her hand holding the comb near her ear, and her face in the mirror smiled.

"Wait. I am leaving here tomorrow," she said. "I'd like to have a farewell supper with you. . . ."

I again climbed Echo's Peak and spent half the day in nature's cathedral, without singing, with nothing to see but a falcon dancing in the sky. The echo, too, remained quiet, not disturbing the thoughts of his familiar singing companion.

The dinner table was covered with a snow-white tablecloth. The granny on one side, the older sister and I sat facing each other. I was at once bashful, happy, lonesome, and sad.

"Please, do begin," she gave a light nod. "Your cook isn't used to being one. . . . I don't know if you are going to like these."

A little shyly she turned her eyes to the plates and smiled. There

SUIMITSUTŌ: PEACHES

the tofu she had made herself trembled, the indigo of the plate pattern almost dyeing its white skin. She grated the *yuzu*[86] for us. The light-green powder softly sprinkled over it, the tofu looked as if about to melt. I put it in the broth and the dark shrimp color swished over it. I then placed it delicately on my tongue. The quiet fragrance of *yuzu,* the sharp taste of the soy sauce, the cold, slippery touch of it all. I rolled it around on my tongue a couple of times and it melted, leaving a faintly starchy taste. On another plate, pert-looking baby mackerels lined up their tails, bodies arched. The parts where their spiky scales had been removed chestnut-hued, their backs blue, the area toward their bellies gleaming, each fish had a uniquely warm smell. Tear a large chunk of its flesh, dunk it in broth, eat it, and a rich flavor comes out.

After the tableware was taken away, fruits were offered. From among the large pears older sister selected a sweet-looking one and peeled it. With strength concentrated in the tips of her fingers to prevent the heavy fruit from slipping down, she made a ring like the *shō* flute out of it. As she turned the pear round and round with her long, arched fingers, the yellow skin went over the back of her white hand and coiled down cloud-shaped. With the juice dripping, she said, I don't like it much, and put it on a plate for me. I took a slice out of it and put it in my mouth and while doing this watched a beautiful cherry being held lightly between her lips, then slip-tumble onto her small tongue. Her jaw, shapely as a seashell, moved comfortably.

Older sister was unusually cheerful. Granny, too, was in a rollicking mood. She even proposed to guess the number of my teeth. As children often do, she hid her face behind the back of the older sister for a long think.

"Not counting the wisdom teeth, I'd say you have twenty-eight teeth, don't you, sir?"

"Everyone has twenty-eight."

"No, that can't be true, sir. The Lord Shakyamuni had more than forty teeth," she said, and wouldn't make any concession.

86 *Citrus junos*: a species of lemon whose rind mixed with pepper and salt is prized for its distinct spiciness.

At this, both ends of older sister's mouth pleasantly rose and revealed her own beautiful teeth. Then, when, continuing some earlier talk, we brought up the subject of birds, granny said the mountains of her province had swarms of white herons. Geese came, and ducks came. Flocks of cranes also came in great numbers. Every year, as if set by some rule, a pair of white-naped cranes came and when they did, the report was passed up to the lord of the province. Storks called, turning their necks. The nest they built on the great cedar of the pacification shrine[87] was woven from twigs and looked like a basket. She chattered on, carried away, so I asked, When did all that happen? and she said, When I was a child.

"Well then they are no longer there."

"But there were so many of them, you see. Besides they give birth to their children every year, don't they?" she stubbornly insisted.

The ends of that beautiful mouth rose sharply and I saw those white teeth.

Older sister was supposed to leave the next morning but for some reason her departure was postponed until night. In the evening when I'd finished bathing, granny seemed to be out on some errand, for the rooms were dark and I was about to step out into the flowerbeds. At that moment a voice came from the round window of the detached room.

"I had to borrow your lamp for a while." Then the older sister came with a white peach on a tray to say her farewell.

"I pray you will be well and happy. When you have a chance to come to Kyoto again, please do visit me."

I stepped down into the garden, sat on a seat among the flowerbeds, and watched the stars turning round toward the sea, toward the sea. The sound of distant waves, the sounds of insects, and heaven . . . that was all there was. The maid brought a hired *jin-rikisha*. I saw older sister, now all ready and beautifully dressed, hurry to my room to return the lamp. In a while, following the maid who was carrying out her luggage, she,

87 *Chinju no yashiro*: a shrine built to pacify and guard the land, the country, the castle, etc. It is surrounded by a forest.

passing by on the porch toward the foyer, stopped, and bowed a little toward me.

"Be well and happy," she said, but I, I do not know why, pretended not to hear.

"Good-bye, be well and happy."

In the darkness I silently lowered my head. The echo of the *jinrikisha* receded into the distance and there was the sound of the gate being shut. Hiding amid the flowers I wiped the tears that endlessly rolled down. Why did I not say anything? Why on earth did I not say a word of salutation? I stood in the flowerbeds until my skin grew cold and, only when the moon, more crippled than the previous night, began to shine from beyond the mountain, did I return to my room. And leaning my elbows on the desk dispiritedly, I held on my palms the white peach faintly reddened like cheeks and comfortably ample like a chin and gently put my lips on it as if to envelop it. And as I inhaled the sweet smell seeping out of its delicate skin, I shed fresh tears.

MANAZURU: WHITE-NAPED CRANES

Bibliography

Aketa Tetsuo. *Edo 100,000-nichi zen-kiroku.* Tokyo: Yūzankaku, 2003.

Akita, George. *Foundations of Constitutional Government in Modern Japan, 1868–1900.* Cambridge, MA: Harvard University Press, 1967.

Baba Kochō. *Meiji no Tōkyō.* Tokyo: Shakai Shisō Sha, 1992; originally, 1942.

Casal, U. A. *Five Sacred Festivals of Ancient Japan: Their Symbolism and Historical Development.* Tokyo: Sophia University and Tuttle, 1967.

Chamberlain, B. H. *Japanese Things* [original title: *Things Japanese*]. Reprint edition. Tokyo: Tuttle, 1971.

Dalby, Liza. *Kimono: Fashioning Culture.* New Haven: Yale University Press, 1993.

Dickins, Frederick Victor. "A Translation of the Japanese Anthology known as Hyakunin Isshiu." *Journal of the Royal Asiatic Society* (1909), pp. 357–91, .

Donald Keene, ed. *Modern Japanese Literature.* New York: Grove Press, 1956.

Doshisha Literature: A Journal of English Literature and Philology (March 1972).

Hibbett, Howard. "Natsume Sōseki and the Psychological Novel." In *Tradition and Modernization of Japanese Culture.* Edited by Donald Shively. Princeton: Princeton University Press, 1971.

Horibe Isao. *"Gin no saji" kō.* Tokyo: Kanrin Shobō, 1993.

Humphreys, Christmas. *A Popular Dictionary of Buddhism.* New York: The Citadel Press, 1963.

Inose, Naoki, with Hiroaki Sato. *Persona: A Biography of Yukio Mishima.* Berkeley: Stone Bridge Press, 2012

Maruya Saiichi. *Chūshingura to wa nani ka.* Tokyo: Kōdansha, 1984.

Mishima Yukio. *Mishima Yukio zenshū,* vol. 22. Tokyo: Shinchōsha, 2002.

Nabokov, Vladimir. "Problems of Translation: Onegin in English." In *Theories of Translation: An Anthology of Essays from Dryden to Derrida.* Edited by Rainer Schulte and John Biguenet. Chicago: University of Chicago Press, 1992.

———. *Speak, Memory: An Autobiography Revisited.* New York: G. P. Putnam's Sons, 1966.

Naka Kansuke. *Inu.* Tokyo: Iwanami Shoten, 1985.

———. *Gin no saji.* Paperback, 48th printing. Tokyo: Iwanami Shoten, 1971.

———. *Gin no saji.* Paperback, revised 1st printing. Tokyo: Kadokawa Shoten, 1974.

———. *Mitsubachi, Yosei.* Tokyo: Iwanami Shoten, 1985.

———. *Naka Kansuke zenshū,* vol. 1. Tokyo: Iwanami Shoten, 1989.

———. *The Silver Spoon (Gin no Saji).* Translated by Etsuko Terasaki. Chicago: Chicago Review Press, 1976.

———. *Tori no monogatari.* Tokyo: Iwanami Shoten, 1983.

"Naka Kansuke to dagashi." http://www.toraya-group.co.jp/gallery/dato2/dato2_047.html. Retrieved Summer 2014.

Ogawa Tameji. *Kaika mondō.* 1874. In Inoue Kiyoshi, *Meiji ishin,* vol. 20 of *Nihon no rekishi.* Tokyo: Chūō Kōron Sha, 1966.

Ohwi, Jisaburo. *Flora of Japan.* Edited by Frederick G. Meyer and Egbert H. Walker. Washington, DC: Smithsonian Institution, 1965.

Papinot, E. *Historical and Geographical Dictionary of Japan.* 1910. Reprint edition. Tokyo: Tuttle, 1972.

Rai San'yō. *Nihon gaishi.* 5 vols. Yomikudashi and annotated by Rai Seiichi. Tokyo: Iwanami Shoten, 1938–40.

Rice, Edward. *Eastern Definitions.* Doubleday, 1978.

Rodrigues S. J., João. "Pilgrims Come to This Temple from All Over Japan." In *They Came to Japan: An Anthology of European Reports on Japan, 1543–1640.* Compiled and annotated by Michael Cooper. Berkeley: University of California Press, 1965.

Ryū Gan'i (Liu Anwei). *Tōyōjin no hiai: Shū Sakujin to Nihon.* Tokyo: Kawade Shobō Shinsha, 1991.

Satchell, Thomas, trans. *Shank's Mare: Being a Translation of the Tokaido Volumes of Hizakurige.* Tokyo and Rutland, VT: Tuttle, 1960.

Sato, Hiroaki. *Legends of the Samurai.* Woodstock, NY: Overlook Press, 1995.

Suzuki, Daisetz. *Zen and Japanese Culture.* Princeton: Princeton University Press, 1959.

Tanikawa Shuntarō, ed. *Naka Kansuke shishū.* Tokyo: Iwanami Shoten, 1991.

Tanizaki Jun'ichiro. *Childhood Years: A Memoir.* Translated by Paul McCarthy. Tokyo and New York: Kodansha International, 1988.

Tomioka Taeko. *Naka Kansuke no koi.* Tokyo: Sōgensha, 1993.

Waley, Arthur. *Monkey: Folk Novel of China.* New York: Grove Press, 1994.

Watanabe Gekisaburō, ed. *Naka Kansuke zuihitsu-shū.* Tokyo: Iwanami Shoten, 1985.

Watson, Burton, trans. *The Lotus Sutra.* New York: Columbia University Press, 1993.

Whitney, Clara. *Clara's Diary: An American Girl in Meiji Japan.* Tokyo and New York: Kodansha International, 1975.

Yampolsky, Philip B., ed. *Selected Writings of Nichiren.* New York: Columbia University Press, 1990.

Yu, Anthony. *The Journey to the West.* Chicago: University of Chicago Press, 1980.

Zengaku dai-jiten. Tokyo: Taishūkan Shoten, 1985.

CPSIA information can be obtained at www.ICGtesting.com
Printed in the USA
LVOW11s2303220915

455210LV00007B/24/P